The taste of desire...

"A fig is like a woman in man[illegible]" said smoothly. "It's unique. Complex. Here, have a bite," he urged. "The textures are indescribable."

While Micki took a dainty nibble, Sebastian took his own advice and bit into the fruit, closing his eyes and enjoying all that he'd described, and all that words never could. The taste of the fig eased onto his tongue and, before he could contain himself, he groaned.

"Enjoying yourself?" she asked, her eyes glittering.

"Not nearly as much as I could be," he answered.

"Why's that?"

His stare locked with hers. The moment had come. "Something's missing from the mix. The fig is exquisite, the wine perfect, and yet..."

She hesitated, then almost unconsciously swiped the fig around her lips, spreading the sweetness over her mouth. "Do you want a kiss?"

He grinned wickedly. "Well, that's a good place to start...."

Blaze™

Dear Reader,

My name is Julie and I'm addicted to soap operas. Okay, maybe *addicted* is too strong a word, but I've been watching them since I was eight years old and the appeal hasn't worn off.

Recently I found a reason to justify my guilty pleasure for *General Hospital*...and his name is Sebastian Stone, the hero of this book. You see, there was a certain *GH* character I thought was incredibly sexy and fascinating, powerful and brooding, ripe for a great story line—one he never got, in my opinion. So I gave him one. Ah, the power of being a writer. He's not the same character, but the same character type...and I hope you find him as irresistible and sensual as I did!

For a man as strong as Sebastian, I needed an equally strong heroine. Enter Micki Carmichael, the recently found runaway sister of the heroine from *Looking for Trouble* (Blaze #92). She's street smart and sassy, but not unaffected by her past—a past she finally comes to terms with, thanks to Sebastian. And I hope you enjoy the reunion with a few characters from other books, too. Bringing them back was a hoot, especially in celebration of this, the ONE HUNDRETH Blaze novel!

As always, I love to hear from readers. You can e-mail me directly from my Web site at www.julieleto.com!

Enjoy,

Julie Elizabeth Leto

UP TO NO GOOD

Julie Elizabeth Leto

TORONTO • NEW YORK • LONDON
AMSTERDAM • PARIS • SYDNEY • HAMBURG
STOCKHOLM • ATHENS • TOKYO • MILAN • MADRID
PRAGUE • WARSAW • BUDAPEST • AUCKLAND

ISBN 0-373-79104-6

UP TO NO GOOD

This edition published by arrangement with Harlequin Books S.A.

Visit us at www.eHarlequin.com

Printed in U.S.A.

This one is for my readers!
To all of you who have written to me over the years by snail mail or e-mail to let me know how you enjoyed my books…
I thank you from the bottom of my heart.

And I can't forget the regular support I get from the readers on my favorite e-mail loops—RBR,
Sensualromance, Temptationreaders, Blazereaders and last but certainly not least, the family at the eHarlequin community! Too much fun!

And last but not least, to Diana Peterfreund.
Your e-mail started me writing again at a time when our entire nation wept. Now you're a cherished friend. Be safe on your travels!

Dear Reader,

This month marks the publication of the 100th Harlequin Blaze novel! I'm delighted that popular Julie Elizabeth Leto has written such a wonderfully sexy story to celebrate this special occasion.

Harlequin Blaze first launched in August 2001 and has been a runaway success. Our talented authors are the reason the line is loved by readers everywhere. Blaze writers create tantalizing plots and intriguing characters, then put it all together in a red-hot read! Month after month they continue to delight, shock and surprise fans.

Here's to the next 100 Blaze books and more! And don't forget to check out all the Blaze news at www.eHarlequin.com.

Happy reading,

Birgit Davis-Todd
Executive Editor
Harlequin Blaze

Prologue

"TELL ME YOUR MOST SECRET FANTASY."

Micki Carmichael swiveled in the surprisingly plush leather seat, nearly sloshing the contents of her complimentary orange juice over the sides of the cut-crystal glass. She'd never flown in first class before. She'd never been on an airplane, period. Made sense she'd be nervous, right? Made sense that she'd jump like a red-handed pickpocket when her friend Danielle, whom she'd thought had zonked out the minute she'd buckled her seat belt ten minutes ago, threw out such an intimate topic of conversation.

Secret fantasy? How about making it from takeoff to landing in one piece?

"Go to sleep, Danielle," Micki answered. "This is going to be a long flight."

Danielle pressed a button in the arm of her chair, extending a footrest hidden beneath the seat and lowering the backrest until she was nearly fully reclined. Micki imagined that before Danielle had run away from home, she'd traveled lots of times in first class. Even if Micki hadn't ditched her home with her grandmother, great aunt and twin sister ten years ago at age fifteen, she never could have afforded to fly in such luxury. The chair she would occupy for the next eight and a half hours was more comfortable than the moth-eaten mattress she'd recently called her bed.

"Oh, yeah. This is going to be a real chore to travel," Danielle said with a luxurious yawn. She peeked one eye open when the flight attendant approached with another tray of assorted juices and coffee. "Add some vodka to that O.J., would you?" she requested.

Micki instantly held up her hand. "She'll take it straight, thanks."

"The vodka?" the flight attendant asked, eyeing Danielle warily.

Micki chuckled. No doubt, Danielle would have preferred only the vodka, but with Micki as her designated watchdog, she'd have to make do with the orange stuff alone. "No, the juice. Thanks."

Surprisingly, Danielle didn't argue or even throw a rancid look her way. Instead, she smiled politely and accepted the glass from the flight attendant, then immediately placed it, unsipped, on Micki's tray. Mumbling, Danielle unhooked her seat belt so she could dig through the bag she'd stored at her feet, rising triumphantly when she extracted a collection of papers haphazardly bundled together. She shuffled through them, pulled one out by its frayed edges, scanned it, then tossed it beside her drink.

"Read it," Danielle ordered.

Micki complied. "This is your birth certificate."

"Yes. And if you'll make note of the line near the center, you will see that you are not my mother."

Micki shook her head. Her pal was notorious for going to great lengths to prove a point. Unfortunately, she had forgotten one important detail.

"And if you'll look at the line near the top, you'll see that you're not yet twenty-one."

"Bitch."

"Whore."

End of discussion. They dissolved into snickers and chuckles, which only got worse when the flight attendant walked by again, a little pale after hearing their earthy exchange. God help the strangers who tried to understand the dynamic between Micki and Danielle. Hell, *they* didn't even understand it. When they'd met five years ago, the differences between them had been so pronounced, Micki couldn't remember why or how she'd hooked up with the kid. Danielle had been fifteen, Micki twenty. Though they'd both lived on the streets of Chicago, Micki had been close to kicking her bad habits and working up her courage to attempt a reconciliation with her family. Danielle, on the other hand, had just escaped her parents, a rich Michigan couple completely out of touch with their daughter. Micki had had a hard time understanding why Danielle had bolted from a house that sported two swimming pools and a full staff, but figured Danielle had had her reasons as much as Micki'd once had hers.

While Micki knew that the unique friendship had kept her on the streets longer than she'd planned, looking out for Danielle had also kept her on the straight and narrow. And so far their connection had also kept hardheaded Danielle out of a coffin. Micki never could have guessed that she'd morph into a guardian angel when, just ten years ago, she'd been just like Danielle—young, alone and on her own in a world that enjoyed chewing up and spitting out misguided teenagers searching for independence.

Independence. Micki rolled her eyes, then checked the seat belt again. Running away from home at fifteen had indeed put her on her own, but the word independence had taken on a whole new, more significant meaning now that she'd finally gone home—or at least, since she'd renewed contact with her twin, Rory. And with her twin's help, Micki now had a decent place to crash and a job lined up. For the first time in a decade, Micki could make choices based on her deepest desires, not on a basic need to remain alive. She could move into an apartment in order to explore new experiences and improve herself, not to escape mutant cockroaches or to avoid an angry landlord chasing her down for rent money she didn't have.

But as bright as the future seemed, Micki couldn't really focus on her tomorrows until she put her yesterdays to rest. First and most important—she needed to deliver Danielle to the care of her brother, the enigmatic venture capitalist, Sebastian Stone. He'd arranged for top-notch, professional care to address his sister's addictions. And he'd seemed more than willing to accept the responsibility for his sister's care.

According to Danielle, her much older brother had also run away from home, though Sebastian had done so by going to college at sixteen and becoming a millionaire in his own right before his twenty-first birthday. Micki couldn't understand how Danielle could idolize a brother she spoke with less than twice a year, but she did. The kid rarely respected anyone more than a minute older than she was. But it seemed if anyone could influence her friend to accept the help she needed, it was "Bastian," as Danielle called him—although according to her, everyone else simply called him "Bas."

Micki had had to move heaven and earth to get the man's phone number. She'd even gone as far as paying Mr. And Mrs. Stone an unexpected visit. When Danielle's parents had refused to intervene for their daughter, dismissing their child's addiction to cocaine as just a "phase," Micki had exploded. She'd pulled every bullying tactic out of her extensive arsenal, figuring William and Dorothy Stone would either call the cops or help Micki contact the brother. Since they feared scandal above all else, they'd given her the phone number and then had the butler politely escort her to the door.

Sebastian Stone had been in China when the call went

through, yet only thirty minutes after she'd contacted Danielle's brother from a pay phone just outside of the ritzy Lansing neighborhood where he'd grown up, he'd sent a limousine to collect her.

Riding home to her sister's place in Chicago in the stretch Cadillac sure as hell had beat the bus. And when Micki had finally arrived at Rory's apartment where she'd left Danielle for safekeeping, Sebastian's attorney had been waiting for her with first-class tickets to Paris and instructions as to when and where to meet Bas.

Sebastian had even sent along a brochure of a beautiful rehabilitation facility in the countryside north of Paris and had included enough spending cash to break the bank. Not that she needed it. Micki could make do with very little, but money had been Danielle's downfall, even after she'd run away. One trip home with a sob story, and the Stones took their daughter back into their mansion, dressed her in designer clothes and ignored whatever troubles had led her to the streets in the first place. Usually less than two weeks later, Danielle had turned back to the streets in Chicago, armed with a wad of cash swiped from her parents' safe or with bounty from a trip to the pawn shop with Mommy's diamond bracelet. Each and every time, she'd steal enough to live on, with plenty left so Danielle could get high, no matter how Micki begged, threatened and bullied her friend to stop.

A rush of dread and fear and anger surged through Micki's blood when the images of the final straw with Danielle replayed in Micki's mind. Danielle had gone missing for a week. Word on the street had been that she'd fallen in with a pusher rumored to work in snuff films. Micki had crashed into the rat-infested hole sometime before dawn, lugging Danielle's semi-conscious body out of the condemned building before anyone stopped her. She'd rushed Danielle to the hospital. She'd saved her yet again, but the doctor on call had convinced her that unless Danielle received quality professional care, she'd be dead before she turned twenty.

Micki squeezed her eyes closed, hoping Sebastian Stone fell farther from the family tree than his sister. If the man suffered from denial or an overactive need to prevent scandal like his parents, Danielle might be lost forever. She wondered if he'd have the common sense to help his sister find a true path to recovery. She knew so little about him. He was wealthy. Powerful. And according to the photograph Rory had pulled up for her on the Internet, devastatingly handsome.

"You didn't answer my question," Danielle said, finally retrieving the juice she'd left on Micki's tray.

"What question?"

"About your most secret fantasy."

"Oh, that's easy," Micki answered, pushing away the image of Sebastian Stone, with his enigmatic eyes and square jaw, masked by an expertly trimmed beard and mustache. "My secret fantasy is that you sleep during the entire trip to Paris."

"Man, you're cranky. Maybe you should have some vodka. You're *way* over twenty-one."

"Twenty-five is not *way* over."

"Is that all you are? Jeez, I could have sworn you were pushing forty or something."

"Thank you, I appreciate that. I look like hell because of you, you know."

"It's not the way you look, it's the way you act."

Micki waved her hand, shushing Danielle as the overhead television screens started playing the safety video. Listening intently, Micki scanned around for exits, even located the little lights running down the aisle. She noticed then that no one else was paying attention. What was wrong with them, anyway? Didn't they watch the news?

Danielle placed a shaky hand over Micki's. "Relax, Mick. You're going to love this flight. And the trip would go a lot faster if you'd answer my question."

"I'm not discussing my secret fantasies with you. Besides, haven't we already covered this at some point?"

Danielle scoffed. "We *never* talk about men, other than you telling me how much you hate them."

"I don't hate men. That would give them all the power. I just don't trust them."

"Who do you trust?"

"I trust me."

"Then maybe your secret fantasy is just about you. Or being with a man you don't have to trust."

Micki swallowed the last of her juice, then smiled weakly when the flight attendant appeared to whisk the empty glass away. She glanced down at her own ratty backpack, shoved beneath the seat in front of her, the one that contained a gift from her sister—a red leather book called *Sexcapades.* She still didn't know what had possessed her twin to present her with such a ridiculous waste of tree pulp, but Micki blamed the raging hormones of a woman who got laid on a regular basis. Her sister was in love and she wanted to share the euphoria. And while Micki denied that she'd ever need such blissfully blind passion in her life, she couldn't help but feel a twinge of jealousy.

Her twin, Rory, had found a man who respected her, who cherished her, who did little things like leave sexy notes tacked to her apartment door or who ordered a pizza and rented a movie after she'd had a particularly tough day at work. Micki hadn't known Alec Manning for long, but she knew enough toads to recognize a prince when she saw one. A prince her sister had snared through the use of a book containing preprinted fantasies—the very book she'd stuffed in her bag, unread.

"What did you and Rory talk about while I was in Lansing?" Micki asked, suddenly suspicious of Danielle's interest in her sexual fantasies.

Danielle's smile was thin, but omniscient. "Girl stuff."

"Makeup and nail polish?" Micki quipped.

"Not exactly."

"Did she tell you about the book?"

Danielle's fawn eyes flashed with such innocence, Micki nearly lost her lunch. "What book?"

"Never mind."

"Oh, you mean the book with the sexual fantasies in it? The one in your bag?"

Micki glanced around, staring down the highbrowed glare of a businessman sitting in the aisle beside her. He was probably getting a hard-on from their conversation.

"I'm not talking about this with you," Micki insisted, gripping the armrests a little more tightly as the engines revved and the plane pulled away from the gate.

"It's either divulge your secret fantasies to me or I spend the next eight hours singing the theme song from every sixties-era television show I've ever watched reruns of."

"You don't know any theme songs from sixties-era television shows," Micki bluffed, hoping she was right.

She wasn't.

"Just sit right back and you'll hear a tale..."

"Okay, okay. Stop before I can't get it out of my head."

Danielle licked her lips, then thanked the flight attendant when she came by offering them soft, downy pillows and rich, soft blankets. Outside the oval windows, the sun dipped toward the horizon. Micki closed her eyes as the aircraft approached the runway. When Danielle again slipped her hand over hers, Micki exhaled the breath she'd been unconsciously holding.

Takeoff was smooth. After thirty minutes, they reached a level altitude. The plane speared straight through the darkening sky, lulling Micki with the mechanical hum of the engines.

Suddenly, she realized that Danielle hadn't yet released her hand. And despite that her friend's eyes were closed, she hadn't fallen asleep. But a familiar, grayish tint formed a pale *O* around Danielle's mouth and the darker rings beneath her eyes seemed more pronounced, even in the dim light.

"Danielle, you okay?"

She nodded, but Micki wasn't convinced. Danielle hadn't had a snort of coke in over a week. No alcohol. No weed. Nothing to take the edge off the D.T.'s. And now they were trapped on a nearly nine-hour flight. There wasn't much to distract Danielle from her misery, so Micki surrendered, snuggled closer to her friend and began to whisper.

"Okay, my most secret fantasy all starts when a man, wearing black, lures me to his posh castle on a high, perilous cliff...."

"WHAT DO YOU MEAN they're going to Paris?"

Idiot! How could such a moron be one of the hottest private investigators in the city? All he'd had to do was find one teenaged runaway, and when he finally did after months of searching, he'd lost her?

"I'm telling you, they checked in at the airport with two first-class tickets to France. How they could afford such a pricey trip is beyond me."

Beyond you, maybe. Only one possible answer existed—Sebastian Stone. He had enough money and power to spirit his sister and her friend to any place on the planet in less than an hour's time. *Damn, damn.* Once again, his interference had ruined a beautiful plan.

"When do they land?"

The itinerary the investigator rattled over the phone provided nothing usable in this quest to reclaim what Sebastian Stone had stolen. But with any luck, another investigator in Paris might have an easier time. Hiding on the streets of Chicago was one thing—hiding in the best hotels in Paris was something else altogether. And if not Paris, then another opportunity would arise. Setbacks had become par for the course, but this time—this time—Sebastian had an Achilles' heel. And exploiting that weakness would lead to Stone's ultimate downfall—one way or another.

1

SEBASTIAN STONE possessed more money than God, or so the saying went. For his part, Bas didn't know why God would want or need money, since He reportedly controlled what men such as Bas truly coveted most—power. But Bas allowed himself a quiet grin as he strolled through the palatial Grand Bernstein Suite at the Hôtel de Crillon in Paris, deeply aware of the decadent luxury around him. If God ever left Heaven for a trip to France, He'd be lucky to book a room as lavish as this.

And if Bas ever made it to Heaven—which was unlikely for such a ruthless venture capitalist as he—Bas imagined the angels might look something like the waif curled on the Louis XV settee. Of course, she'd have to trade her skintight, black leather pants and shimmery tank top for something modest and white, but even in her tough street clothes, she looked nothing less than angelic.

And yet Bas's response to his sister's friend was nothing short of sinful.

The heels of his freshly polished shoes crackled over the parquet floor, stirring his guest from her involuntary nap.

"Sorry," she said, wiping sleep from her sapphire eyes. "Didn't mean to conk out on you. How's Danielle?"

Bas bit down a smile, amazed at how much he fought the urge to grin since Michaela Carmichael had barged into his life. With one demanding phone call, the woman his sister called her best friend had turned his life upside down.

Because of her revelations about the dire circumstances of his sister's addiction, he'd cut a crucial business meeting short to fly to Europe. He'd allowed competitors time to usurp two other promising deals while he'd researched drug rehabilitation facilities. In less than forty-eight hours, he'd had a total of three hours of sleep...probably lost a few million dollars...and, still, he wanted to smile.

Unfortunately, such an outward show of happiness contrasted with his image. He maintained a serious mien. "She's settled in her room, asleep finally. Likely, not for long." He leveled his gaze on her. "Please don't apologize for your exhaustion. You traveled a long way to bring Danielle to me."

Michaela stretched full and long like a dark-coated feline, a pampered pet concerned with nothing but her own comfort and pleasure. However, after his long talk with Danielle, Bas knew this woman rarely put her own needs first. According to his baby sister, Michaela "Micki" Carmichael had put her generously curved ass on the line for Danielle more than once, most recently saving her from nothing less than an ugly, lonely death.

"What's a little international travel to help a friend?" Micki cracked, her sardonic tone already becoming an expected response though they'd met less than four hours ago.

"According to Danielle, you've done more than travel for her. You saved her life."

She shook her head, her bluish-black hair streaking across her face in sleek, glossy slashes. "I just treated her like I would treat any friend, okay?"

Bas nodded, but knew she lied. He didn't normally respect false gestures of humility. But Danielle had warned him about Micki's inability to consider what she'd done as self-sacrificing. In Danielle's eyes, only Bas could ensure that Micki was amply compensated for finally convincing

Danielle to get off the streets and, soon, into a drug rehabilitation facility.

According to Danielle, Micki had been the one to track her down every time Danielle disappeared on a binge. Micki had chased off the vultures who'd lured Danielle into swapping sex for drugs. Micki had traveled, alone, to Lansing, facing off with Bas and Danielle's parents, forcing them to give up Bas's closely guarded cell phone number. She'd nursed her through the horrible side effects of detoxification. She'd even made sure Danielle ate, force-feeding her soup through a straw when necessary.

Michaela had kept his sister alive and, for that, he owed her more than money. Which was good, since Danielle insisted Micki wouldn't take one red cent, no matter what exorbitant amount he offered. He believed her, since shortly after introductions, Michaela had returned the cash leftover from their trip to Europe.

"I've arranged for a car to take Danielle to the rehabilitation facility in an hour."

"An hour?" Michaela jumped to her feet. "That's so soon."

"The head psychiatrist thinks delays could compromise Danielle's recovery." Bas sat on a high-back, curved leather chair, enjoying the feel of the polished texture against his fine cotton shirt. He longed for a snifter of cognac, perhaps a fine Montecristo cigar, but he considered the indulgences counterproductive and rude, in light of his sister's problems.

"I explained to the administrator what you went through to convince Danielle to get help in the first place. He's afraid if she finds too much comfort here, reuniting with me and living in the luxury of this hotel, she won't want to follow through with treatment. You and I both know that she needs professional intervention."

Micki snagged her bottom lip with her teeth. The bold red hue she'd worn earlier had nearly faded completely, leaving her generous lips pink and puckered. Most women would look washed out, exhausted, after the long trip and insufficient sleep. Michaela, on the other hand, wore the intense concentration of deep thought.

"May I say goodbye?"

Bas shifted in his seat. "Of course. You can ride with us to the facility and accompany me when I meet with the doctors."

She paused, glancing sightlessly out the window behind her. "I don't have any right," she mumbled.

"I'm not my parents, Michaela. You've been her family for the past five years, more so than anyone who shares her last name. I won't deny you that role now."

Her eyes met his, coated with a glossiness that undoubtedly stemmed from her lack of sleep. This one wore her emotions as closely guarded beneath her skin as he did.

"Thank you."

He nodded. "She'll likely wake up again soon. She's having trouble keeping still. Why don't you check on her?"

Michaela cursed, causing Bas to raise a shocked eyebrow she either didn't notice or simply didn't care about. "I was so sure we'd gotten over the worst part of the shakes. But they never really go away. Did you put someone outside in the hall like I suggested? Even in a strange city, she might get desperate enough to sneak out for one last fix. I didn't let her drink on the flight. She wasn't happy."

Beneath his expertly tailored suit, Bas fought to control the emotions that shook him. He closed his eyes and nodded, barely able to stand the guilt he felt about his sister's condition. While he planned to lambaste his parents for the lies they'd told him, convincing him that his baby sister had been tucked away at an exclusive private school instead of living on the streets of Chicago, he couldn't assign all the blame on them.

When was the last time he'd gone home? The last time he'd seen Danielle with his own eyes rather than blindly accepted the reports his parents gave him during their monthly phone calls? He'd been so wrapped up in maintaining his billion-dollar portfolio that he'd lost touch with the one person who'd never expected anything from him but an occasional approving smile.

"I've done as you suggested," he said.

"Good," Michaela answered. "I'll stay with her until we leave, if you don't mind."

"Not at all. I'll be here."

She stalked past him on her high-heeled boots, then turned with such a quick motion he wondered if she'd ripped a tear in the antique rug.

"You should get some rest, you know. You look like shit."

Again, her language evoked his surprise. And his amusement. Except for Victor, his pilot and valet, no one had the audacity to speak to him with such earthy candor. "I'll rest once Danielle is safe."

"Yeah," she said, vacillating from foot to foot, wariness ricocheting in her crystal-blue eyes. "Me, too."

With surprising quiet, she crossed the room and disappeared through Danielle's door.

"Fascinating, isn't she?"

Victor emerged from a shadowy corner. How the man managed to conceal his bulk in such an open, airy room justified, at least in part, the obscene salary Bas paid him.

"I can't decide," Bas answered. "She's either a perplexing combination of street smarts and a warm heart, or she's a prime example of a con artist attaching herself to a woman connected to large sums of money." He paused, doubting the latter explanation applied to Ms. Carmichael. And while Bas trusted his instincts, he trusted the work of his private investigators even more. "Have you anything to help me decide?"

Bas held out his hand. Victor slapped a rather thin dossier across his palm, then turned toward the bar where he chose a decanter of Hennessy X.O., Bas's favorite cognac.

"Not now, Victor," Bas directed, flipping open the folder and scanning the page inside.

Victor replaced the brandy and stepped to his side. "Not much in the file, boss, but we can dig deeper. There's an arrest for loitering. A hospital stay. The address where she and Danielle crashed, which Danielle paid for with money she lifted from your parents. There's a picture."

Bas scowled and tossed the photograph of the rat-hole aside. Apparently, while Danielle had racked up a rather lengthy rap sheet with crimes ranging from petty theft to prostitution, Michaela Carmichael had remained relatively clean while living in an apartment marginally fit for human occupation.

Flipping the page, Bas narrowed his gaze, reading the concise report with great interest. A woman as resourceful as she was stubborn? Fascinating. And attractive, too—in a hard-rock, bad-to-the-bone sort of way. Overtly sexual. Unrefined.

Intriguing.

He scanned a clipping from a small community newspaper, detailing Michaela's disappearance from home at age fifteen. He read the decade-old pleas from her grandmother for information, for her return. He scanned a grainy, yellowed photograph of her forlorn twin, Aurora.

"Did you check into her sister?"

"Clean as a whistle," Victor responded. "Not so much as a parking ticket. Lives in the city now, but stayed with her grandmother in the 'burbs until just a month ago. Helped nurse the old broad through cancer."

"Regular yin and yang, aren't they?"

He moved on to Michaela's elementary, middle and high school records. Average grades. Deplorable behavior. More than one notation from teachers bemoaning her wasted intelligence and insolent attitude. A copy of the arrest report, filed three months ago, with a special notation from the arresting officer recommending community resource intervention.

The last page, he lifted from the others. A letter of recommendation, addressed to a Shaw Thomas, written recently by the administrator of a homeless shelter, detailed Michaela's contribution to their free day-care program. *Even when she's had nothing of her own, she's shared her time and attention with needy children.*

Bas slipped the letter back into the dossier, along with the other documents. According to both reports and his instincts, Michaela Carmichael was exactly what she appeared to be—a genuine kind heart hidden behind a streetwise exterior. A woman who'd saved his sister. More than once.

He shut the folder and handed it over his shoulder to Victor, who would make the personal information disappear with the same efficiency as it had appeared in the first place. "That's quite enough. She is who she and Danielle both say she is."

"What'll you do with her now? I mean, she brought Danielle to you when no one else would or could. Couldn't have been easy to stand up to your mother and father the way she did. She deserves something, right?"

Bas's scowl deepened. Victor's sentiment matched what Danielle had said to him nearly word for word, and he had no doubt the similarity wasn't accidental. Danielle and Victor had taken an instant liking to one another, and he hadn't missed the conspiratorial gleam in both their gazes.

But Bas needed no help in understanding the depth of what Michaela had done for his sister or how formidable his parents could be when it came to covering up family embarrassments. So why did everyone seem so devoted to making sure he repaid Michaela for her help?

"She deserves quite a bit," he responded.

"A night on the town in gay Paris?" Victor suggested.

Bas smirked. Victor sounded like he was quoting a line from an old musical.

"More than that, my friend. After Danielle is safe in the clinic, we'll all get a good night's rest. In the morning, I'd like you to go straight to the airport and prep the jet. We're leaving Paris first thing."

"We're going somewhere else? What could be a better reward than a few days in France?"

Bas stood and proceeded toward his bedroom to catch a short nap. As much as he appreciated the beauty, history and romance of France, he wondered if there wasn't a more suitable place to show Ms. Carmichael his appreciation for all she'd done. Trouble was, for the first time in forever, the choice wasn't up to him. At Danielle's rather outrageous request, Bas had agreed to let Michaela choose her reward, no matter the price. To him, or to her.

FILLING HER LUNGS with air, Micki slipped inside the darkened bedroom, trying to shake the tension quaking through her body. Lord, but she'd never met a man like Sebastian Stone. Expertly controlled power simmered beneath the surface of his tanned skin, giving his pewter eyes an intense gleam. So well-dressed in his tailored suit, he moved with the grace of a man who knew his true strength. His hair, though professionally cut, shot away from his face as if his hand, for the thousandth time, had forked through the dark brown strands in deep thought. And though Micki had known him for less than a day, she doubted he'd ever allow himself such an expressive gesture. This man controlled everything—from his actions to his words to his emotions. Likely, he dictated the actions, words and emotions of everyone around him, too.

Micki had an inherent distrust of men who wielded such awesome power. And yet she could easily imagine Sebastian dressed all in black, enticing her into his castle on a hill.

She'd shared only that one fantasy with Danielle, and yet the woefully romantic images of a lost princess and a mysterious lord had kept them entertained for an hour until Danielle had finally fallen asleep on the plane. Too bad Micki hadn't been so lucky. The sensual musings had kept her awake nearly the entire trip.

A lord and a princess. A powerful man and a vulnerable beauty. Only in Micki's version, the princess didn't submit to the potent prowess of the dominant nobleman. Instead, she found her strength by capturing him. What would it take for a waif like her to catch a man like Sebastian Stone?

When she'd first confessed this scenario to Danielle, the man in her fantasy hadn't had a face. Now that she'd experienced Sebastian's incredible magnetism, an invisible tug jerked from deep within her. A pull inherently sexual—and intrinsically intimate. She tried to laugh her physical reaction away, but the sound caught in her throat and emerged as a moan, spawned by the electric shiver racing up and down her spine.

God, she'd ignored her sexual needs for so long. Smoothing her hands down her body, Micki's flesh tingled, warmed. Yearned. She tried to imagine the last time she'd allowed a man close enough to touch her, much less arouse her. Unlike any other man she'd ever met, Bas Stone had awakened her dormant libido with little less than a glance and a half smile.

Micki slipped off her noisy boots and tucked them behind a chair. Hours seemed to have passed since she came into the room, but only minutes had ticked by, right? A sound echoed from the bed, halfway between a groan and a sigh. With only the light from a small lamp to guide her, she crossed the room, stopping when the surroundings suddenly struck her as wholly unfamiliar.

This wasn't Danielle's room. Her room did not have long, sheer curtains fluttering from the bedposts. Or an open window that billowed the gossamer fabric. And if a window was open, where were the sounds of the busy Place de la Concorde, situated below their suite? Micki squinted as she walked closer, batting the flapping material away from her face.

"Danielle?"

"Michaela?"

Micki broke through the cloud of curtains, shocked when the sound of her name started with a soft feminine voice, then ended with a man's distinctive tone. She was only half-surprised to see Bas in the bed, naked from the waist up, a dark burgundy sheet drawn around lean hips and a washboard stomach, a dreamy stare in his eyes.

This most certainly wasn't Danielle's room. She should have known the moment she entered, since the combined scents of musk and smoke and fine cognac taunted her from all sides. She should have known.

She did know. And yet, she'd come.

Wait a minute.

With a wry smile, Micki reached over and pinched her arm.

She felt nothing.

Holy shit. I'm dreaming.

She moved to slap her face, then stopped. She wanted to wake up…why? Images of the afternoon flickered in her mind. The reality of taking Danielle to the rehab center. Having dinner in the limo on the way back. Her quick retreat to her own bed. All the events of the day seemed more like dreams than what she experienced now. She couldn't remember the last time a dream had formed so vividly in her subconscious. She inhaled the subtly spicy scent of Bas's distinctive cologne, and her mouth watered.

Why would she want to wake up? Ever? Talk about safe sex. She glanced down at her body, fully clothed, but with only a flash of a thought, her jeans and T-shirt faded to nothing, leaving her bare, revealed.

Aroused.

Dream Bas scooted closer. "God, you're beautiful."

"Bet you say that to all your dream girls," she quipped, and, for a split second, a gray haze descended around her and the feel of the sheets—the soft white ones that covered her bed, not the burgundy ones around Sebastian—rustled against her skin. She was going to wake up!

She relaxed, released her disbelief. Safe in a dream, she could believe in desire. She could succumb to a man's seduction without worrying what else he had in store for her, what fate she might face if she dropped her protective walls, even for a moment.

In the dream, Bas would do only what she wanted, when she wanted. And for now, the dream was all she could have.

Yes, she and Bas were both consenting adults. Yes, something potentially electric sizzled between them. But he was Danielle's brother—rich, powerful, indebted to her for the sacrifices she'd made for his sister.

Micki couldn't ignore that he was also out of her league. He was Harvard and Paris and Dom Perignon. She was

State Street and Chicago and Old Style beer. Not that the disparities made her any less than him. Bas was no better and vice versa. But she couldn't deny that at the bottom line, they were creatures who thrived in two different universes.

Except in the universe of dreams. Here, they were equals. Matched. Or at least, they could be if her imagination cooperated.

"So you think I'm beautiful?" she asked.

The hungry look in his gray eyes tightened her nipples to hard peaks. "I have eyes, don't I?"

"What else have you got?"

This time, her sassiness spawned a thick, hard reward as he tossed aside the sheet and proudly revealed his erection. "I have what you need."

"Dicks are a dime a dozen," she said, even if the unfettered sight of him caused an intense throb to pulse between her legs. "I want more."

"You can have more. You can have whatever you want. Just tell me."

Even with words of surrender, Dream Bas spoke with utter power and fortitude. Had she been awake and facing the real man, she would have believed him in a heartbeat. So why not give in while ensconced in the safety of la-la land?

"Why don't I just show you?"

She climbed into the bed, straddling her lover as if she had no inhibitions, no past hurts, no list of reasons why she couldn't tell a man what she wanted and expect to have each and every wish fulfilled. Her former life didn't exist here, in the safety of this imaginary bed, with this imaginary man—the world-famous venture capitalist whom, in reality, she'd never dare pursue.

The minute her sex met his, moisture seeped from her

flesh. The rapid pulse of unexplored need shot fire through her every nerve ending. He groaned, grabbed her hips with hard hands, then splayed his fingers on her buttocks and pressed her even closer.

She looked down, but didn't have to voice what she wanted him to do. He flicked his stiff tongue across her tight nipples until she cooed with pleasure. One moment, his mouth surrounded her breasts, suckling and laving her to sweet delirium. The next, she was on her belly while he kissed every inch across her shoulders, then down her spine. In a red flash of light, she was on her back, her knees spread, his lips poised just above her sex, his hot breath teasing her dark, moist curls.

"I want to taste you, Michaela."

She swallowed her response. Even in the dream, she didn't know what to say. *Please* sounded so desperate, even if desperation described precisely what she felt.

"You're so hot," he added.

"Hot for you," she answered.

But before she could feel his mouth against her mons, Bas was back on the bed, reclining on the pillows, gently tugging her hands forward, luring her to climb atop him as she had before—only this time, to take him inside her.

"I can't wait any longer," he claimed, his voice hoarse, needful.

"Why wait?"

She shifted, then shouted when his hard shaft slipped inside her with liquid ease. She tried to feel him—all of him—but the sensation was, at the same instant, intense and elusive. There, but not there. Real, but not real. Still, it was real enough that when she moved, just once, she orgasmed with keen intensity.

She cried out, maybe even screamed. She tossed her head back and milked every sensation she could capture from his body into hers. In the next instant, she woke. Her eyes flashed open briefly, but the warm sheets and the phantom scent of Bas's cologne quickly lured her back to sleep.

Only this time, a contented smile curved her lips.

2

Bas paused outside Michaela's room. Was that a moan he'd heard? He glanced at his watch—2:00 a.m. Was she asleep? He should have gone to bed a long time ago, as she had. After they'd returned from dropping Danielle off, having eaten dinner in the back seat of his limousine of all places, she'd disappeared into her room with a breezy good-night. He'd allowed Vic to serve him a cognac, but the ache of Michaela's absence had instantly struck him. He'd been with her for less than twelve hours, but she'd stolen into his psyche like a thief. And though he'd barely slept in the past three days, he knew that once he did, she would haunt his dreams.

He blamed Danielle, of course. In the short conversation they'd exchanged upon their reunion, she'd sufficiently lured and baited him with carefully chosen details about her friend. And true to her genetic makeup, Danielle had worked the pitch like a pro. And because she was his little sister—and would be no matter what trouble she found herself in—he'd fallen for her presentation hook, line and sinker.

First, she'd detailed the journey from her frustration with their parents to her life on the streets. She'd been brutally honest in her descriptions of her drug addiction. Then she'd described how their parents had at first ignored her problems, then downplayed them. Finally, she'd revealed Michaela's role in her redemption. How the older, more experienced runaway had chased off the pimps, found them a place to live, showed her the ropes of free medical care and shelters—and even taken a job every so often so they could eat decent food.

Danielle added that Michaela could have found a real job with a real apartment and real independence at any time, but Danielle's addictions had kept them chained to the streets. Michaela had promised she wouldn't abandon her—no matter how low she drifted—not until Danielle had the help she needed.

Stripped of Danielle's melodramatic presentation, the truth remained, hard and black for Bas to ponder. Danielle owed Michaela her life, and the least he could do was ensure that she had a few weeks of pampering before she started her new life back in Chicago. *Pampering.* That was the exact word his sister had first used. So innocent and unassuming—practically innocuous in his world of luxury and overindulgence.

And then, after she had him sufficiently ensnared, she'd launched her final sortie.

"Make her fantasies come true, Bastian," she asked, climbing beneath the covers of her bed after her frantic pacing had finally worn her down to exhaustion.

"Pardon me?" he'd asked.

Danielle had snuggled into the plush pillows, her paleness offset by the rich ivory comforter and amber-shaded lamp. "Micki's had it rough. She's been away from her family for ten years, until just a few weeks ago. But instead of sticking around Chicago and making a life for herself, she rode a bus to Michigan, faced off with Mom and Dad, tracked you down, then jetted off with me to make sure I arrived safely. I can't bear to think of her going back now, not without having something special to remember."

Bas had dropped his guard, falling into his sister's trap

like a junior broker on his first day out of Wharton. "I'll make sure she has a luxurious few days in the city before she returns."

Danielle shook her head. "Not good enough. Paris is great, but wandering around looking at old paintings and crumbling cathedrals isn't what I had in mind. I want more for Micki."

"There's an excellent spa not far from here...."

Danielle had blown out an exasperated breath. "A spa? There are spas everywhere. Think bigger, Bastian. She's not a kid. Her dreams are life-size. And she'll need a real man to make them come true."

She'd been barely more specific than that, mentioning he should add a little more black to his wardrobe before he made her friend an offer she couldn't refuse. She'd talked about a princess and a lord. Then, Danielle had thrown out some vague comment about a book of fantasies Micki's twin had given her. Immediately after, she'd feigned sleepiness so he'd leave her to nap. When he'd laid his hand on the doorknob, she'd pulled out her final ace.

"Promise me, Bastian," she whispered, again using the name no one ever called him but her. "Do this one thing for me, so I can go into rehab without feeling guilt for what I've put her through. Promise me. Promise you'll make Micki's fantasies come true."

If he'd ever doubted, Sebastian Stone knew at that moment that he did indeed possess a capacity for love. The stone casings of his heart cracked in his chest. He'd neglected his sister for too long. Now, for Danielle, he'd do anything. She was his only real family—the only person who shared his blood and who shared the pain of their cold and loveless upbringing.

He'd clutched at his chest, pressing the air from his lungs in order to speak. "I promise, Danielle."

Now, through the door that had been across from Danielle's in the suite, he heard another moan, higher pitched than before, just the right tone to slip beneath his jacket and make him shiver.

Michaela.

He couldn't deny how she intrigued him. His mind questioned why she had abandoned her family for poverty and desperation. His body reacted instinctively to her generous curves and rough-hewn beauty. The idea of pleasing her appealed to him on many levels. He'd been so bored lately with women and lust, any woman who generated this much interest from him deserved at least one night of fantasies come true—sexual or otherwise.

He gripped the latch on her door, assuring himself that he only wished to ensure her comfort before he retired for the night. The bedside lamp still burned brightly beside her, throwing golden light across her bed. A half dozen pillows buoyed her head and shoulders. Her ink-black hair with fading slashes of blue gleamed against the white sheets and streaked across her strangely flushed cheeks.

And a red book lay open against her chest.

The mysterious book of fantasies?

Bas padded quietly across the room. The red leather book had no title, so he suspected it was a diary of some sort. Had she committed her fantasies to a journal? And if so, did Danielle expect him to steal a peek in secret, or would bold, brash Michaela share her most private wants willingly?

He flipped the switch on the lamp, but the moment the room crashed into darkness, she groaned again. Only this time, this close up, Bas recognized the pleasured sound. He adjusted the lamp to a dim setting, illuminating her just enough so he could watch her move, tossing beneath her sheets. The covers slipped, revealing her threadbare T-shirt and the tightly puckered nipples underneath.

"More," she moaned.

Bas arched a brow, felt a wave of heat creep between his skin and his suit.

She turned again. The book slipped and would have crashed to the floor if not for his quick reflexes. He held the first page to the light.

Sexcapades?

Not a diary, but an instruction manual for adventurous lovers seeking new ways to enjoy their sexuality. He noted the copyright date and publisher, surprised that a legitimate company such as the one listed there would distribute something so lurid. And yet, he couldn't deny his curiosity. He flipped through the pages. Most were missing, torn from the perforations. The ones that remained in the book had been broken open through the glued seals.

The titles were provocative, the instructions within downright erotic.

But, apparently, not as erotic as the dream Michaela was having.

He couldn't help but watch as her hands moved beneath the covers. He watched as she touched herself. He listened raptly as she cooed and groaned while her hands subconsciously explored her erogenous zones. Her neck. Her breasts. Lower. His fingers and palms ached to touch her, but he fisted his hands and stepped back.

What was he, some sort of sick voyeur?

No, just a man fascinated by her vulnerable sexuality.

He turned and stalked toward the door, but she cried out, stopping him in his tracks. He couldn't resist turning, watching as her knees parted beneath the sheets, as her hips bucked. He closed his eyes, wondering if she'd dipped her fingers inside to pump herself to orgasm, or if a man existed in her dream, driving her to maddening pleasure.

With the final cry, her eyes flashed open. Bas's breath caught and he glanced aside, unable for the first time in recent memory to form a quick explanation for his behavior. By the time he turned back, she'd curled onto her side, a sated smile on her sleeping face.

She hadn't seen him. Hadn't known he'd watched. But he had, and the image and sound of her orgasm echoed in his mind. He was rock hard, short of breath. And now that he knew the brazen sensuality of this woman while asleep, he knew he could never deny himself the thrill of bringing her such delight in the light of day.

He returned to her side one last time, dousing the lamp and returning the *Sexcapades* book to the enviable place near her belly. He didn't know why his sister deemed him worthy of such a reward for his inattentive behavior, but he decided then and there that if he could make Michaela's fantasies came true, *he'd* be the one to have received a gift.

MICKI STIRRED, not quite sure what had lured her out of her deep, dream-filled sleep. Confused by the dark room, she fought the dryness coating her eyes. She didn't have shades in the Division Street walk-up she shared with Danielle. Why was it still so dark? And where were the trains? The "L" rattled past her window every hour on the hour, except in the mornings when the heavier commuter traffic shook her windows every fifteen minutes, forcing her to wake up and start her day whether she wanted to or not. And yet this morning, her muscles melted into her bones with complete relaxation, as if she'd slumbered for days.

When she grabbed the silky coverlet cocooning her in luxuriant warmth, she remembered. She wasn't in Chicago anymore. Like Dorothy, she'd traveled on a whirlwind somewhere over the rainbow. A delicious dream, brimming with fantasies and triumphs, skirted the edges of her memory. She shifted her legs, and when a moistness in her panties kissed her intimately, she remembered even more. While asleep, she'd made hot kinky love to the most powerful man in Oz.

When she sat up against the cascade of down pillows perched against the carved headboard, she spotted that wonderful wizard sitting in a high-backed chair at the foot of her bed. Watching her sleep? Watching her wake.

She flipped on a lamp, casting a soft, golden glow over the room that barely made her blink.

"Good morning."

Sebastian's throaty voice rolled over her like another layer of silk, capturing her response. She managed to glance beneath the covers, relieved to find herself dressed, at least, in her ratty Cubs T-shirt. Still, Micki had a habit of responding to pure exhaustion by tearing off her clothes and climbing beneath the covers naked. And after her dream, she wondered how the covers remained on the top of the bed at all. She could have sworn she'd kicked them to the floor.

"What are you doing in here?" she asked.

"My jet is waiting for us at the airport. Consider me your wake-up call."

"You were watching me sleep."

"Guilty as charged," he responded, without the least hint of apology in his steely gaze. "You're a restless sleeper."

She shivered. Just what had he seen? Had her erotic dream occurred hours ago or moments? "And you're scary. Danielle should have warned me her brother was some sort of freakin' Peeping Tom."

"Danielle wouldn't know, would she?"

Micki yanked the sheet tighter at his dire tone—until one corner of his mouth lifted. A smile? Not exactly. Amusement? Absolutely.

"Nice," she commented, dropping the sheet all together. "I'm trapped in a room with a guy who has a warped sense of humor."

From his surprised expression, she wondered if people considered him to have any sense of humor at all. "You have nothing to fear from me, Michaela. You saved my sister's life. I owe you."

"Yeah, well, I take tens and twenties," she quipped, turning to beat a little more softness into the pillow behind her.

Sebastian slowly shook his head. "That's not what I heard."

She narrowed her gaze, trying to read meaning into his inscrutable smile. Was it a smile this time? Really? More like a nearly imperceptible curve on lips centered within a square mustache and beard, both cropped short and expertly trimmed. Everything about the man denoted mystery. From his dark hair to his smoky eyes, Sebastian Stone's face revealed nothing more than he wished to. Even his clothes explored the spectrum from dark gray to inky black—his shirt, buttoned to the neck but without a tie, to his expertly tailored jacket and his equally perfect pants.

A man in black.

Her words, spoken just yesterday on the plane as a way to amuse and distract Danielle, rushed back to haunt her.

My most secret fantasy all starts when a man, wearing black, lures me to his posh castle on a high, perilous cliff....

She swallowed deeply. She'd thought Sebastian Stone was the perfect fantasy man—when relegated and kept in the realm of her fantasies. But he fit the bill in the real world, too. Too bad she couldn't think of a way to meld the two. Or could she? She glanced around the covers, but didn't move. Where was that book?

"Did you say the plane was waiting?" she asked, diverting his attention while she pawed beneath the sheets.

"Yes, Victor has everything prepared." He glanced at his watch. "We should leave here in no less than twenty minutes. Can you be ready by then?"

Micki could be ready in ten, but that didn't concern her.

"Where are we going?" she asked.

Again, that barely-there hint of a smile teased within the shadows of his mustache and beard. "That depends entirely on you." He stood, and with nonchalant grace, smoothed any wrinkles that dared creep onto his slacks. "Perhaps you should consult your…reading material."

He gestured toward her lap, where the red leather book her sister had forced into her possession nestled in the golden comforter. So that's where the dream had come from. The night before, she'd slipped into her bedroom, expecting to be exhausted after the flight from the States and the whirlwind trip to the facility now caring for Danielle. Then they'd zipped around Paris, grabbed dinner, completed a spontaneous tour of the City of Lights from the back seat of Bas's limousine, with Vic as the guide. The minute they'd returned to the hotel, Micki had disappeared into her room, unwilling to spend one more minute trying to ignore Bas's potent male power and unfathomable grin.

And yet, after all the excitement and travel and emotion, Micki couldn't sleep. Instead, she'd snuggled in bed with the book her sister had given her, cracking open the sealed invitations for fantasy sex without dislodging them from the bindings. The naughty scenarios she'd found inside ranged from the ridiculous to the fascinating, the tame to the torrid.

And as much as she'd hate to admit it to her sister, Micki

had been utterly engrossed. Before this morning, she couldn't have imagined herself in any of the settings or situations detailed in the book. First of all, she had no lover nor any prospects. Second, the fantasy role-play had reminded her way too much of Jazz.

Jazz. Jazz Jericho. God, hadn't she forbidden herself to think of that loser? Ever?

With practiced skill, she banished the jerk from her mind—then realized, while staring at Sebastian, that she might have gone one step too far. When she'd stopped thinking about Jericho, she'd stopped thinking about sex. She'd banished the natural act from her life all on account of one charming, manipulative and scheming creep. Jazz Jericho, part-time hustler, full-time prick, had ripped all the sweetness out of sex for her.

But a refined power broker like Sebastian Stone? He could be the one to put it back.

Bas touched the corner of the book, then moved to flip open the cover. Micki fought the urge to snatch the book away and hide it beneath the sheets, but what would be the point? He already knew it was there…and from the guarded look in his eyes, he knew what it said, too.

"Did you peek?" she asked.

"*Sexcapades,* is it?"

She expected mockery in his tone, but heard none. The question was matter-of-fact, yet not entirely without emotion—and not entirely without a subtle admission that he had indeed glanced inside the red leather covers. She expected a class-act guy like him to find the book frivolous. Common. But did she really spy keen interest in his gaze?

"Yeah, that's it," she answered. "Heard of it?"

He chuckled. "Not until yesterday. Danielle mentioned that you had a book of fantasies, but she didn't tell me the title."

Boy, her friend had a big mouth. "What else did Danielle tell you?"

"Enough to pique my interest."

He fetched the complimentary hotel robe from a chair beside her bed, then laid it out beside her. "But I should make one thing clear from this point. It's not what Danielle told me about you...or the book...that fascinates me, Michaela. It's what she asked of me." He paced alongside the window, his manner more a casual stroll than a nervous tick. He hooked his hands behind his back, as if pondering some great mystery. "More specifically, it's the fact that I'm incredibly charmed by my sister's request in regards to you. Common sense tells me that I should at least be wary. Possibly insulted. But I'm neither. I'm just...intrigued."

Oh, God. Micki was going to regret the question she was about to ask. Danielle could dream up some incredibly wacky schemes, if given the right incentive.

Still, she had to know.

"What did she ask you for?"

Sebastian turned, his gaze so intense that Micki checked one more time to make sure she was dressed. His stare seemed to seep right through the one-thousand-count threads of the comforter, beyond the tattered-thin material of her shirt. Her nipples peaked in instantaneous response and a subtle warmth pooled in her belly. And he was still at least two feet away.

But the distance didn't last. He sat on the bed beside her again, his eyes trained on hers.

"An amazingly simple request. And one I think we'll both thoroughly enjoy."

She didn't think he'd be so bold as to touch her, but the moment he did, she wondered how she could be so wrong. His index finger snaked up her arm from her wrist to her shoulder, fingering the bare flesh just beneath the sleeve of her T-shirt. And since retreating when under assault—even this type of subtle sensual attack—wasn't in her nature, Micki willed herself to remain perfectly still.

On the outside. Deep within, electric impulses ricocheted from nerve ending to nerve ending, coloring the insides of her eyelids with flashes of white light. His scent taunted her with essences she couldn't precisely name—exotic spices and rare oils—enhancing her sensory reaction to everything he said, every move he made.

"I can't wait to hear what it is," she managed, her voice a raspy echo of fear and need and determination.

"Then, I won't make you wait."

Since the moment he'd spoken his first cultured hello, Micki had noted that Sebastian's natural tone lingered just above a whisper. But now, his voice skimmed the depths of his throat, heavy with intentions she couldn't possibly predict.

"My sister wants me to make your fantasies come true."

3

"AND I INTEND TO DO just that, Michaela, starting right now."

"She wouldn't have asked you something so private," Micki insisted, but Bas saw the doubt in her eyes. It was the same uncertainty he exploited daily in his business dealings. Normally, he craved the moment when he recognized this exact look in his opponent's gaze, but on his sister's best friend and savior, the expression made him pause.

He stepped away from the bed. The loss of contact between his hand and her soft skin deepened his scowl. "I'm afraid she would."

"It's the drugs," Micki said quickly, scrambling out of the bed, the hotel robe clutched tightly in her hand. "She sometimes imagines some pretty wild things."

"You told me yourself she's been clean for nearly two weeks," he pointed out, not entirely unamused by Michaela's discomfort. Just yesterday, he'd guessed that nothing would ruffle her tough-girl persona. She'd stepped into the five-star hotel on tattered, high-heeled boots looking and acting like she owned the place. She'd discussed Danielle's care with the hospital administrator as if she too possessed multiple degrees from the finest universities in Europe. And even when she insisted Vic pull their limousine to the curb so they could grab a dinner of crepes and souvlaki from a street vendor, she'd displayed a quirky style embedded in a foundation of perfect manners.

She was a contradiction. A puzzle. A challenge. And Bas Stone couldn't resist a challenge any more than Michaela Carmichael could resist speaking her mind.

"Yeah, well, apparently she either sneaked out and grabbed a hit while we weren't looking or hallucinogens last longer in the bloodstream than I thought."

"She wasn't taking hallucinogens," Bas reminded her.

"What do you know? Before yesterday, you hadn't spoken to her since before the new millennium."

Touché, he thought, though she wasn't one hundred percent accurate. Bas had chatted with his sister just at Christmas. He'd been somewhere over Sydney, making his annual holiday phone call from his cellular phone while en route to closing a deal. What he hadn't known at the time was that Danielle had only just arrived home that afternoon, after a year-long disappearance, because she'd run out of money. Shortly after their conversation, she'd escaped the house in Lansing, her expensive presents in tow, hocked them at a nearby pawnshop, then returned to her life on the streets.

But now, thanks to Michaela, Danielle had made a bold step toward recovery. The doctors had assured both of them that Danielle's initial psychological evaluation seemed promising, though, naturally, no one offered guarantees. No one but Bas, that was. He'd promised his sister that he'd make Michaela Carmichael's fantasies come to life and he intended to follow through.

"Thanks to my sister, I now know a great deal. About her. And about you. I chose this attire in honor of your fantasy, Michaela," he said, indicating his black shirt, slacks and jacket with an understated sweep of his hand. "Do you want me to elaborate or do you remember the details yourself?"

She tied the sash on the robe with a curse. "Thanks, but

I'll pass. Who knows what nonsense Danielle has filled your head with? Look, Mr. Stone, I'm not going to deny that you're one smart-dressed hottie. Takes one hell of a confident man to wear Versace in the daytime and not look like Vlad the Impaler, but I'm not looking for someone to make my fantasies come true. As soon I get back to Chicago, I'll find a way to do that on my own, thank you very much."

"I understand you have a job waiting for you."

"You understand correctly."

"A bartender position at a club called Dixie Landings."

"Yes, and my boss expects me there very soon."

"A week, I believe is what Mr. Thomas told me."

She snagged a croissant from the room service tray he'd wheeled into her room just before she'd awoken. "You spoke to Shaw?"

"Interesting man, this Shaw Thomas. Sounds like a good, old-fashioned Southern boy, yet he appreciates the art of the deal."

Michaela stalked toward him, waving the curved pastry like a weapon. "What deal? What did you do?"

Bas allowed himself a small grin, knowing he could have done so much more than he had. Bas had thought of giving Michaela the club as a present. Unfortunately, Shaw Thomas hadn't seemed like the type of man who would sell his business on a whim, no matter the price. Besides, Micki wouldn't know what to do with the cash-cow operation and would likely run it into the ground within a month. Bas was a generous man, but he couldn't stand to see a lucrative venture go to waste.

"I simply verified that Mr. Shaw did not expect you to begin your employment at his club until next week. That gives me six full days to fulfill my promise to my sister. I suggest you get dressed first." He nodded toward the armoire in the corner where he'd ordered the concierge to hang the clothes Vic had ordered for her. "Unless you have other ideas of how we should spend our morning?"

He eyed the bed, and as he expected, she answered his innuendo by throwing the croissant directly at his face. Luckily, Bas had been blessed with quick reflexes.

"Your sister didn't tell me you were a chauvinistic pig."

"As you pointed out, we haven't been the closest of siblings." This time, Bas didn't fight his grin, infuriating her until her blue eyes flashed with pure rage.

"Listen, here, Buster. Don't for one minute think that I'm dependent on you to get out of this foreign wonderland. I survived ten years on the Chicago streets relatively unscathed. I can sure as hell ditch you right this minute and find my way back to the States on my own!"

"You have no money," he pointed out, doubtful that detail would make any difference.

"I never have any money, so that's not even a consideration."

"No, but my sister asked you to stay with me, didn't she?"

Michaela opened her mouth, briefly, before snapping her pouty pink lips shut.

"My sister might have a problem with drugs, but she apparently is a clearheaded judge of character and an amazing manipulator. She knows I'm a man of my word, so she made me promise to make your fantasies come to life. I got the impression she convinced you to make a similar pact."

Michaela didn't speak, but her eyes verified his suspicion. After he'd had time to consider his promise to his sister, he'd taken her aside at the clinic and questioned whether her friend would even want him to make fantasies came true. Danielle assured him that he shouldn't worry.

The glint in Danielle's red-rimmed eyes had been enough to convince him that his sister had inherited more of his devilish traits than he'd first guessed. She'd had a plan up her sleeve all along, and apparently both he and Michaela had fallen into the trap.

"I only promised her that I'd hang out with you for a while. Get to know you. Report back about what kind of man you were. If you could really be trusted not to screw with her mind the way your parents do."

Bas nodded, his chest tight. Yes, his parents. Dorothy and William Stone had made some serious parenting mistakes in his upbringing, but none that had sent him into a downward spiral of drugs, prostitution and homelessness. They'd coddled him, protected him, had done everything in their power to ensure that their only son with the genius IQ followed a straight and narrow path to financial success. And he had. But at the expense of a loving family life, of friends and school pals.

Of course, now he had Vic. He often wondered how he'd acquired such a good and loyal friend, but he didn't delve too deeply into finding the answer. Some things were better left unexplained.

Unlike his attraction to Michaela. Yes, she was beautiful and smart and fiery—but to note that she "wasn't his type" constituted an understatement of global proportions. Still, he couldn't turn down the opportunity to spend time with her and indulge whatever fantasies she possessed—his sister had been stingy with that information beyond the color of his clothes and the existence of the book.

"I can assure you that I have nothing in common with my parents."

She crossed her arms over her chest. "We'll see, won't we?"

"Yes, I suppose we will. Now, do you prefer to stay

here in Paris, or shall we get further acquainted during our return flight to the States?''

Her gaze darted toward the drawn curtains. For an instant, he thought he spied a brief flash of longing in her eyes, but the expression disappeared before he could be sure.

''I don't care,'' she said, rolling her shoulder in a nonchalant shrug. ''Whatever you want to do.''

Bas chuckled, strolling to the window and tugging the curtains aside. Across the tops of emerald green trees, the sun gleamed gloriously off the roof of the Grand Palais. The Eiffel Tower rose proudly just to the left and the busy Place de la Concorde bustled beneath them.

''You're sure about that? This is Paris, after all. City of Dreams.''

She scowled. ''City of Lights. I may have been homeless, but I'm not entirely uneducated.''

''If I thought you were before we met with the hospital administrator yesterday, I don't anymore. You have a keen mind. One that couldn't possibly miss the rare opportunity we each have, right here. Right now.''

When her doubtful look blossomed with the glow of interest, Bas felt his blood surge with the truest, most concentrated form of desire he'd experienced in some time—perhaps in his entire life. Not only was she bold and beautiful, but Michaela Carmichael hardly hesitated when chance and prospect knocked on her door. She joined him beside the thick-planed glass, but gave the scene only the most cursory glance.

''You talking about Paris, or about us?'' she asked.

''Both, though I've seen Paris.''

''You haven't seen it with me.''

''This is true. I've no doubt you could shed new light on the city.''

She rewarded his compliment with a tiny quirk of a smile.

"I don't see the point of hanging around though. We can't see or contact Danielle for a while, right?"

"Thirty days, then we'll be allowed a phone call. A visit after two more weeks. But only if she abides by all the rules and makes progress in her recovery."

Michaela nodded. "And you'll make sure I can talk to her when the time comes?" she asked.

He reached into his jacket and extracted the slim packet Vic had put together on his orders this morning. "Inside, you'll find a round trip ticket from Chicago to Paris, a generously charged long-distance calling card, the name, address and phone number of the clinic, a copy of the letter I gave to the doctors authorizing you to speak with my sister when they allow it and a hotel voucher for a small inn fifteen minutes away from the rehabilitation center." He extended the envelope toward her, but she hesitated.

"This is mine? Now? No strings attached?"

Yes, Bas thought with a smile. With a heavy dose of formal education and maybe a tad more spit and polish, Michaela Carmichael had the makings of a sharp business-woman.

"No strings. Look it over. You'll see I'm telling you the truth."

She did so, riffling through the papers twice before she dashed to the armoire and opened her backpack, then stuffed the papers between the pages of a red leather book. Ah, the book. He was inherently glad he'd peeked inside, though he'd be damned if he'd admit it aloud. Inside, Michaela's secret fantasies lived, untapped. Untried. But not for long. Yes, many of the fantasies had been ripped from the book, but Danielle had explained that Michaela had received the book after a long list of women had stolen their desires from between the red leather covers.

"So, what will it be, Michaela? Paris or back to the States?"

"Paris is tempting, but since I already have a ticket to come back whenever the heck I want, let's bail. I'm dying for a cheeseburger."

A smile took over his face before Bas could tamp it down. "I know the perfect place."

He walked toward the door, wondering about nothing more significant than pinpointing the last time he'd indulged in American fast food and if he still liked his onions grilled rather than raw. Such a simple thought, but one that suddenly took on great importance.

"Hey!"

He turned back to find Michaela strolling toward the bathroom, her robe discarded, her hair fluffed by fingers intent on torturing him with glossy strands mussed in sexy disarray. "For the record, my fantasies entail a hell of a lot more than a cheeseburger with a handsome guy in a dark suit."

He grinned and gave her a slight bow. "I'm counting on that, Michaela. More than even you could guess."

MICKI COULDN'T HELP but stare. As of this moment, she'd been on exactly two airplanes in her entire life and the experiences couldn't have been any more different. She'd thought first class on the international flight had been fancy, but commercial airlines had nothing on Bas Stone and his private jet.

"Anything I can get you, Ms. Carmichael?"

Looking like a prizefighter stuffed into a pilot uniform, Victor Campisi rounded the hand-carved bar that stretched down a generous portion of the aircraft. At least one or two private rooms existed in the back, and the other wall sported a comfortable collection of couches, plush chairs and glossy tables. "We have just about everything you might want."

Micki bit the side of her mouth to keep her grin in check. "Got a cheeseburger?"

Vic's smiled, apparently in on the joke. "Impatient, aren't you?"

"Actually, no. But I am kind of hungry." And she was wondering just exactly where "the perfect place" for a cheeseburger might be.

Vic nodded, then somehow managed to dip his bulky frame beneath the bar and then emerge with a sterling tray sparkling with assorted goodies. He mixed her a drink, then presented the snacks with great flourish, totally wowing her with his refined mannerisms.

"A specialty relish tray, my lady. A collection of various delicacies that I thought would be a nice prelude to a burger and fries. Should be enough to tide you over until take-off."

Micki eyed the offering with interest, but found it hard to believe Bas Stone had a thing for pickles.

"What is this?"

Vic licked his lips. "These bread-and-butter chips are from a country store just outside of Nashville. The owner cans them herself. This is pickled watermelon rind, jarred at a small factory on the Louisiana border. This raclette cheese is from the village we visited yesterday. Oh, and these grapes were flown in from Italy just this morning. Sweetest things you ever tasted."

Pickles, cheese and fruit, Micki concluded, that somehow managed to be elegant, eclectic and homey all at the same time. She reached toward the watermelon rind, intrigued by the glossy green color, then stopped when she heard Bas's voice from the cockpit.

"Patch me through," he ordered.

Vic ignored him, so Micki guessed Bas was either on the phone or using the plane's radio.

"Which of these is Mr. Stone's favorite?"

Vic narrowed his gaze. "Don't know." His smile stretched the scar that extended across his chin. "These are my favorites."

He wiggled his dark, bushy eyebrows and Micki laughed, then accepted the cocktail fork he handed her and skewered the rind. Sweet and sour flavors exploded on her tongue, soothed by a crunchy but soft texture that was surprisingly good.

"That's awesome," she concluded. "Thanks."

Vic gave her a humble nod. "Most people go for the pickles or the cheese. They are more familiar. You went for the most unusual item on the tray."

Micki rolled her eyes. "It wasn't exactly octopus legs or anything."

Vic licked his lips. "I had some awesome octopus in Spain last summer. Served on a bed of rice in its own ink. Amazing."

Micki didn't hide her disgust, and put back the black olive she'd just chosen. "That's disgusting, Vic."

Deep thought drove lines into Vic's face, which Micki noticed would have been incredibly handsome if not for the scars and crooked nose. Vic had been around the block. And for that, he won her instant respect.

"Sounds gross, doesn't it? But it really was good. I bet you'd be the first one to take a taste."

"Maybe if I hadn't known what it was," she answered, doubtful. Still, Micki had been known to scarf down all kinds of odd meals, just to have something in her stomach.

Octopus probably wouldn't be so bad, not if so many people considered it a delicacy.

"You're an adventurous woman. That's good."

Micki scoffed. Usually, her adventuresome attitude toward food could be directly attributed to extreme hunger. Her adventuresome attitude toward the rest of her life usually ended with her in deep trouble. "Good for who? The darkest moments of my life can all be traced back to my need for excitement."

With a shrug, Vic invited her from the bar to the sitting area, then placed the relish tray on the table across from her plush seat, threw down a cocktail napkin and served her drink. "Probably the brightest moments, too, if you take a minute to think it over."

"What are you, a butler slash pilot slash shrink?"

His grin was his only response. "That's a vanilla Coke. I hope you like them."

Micki almost launched herself out of her chair. She loved vanilla Cokes. Vanilla Cokes were her favorite drink in the entire universe. She grabbed the straw and lifted the drink to the light, stirring the dark liquid until she saw the telltale signs of the sugary vanilla syrup swirling in the carbonated cola.

"How'd you…?"

But Vic had already disappeared beyond the doors that separated the main cabin from the cockpit. In the moment the door was open, she heard Bas's voice soften to a whisper, raising the hairs on the back of her neck. Glancing at the drink, she waylaid her anticipated first sip long enough to follow the instincts she'd learned a long time ago not to ignore.

Bas's voice hadn't raised her hackles because of the throaty, sexy tone. Something was wrong. Something he didn't want her to know about.

The door that separated the cockpit from the cabin on this custom-built aircraft was no thicker than an inch. The reverberation of Bas's anger stabbed through the metal and straight into her spine.

"I won't be delayed."

He must have flipped the switch to allow Vic to listen to the other end of the conversation.

"I'm sorry, Monsieur Stone, but the airport cannot ignore such a threat. We order you again—evacuate the aircraft. Immediately."

4

MICKI DIDN'T BOTHER PRETENDING she hadn't heard. Someone had threatened the plane? They could die right here, right now? The concept seemed too large, too overwhelming, so she whittled it down to the basic message.

Get out.

Bas stormed from the cockpit, nearly pinning her with the door. He snatched her wrist and tugged her through the cabin without explanation. If he'd been annoyed at her obvious eavesdropping, he wasn't going to waste time chastising her now.

"Grab your bag. There will be a delay before takeoff."

Micki followed him, slinging her bag over her shoulder while he worked on opening the door. His calm, polite attitude amazed her. Man, once those manners were inbred so deeply, she figured they'd never shake free. From the cockpit, however, she heard Vic cursing a blue streak as he powered down the engines.

While Bas worked the lock, Micki glanced at the drink she hadn't touched, then decided she had nothing better to do while she waited for him to orchestrate their escape from whatever they were escaping from. She grabbed her glass and took a long, sweet slurp. The flavors danced on her tongue, then slid down her throat like an icy memory of childhood. If she was going to die on this plane before it even left the ground, the least she could do was grab one last shot of comfort. Only recently she'd learned that the fortification she used to obtain with alcohol could be substituted with a hearty dose of nostalgia.

She rushed to the door just as Bas lowered the retractable stairs. In the distance, a black car sped toward them, tiny flags flapping on either side of the windshield. Other than knowing the insignia was neither French nor American, Micki had no idea which country owned the sleek black sedan and why it was speeding to the rescue like a bat out of hell.

Bas escorted her to the bottom of the stairs, then handed her over to the limo driver, a giant of a man even broader and bulkier than Vic. He spoke a few words in some Slavic tongue Micki didn't recognize and Bas answered with equal speed and diction. She guessed she should have argued or protested or at least asked what the hell was going on. But Micki had learned that silence was often her best defense, particularly when Bas, a man she suspected didn't know the definition of fear, now had the emotion gleaming ever so subtly in his grayish-green eyes.

She slid into the back seat. Her backpack slammed against her shoulder, shocking her system with pain. Yet when the driver moved to shift the car into gear, she hurdled herself halfway through the open divider window to stop him and shouted, "No! Wait."

"Mne prikazano vas ot suida u visti."

Micki cursed. Why couldn't the guy speak Spanish? She had a working knowledge of Spanish. Hell, she could say a few key phrases in Creole, Korean and Cabrini Green jive. But this? She had no clue. So she kept it simple.

"No!"

At her command, the car remained in place. In a heartbeat, she climbed completely through the window to the front passenger seat and by the time she'd twisted out of her somersault and impaled the driver with her most determined look, she knew she'd won his admiration. Or at least, his compliance. He let loose another string of unintelligible words, but he didn't move. He did, however, shove her to the floor with his hand and an insistent succession of words.

Oh, God. Was the plane going to blow?

She peeked through the windshield briefly before Boris pushed her back down, a plea in his hard black eyes. From across the tarmac, a parade of police cars wailed toward them, then halted in a circle around the airplane, an armored truck in the center. The uniformed squad piled out and rushed toward the plane, Bas and Vic waiting for them on the stairs. After a brief interaction with a cop toting a fairly impressive load of firepower, Bas hurried toward the limousine.

As the authorities filed into the plane, Bas opened the front passenger door.

"Why is this car still here?" he asked, tilting his head so he could see her clearly balled beneath the dashboard.

"Because I don't speak German?" she guessed, punctuating her impertinence with what she hoped was a charming smile.

The corner of his mouth quirked, but she wouldn't call his reaction amused. The man was a tough nut, all right.

"Get up, Michaela. As much as I despise retreat, I guess I'll have to ensure your safety myself."

She accepted his proffered hand and, in an instant, she was in the back seat again, this time with Bas beside her. Before he'd even closed the door, the limousine sped away, leaving Vic and the aircraft behind.

"What about Vic?"

"He designed and refurbished the interior of that aircraft himself. He isn't about to let some overzealous French policemen tear it apart in search of a threat that likely doesn't exist."

He sat forward and conversed with the driver, who nodded obediently and turned the car sharply to the left.

"It's very rude to speak in a language not everyone understands," Micki said as she slid back into the center of the seat, mimicking something she'd heard her grandmother say once.

"Then you should learn Russian," he answered. "Might save your life some day."

"Do you think you can speak English long enough to clue me in on what the hell is going on?"

Bas peered through the front windshield, then glanced through each of the side views, as well as the rear. "We received a threat to the aircraft. I'm moving you a safe distance away."

"What kind of threat?"

"The kind that causes an unexpected delay."

After the limousine slipped into a dark hangar at the end of an apparently unused runway, Bas relaxed and resumed a calm posture in the seat beside her. He took his cell phone from his pocket and checked the signal while the driver turned the car around, facing the limo toward the opening. In case they had to escape again? In case they'd been pursued?

"Victor will call when it's safe for us to return," Sebastian added.

Though sunlight gleamed inside the hangar from the open bay doors behind them, the interior of the car was dim. Tinted windows filtered out most of Micki's view, but Bas flicked on a light above what appeared to be a fully stocked wet bar and continued to punch numbers into his cell.

The seats weren't leather, she noticed, running her hands over a fabric she'd best describe as suede. Crystal glasses twinkled from a bar stocked with several different brands of vodka, most sporting what she assumed were Russian labels. The entertainment system installed across from them made the window displays at an electronics store look like factory rejects.

"Whose car is this?"

"The Russian ambassador to France. He took off just a few moments before we received the call, so the tower requested their assistance in ensuring our immediate evacuation from the plane. Luckily, Ambassador Grikov is an acquaintance of mine."

Bas conversed once more with the driver, who said what Micki guessed was, "Yes, sir," and then the Russian exited the car.

Alone, the atmosphere crackled with carefully checked fear and forced intimacy. Micki shifted in her seat, aware of her heightened senses. The soft suede caressed her bare arms. Her mouth still tingled with the sweet and sour flavors of the soda and the crunchy pickled watermelon. Her ears registered the hollow echo of the limousine's engine in the cavernous hangar, the gentle hiss of the air conditioner, which blew fingers of coolness across her heated skin. She took a deep breath to calm her rattled nerves, and instantly recognized the error. Bas's cologne, a refined mixture of crisp, yet earthy scents, spiked her awareness. Man, the guy smelled good.

"Does this happen to you a lot?" she asked, forcing a casual tone she knew Bas wouldn't buy for a second.

"Death threats? Depends on your definition of *a lot.*"

"More than once a year?"

"Sometimes."

A terrified laugh exploded from Micki's chest.

"I didn't say that to amuse you," he said.

"No, just to scare the hell out of me. Congratulations."

Bas scooted toward her, snared her hand in his. His grip

was tight, possessive—not comforting, as she'd expected, but intense, like the man himself. "You've no need to be frightened. Your safety is my first priority."

She knew she should have pulled her palm from his grasp, but the feel of his skin, a contrast of hard and soft, was too seductive to deny. His heat pressed against hers, igniting a sizzle that flew up her arm, to her breasts, then deeper. The air in the car thinned, despite the wind blowing out of the air-conditioner vents.

She tried to tug her hand free, but he held her still.

"Finding out who threatened you," she said, hoping to distract him long enough to escape, "and why, should be your first priority."

He glanced down at the pairing of their hands. Did he feel it, too? This attraction between them was strong, undeniable, but couldn't come at a more inconvenient time.

"Of course."

He didn't release her. Electricity continued to shoot to every zone of her body—all from his steady touch.

"And if this has happened before," she continued, "I also think you should probably tell me, since I'm supposed to be hanging out with you for at least as long as it takes to get back to the States. I tend to appreciate knowing when my life is in danger."

He nodded and, with clear reluctance, let her go.

The break allowed her brain to fully engage. "Oh, and Danielle!" she added. "If someone is trying to hurt you then she…"

Bas broke the last contact between them by leaning back into the seat, forcing what distance he could. "Danielle is safe. Make no mistake about that, Michaela. I've arranged not only for her to remain at the clinic, but also for security to ensure that she does not attempt escape. The team watching her is well aware of the previous threats against my life."

"When was the last time you had one?"

"This is the first in nearly eight months."

"And you don't think it's a coincidence that your psycho stalker comes back at the same time your sister returns to your life?"

Bas relaxed his shoulders into the curved seat, but Micki saw that his outward signs of calm were just that—outward signs. With no depth. No substance.

"If someone wished to hurt me by attacking my family, they would have done so by now."

"Yeah, well, maybe they guessed that hurting your parents wouldn't be much skin off your nose," she mused. "And your sweet little sister wasn't home long enough to snatch."

"You have a devious mind, Ms. Carmichael."

"Thank you."

"You'll make a fine stalker someday. I'll have Victor draft a letter of recommendation."

It took a minute, but by the time Micki turned and glared into Bas's intense gaze, she realized he was kidding. In the face of mortal danger, serious and scowling Sebastian Stone had cracked a joke.

"You're an asshole," she concluded.

"I've been called worse."

"Yeah, so have I."

"Then we have more in common than either of us realized."

She decided to leave that one alone. For now. What they had in common amounted to raging hormones. Not that this was a bad thing.

Moistening her lips, she suddenly wished she'd taken the vanilla Coke with her off the plane. She was wicked thirsty, but figured while trapped with Bas in the back seat of his car, she had two drink choices. Vodka or Bas. Either one would supply her with more intoxication than she needed at the moment.

"Care to tell me more about these threats on your life?" she said, pressing further. "My criminal mind may lend additional insight."

Beneath his trimmed mustache, his lips formed a deep frown. "Or you could just decide it might be better for your health to get as far away from me as you can."

"Crossed my mind," she commented, though the prospect of letting some nameless, faceless psycho spoil her potential fun with Sebastian didn't sit right.

"However, I promised my sister I'd see to more than just your safety," he reminded her in a low tone.

"Then tell me about the threats. If I decide to bolt, I'd like to make a fully informed choice."

Bas folded his arms over his chest, his tone even and matter-of-fact. "I receive no less than three threats a year, no more than five. Some are very specific, others quite vague."

"For example?" she prompted.

"Oh, let's see. One said something along the lines of 'Die, Capitalist Pig.' Others are more esoteric, like, 'One day, you'll pay.' Usually, they reach me in Europe, though once in Southeast Asia. There is no pattern. Sometimes the threat comes in the form of a speculative message on my private phone line, other times in the form of e-mail. This one was a fax sent directly to the control tower. Once, this deranged individual, if it is indeed one person, sent a lock of hair to the office of my Italian attorney."

"Your hair?"

He combed his expertly shorn locks with his hand. "It

wasn't human hair. Canine, according to the tests I ordered."

"They sent dog hair?" she asked, shocked. She'd never actually owned a pet herself, but she'd befriended strays while living on the streets. The idea that someone would threaten to harm an animal chilled her blood. "Do you have a dog, because if this wacko killed your pooch, I am *so* out of here."

"I've never owned a dog in my life."

"Not even when you were a kid?"

"Michaela, you'll soon learn that I've never been a kid."

The cell phone tucked in Bas's jacket pocket trilled and he answered instantly. From what she could hear of the conversation, the search of the aircraft wasn't resulting in any potentially explosive discoveries, which, surprisingly, didn't relieve the accelerated pounding of her heart.

"Victor reports that, so far, they've found nothing to indicate the threat was real," Bas told her after disconnecting the call. "We'll wait here until the police give us clearance."

"It was a bomb threat?" she asked, not entirely sure she wanted clarification.

"Of sorts. The message itself was rather vague, but, in this day and age, even vague threats require investigation. Particularly when the person threatened is someone like me."

"Because you've made a lot of enemies?"

He grinned. "Because my status as celebrity businessman, as much as I've tried to cast off that mantle, makes me a target for mentally ill people with delusions of attaining grandeur through violent acts."

"And because you've made a lot of enemies."

"That, too."

She nodded. "Okay, so you've obviously earmarked some of your wealth toward protecting yourself."

"Apparently not as much as I should. That will be remedied so long as you're in my company."

"I don't want a bodyguard," she insisted.

"You do realize that is Victor's primary job?"

"I thought he was your butler. And your pilot."

"He's a jack-of-all-trades, so to speak. Victor Campisi is a former heavyweight Olympic boxer and decorated Army Nightstalker. We met during a rather tense negotiation between an American company I represented and a Saudi sheik who'd hired Vic immediately after Desert Storm. He watches my back and I pay him handsomely for it."

"And he's your friend."

Bas glanced aside. He probably hated admitting that he needed friends as much as admitting he actually had one.

"Yes, he's a friend. I trust him with my life."

"But do you trust him with mine?"

He scooted closer, pressing nothing but his scent against her, whetting her appetite for another taste of the sensation of his skin. Her mind focused so completely on the question of whether or not he'd touch her again, she almost didn't hear him when he said, "I trust *me* with your life. I'm very resourceful."

She met his gaze, which fairly twinkled with confidence.

"And trustworthy?" she asked.

He glanced sideways. "I'm no Boy Scout, but my word is good on several continents."

"Not that you'd ever do business without a written contract."

He shrugged, but when the shoulders moved beneath a three-thousand dollar suit, the movement wasn't as lackadaisical as he might have thought.

Micki allowed herself a moment to imagine Bas in different clothing. Then, in no clothing at all, as she had in her dream. No matter how she sliced it, the man turned her on. And for the life of her, Micki couldn't remember the last time she'd found a man attractive. At least, not while sober. There was Jazz, but she'd been pretty screwed up when she'd fallen into his clutches.

Maybe now she really was ready to explore the aspects of her personal life she'd ignored back when surviving was her daily goal. *Living* was now Micki's primary focus. And with Danielle tucked away in the best rehab clinic money could buy, Micki had no one to worry about but herself. Though, strangely, she worried about Bas, too. He might have become accustomed to death threats, but even after ten years on the street, Micki had never gotten used to violence. The man needed a serious lesson in self-preservation.

"My word is good," he said. "That doesn't mean everyone else's is."

"Oh, and you're humble, too," she quipped. "What a winning combination you have going."

"Humility doesn't make success," he replied.

"Depends on your definition of success."

"How would you define it?"

Micki pursed her lips, suddenly wondering why she was engaging in such a cerebral topic with a man who most certainly could fry her with his mastery of language and advanced thought. Particularly when her blood still thrummed from their mad dash into the dark hangar. Why were they talking at all, anyway? The man had promised to fulfill her fantasies, yet here he was asking her to construct a definition of success instead of seducing her out of her clothes.

She glanced at her backpack, knowing the secret to success was hidden beneath her denim jacket and sink-washed panties. "Success is getting what you want."

"At all costs?"

"Sorry, you're the corporate raider, not me."

"I'm not a corporate raider. I'm a venture capitalist."

Vaguely, she knew there was a difference, but figured he could save that explanation for later. Much later.

"Still, I think true success means that all parties involved are pleased with the outcome," she concluded.

"Win-win, you mean?"

"Absolutely. Take this book, for instance."

With a deep breath to propel her forward, Micki grabbed her backpack, unzipped the pocket and withdrew the book her sister had given her only a few days ago. Good old *Sexcapades.* After sitting on the reception desk at Divine Events, a party-planning business where her twin, Rory, worked, the book had become a little thin. The perforated edges had been incorporated into the design to allow lovers to tear out a secret fantasy to share, but according to her sister, customer after customer at Divine Events had surreptitiously stolen pages to take home with them. After Rory had succumbed to her own curiosity, she'd ended up in love and on the road to marriage.

Micki wasn't looking for anything so life-altering. In the past month, her existence had already done a one-eighty. No, Micki just wanted exactly what Danielle had decided she needed—escape. Fantasy. A chance to be someone else, someone who didn't worry about paychecks or rent payments or grocery bills, at least for a little while.

And since Bas had agreed to fulfill her fantasy, why not go for the gusto?

"You're sure we're safe from your stalker?" she asked.

"One vague threat on my aircraft—with no evidence that any of the threats over the years have been related—hardly justifies the term stalker. But I will take every available measure to ensure your safety. And my own. Not just because of Danielle, either.''

That piqued her interest. She hugged the oversized book to her chest. ''Oh, really?''

Bas slid into her personal space, his cologne so intrinsic that she couldn't differentiate between the cool essences that came from a bottle and the hot muskiness that came from the man. ''I'm a man who gets what he wants, Michaela. And I want you.''

5

AFTER RUNNING THE PADS of her fingers along the sleek casing of the portable fax machine she'd used minutes ago to send the threat, she tapped an ominous tattoo on it with her glossy nails. Wonder how gay Paris was for Sebastian Stone now, with his plane under the scrutiny of the French government? She hoped they tore the custom seats out by the hinges and tossed his eclectic wine collection onto the tarmac. He deserved the discomfort, the fear, that her ominous message had undoubtedly stirred. She needed him to be on guard—alert. Only then, would her plan come together.

The cell phone chirped, a sound she'd programmed in when she'd first bought the device. Every time she received a call, the peaceful birdsong prepared her for the ugliness that undoubtedly spewed from the other end. Investigators failing her. Creditors demanding payment. Her family insisting on her immediate repentance and return. Nothing but disappointment ever greeted her through the phone. She wondered why she bothered answering.

She wondered…until she heard the triumphant chuckle on the other end of the line. "Your plan worked perfectly."

"Tell me his plane is in a million pieces all over the runway at Charles de Gaulle," she insisted.

"Not exactly in pieces, but there are a swarm of police crawling through every nook and cranny."

A surge of power shot through her veins. Finally! In all

these years of threatening, never once had she disturbed Sebastian Stone's world for more than an instant—not with his dog-loyal bodyguard forever at his side. This was a small step, a nuisance, she knew. But the nature of the threat—a bomb on his plane—was only the beginning of her plan to turn Stone's world of order and control into topsy-turvy madness. Only then would she get what she wanted.

"Where is he?"

A pause. "Took off in a dignitary's limousine with some woman. Looked like the friend of the sister."

"The sister is at the clinic?"

"Yes. Very heavily guarded. I don't think anyone could get to her unless we get them in as a patient."

She waved her hand at the phone. "I don't care about her any longer. There are other ways to accomplish my plan. Where's the bodyguard?"

"Still on the plane. Refused to leave. Almost decked the commandant when he ordered the fuselage stripped."

Her heart froze. She'd only been half joking about the plane being torn apart. Leave it to the French police to go too far! "They're stripping the plane? That will delay their departure!"

"Wasn't that the idea?"

Yes and no. She wanted to insert an air of danger into their flight back to the States. She wanted Sebastian Stone on guard, fearful. He'd keep the woman close, and the bodyguard closer. And he'd make a mistake. Then, she'd make her move.

"They won't find anything," she said.

"Not anything we put on board. I don't think the body-guard will allow any damage. They'll likely file a new flight plan in a few hours."

"And when they do, you'll discover their destination?"

''Of course,'' the investigator answered, clearly miffed at her pessimistic tone. ''I know what I'm doing.''

''That remains to be seen.'' With a sniff, she disconnected the call, hoping the American expatriate she'd hired would have the sense to call her with the flight information as soon as he had it in his possession. If only the man knew how many of his kind had failed her before, how much of her depleted legacy she'd spent on this ultimate quest for justice. Well, he didn't have to know anything except that he wouldn't be paid in full until Sebastian and his oddly growing entourage landed in the United States.

Nothing more could be done now. She tapped the glass on the cab's window and motioned for the driver to return her to her hotel. In a few hours, she'd know where she had to go next, where the final showdown would take place. As they took a curve over a bridge above the filthy green Chicago River, she rolled down the window.

She tossed the fax machine out of the car, rolling her eyes when the driver started shouting at her in Vietnamese. She waved her hand at him, then adjusted the veil hanging fashionably from the brim of her hat. His fury was inconsequential. He was inconsequential. The only man who meant anything to her—who'd ever meant anything to her—was currently stranded on a runway in France, because she wanted him to be.

But soon, he'd return to his home country. And when he did, she'd finally reclaim what he'd taken from her. Once and for all.

''OH, YOU WANT ME, DO YOU? And just how much are you willing to give to get me?''

For an instant, Bas had thought Michaela Carmichael would be shocked by his admission. His misjudgment verified that he might have met his match with this sassy sprite of a woman. He'd made his millions from his knack for thinking one step ahead of both his business partners and his corporate rivals. He knew the content of their next thought before the idea formed in their minds. But with Michaela, he had no idea what to expect.

Lucky for both of them, he rather liked the novelty. Not nearly as much as he enjoyed the soft flutter of her skin against his, but he'd have more of that soon. Very, very soon.

"Tell me what you want," he said, certain he could—and would—fulfill any request.

She leaned back against the seat. "That's a tall order. I want a lot. And from what you've told me, you're bound by your promise to your sister to give me my heart's desire."

Bas cleared his throat and sat forward, his elbows on his knees. In the tight confines of the limousine, her body warmth seeped through the threads of his tailored suit, injecting him with heat. He adjusted the air-conditioning vent to blow straight at them.

"I promised Danielle that I would make your fantasies come true, yes," he verified. "And I intend to keep that promise. But let's be clear. If I didn't want you for myself, I would have found a loophole in that vow and exploited it."

Michaela narrowed her gaze, skewering him with glints of sapphire blue. "What do you mean? You would have broken your promise if I didn't meet with your approval?"

"What I mean is that I want you because *I* want you. My sister's request only made my pursuit easier."

Bas may have been a notorious shark in the business world, but he played on the up-and-up whenever possible, particularly with women. Yes, he took lovers with less frequency lately, and the attractions he did pursue usually went no deeper than the woman wanting to have sex with a billionaire and Bas simply wanting sex. Everyone walked away satisfied.

From Michaela, he had no idea what he wanted. Not entirely. The sex was a given. No man could possibly resist her compelling combination of strength and sass. But beneath her street-tough exterior, she possessed a latent sensuality, a vulnerability that a less observant man might have missed.

And yet something more nipped at the edges of his consciousness—something subtle, unnamed. A possibility that, with her, he'd experience something new. Not love, of course. As far as Bas was concerned, love wasn't even remotely possible. Years ago, he'd accepted that he was incapable of putting a woman's needs above his own for more than a short time. He was too driven, too intensely committed to his career. But caring for a woman, genuinely respecting her for who she was outside his bed—that appealed to him.

"So you understand?" he asked.

Michaela pressed her lips together, but nodded. "Yes. And thanks for telling me. Takes the edge off the outrageous request I'm about to make."

With a rip, Michaela tore a page from *Sexcapades* and then dropped the book on the floor. He bent to retrieve it, but she stopped him halfway.

"Don't. Leave the rest here. We won't need them. Maybe Boris has a hot date later with some French mademoiselle."

Bas did as she requested, but couldn't fight a twinge of disappointment. "Only one fantasy? We have seven days, Michaela. Surely you don't want to limit yourself."

She laughed, slapping him lightly with the torn page.

"You're full of surprises, Sebastian Stone. You have a wicked sense of humor you don't like anyone to see."

"I let you see," he pointed out. He spoke lightly but inside was floored by the ease with which they sparred and teased each other, when others evoked only the most serious responses. Yes, he toyed and teased in pursuit of seduction, but always as a means to an end.

But with Michaela, the repartée came naturally, with no greater purpose beyond the enjoyment of interaction.

"Yes, you do. Makes me have hope for you, yet."

She started to hand him the torn page when his cell phone rang. He apologized and took the call.

"The plane is cleared for takeoff," Victor informed him.

"Anything suspicious on board?" he asked.

"Nothing. The head of the Paris bomb squad surveyed the entire plane himself. He saw nothing to concern him."

"You checked the instruments and engines?"

"Checked and double-checked. Nothing's out of place, Bas. And the plane had a twenty-four-hour guard posted the entire time we were at the hotel. I interviewed the guards and the airport security force. They insist no unauthorized person had any opportunity to get within twenty feet of the plane."

"What about authorized persons?"

Victor paused. Though both he and Bas went to great lengths to investigate each and every employee they brought on board, from the cleaning crew to the head mechanic, they couldn't be sure of loyalties. Not when Bas wielded so much power over so many people. Not to mention the fact that he rarely remained in one place long enough to engender true loyalty among his staff. Yes, they loved their paychecks, but a madman could offer more money.

"I'll pull the security tapes," Victor suggested. "I can review them before takeoff if you wish."

Bas paused. His instincts told him that the incident had been no more than a scare tactic, with no substance. Had only he and Victor been on the plane, even the scare tactic would have failed. But with Michaela involved, his harasser had gone too far. He'd find out who'd arranged this threat. He'd make them pay.

"What's your gut say?" Bas asked.

Victor barely stopped to think. "My gut says we've got better things to do than stick around here any longer. I've got a medium-rare burger with my name on it waiting for me in New Orleans."

Bas laughed. "Agreed. Refile the flight plan and make sure the airport clears us to take off immediately."

"Consider it done."

Bas disconnected the call, then turned to Michaela, who'd spent the duration of the phone call folding the *Sex-capade* into a neat little square. "Ready to show me the price I must pay for you?" he asked.

She smiled and a thrill shot through Bas unlike any other he'd experienced in…well, ever. But in an instant, her grin disappeared, replaced by a practiced poker face if ever he'd seen one.

"Well, I was. But now I think I'll wait. Anticipation can be a powerful bargaining chip."

Bas eyed her narrowly, their gazes locked. Only when an intense heat warmed her thigh did she realize he'd laid his palm over her leather jeans, his fingers skimming the snug inner seam. "What do you know about negotiation?"

She swallowed, then grinned, enjoying her body's reaction as much as she enjoyed his. She could see the heat in his gaze, feel the slight increase in his breathing rate.

"Nothing I learned at business school," she said, glancing at his hand.

With a nod, Bas slipped across the seat, lowered the window and waved for the driver to return. "Business school can be a very rough, highly competitive place. You'd be shocked by the lengths some people go to in order to succeed."

She laughed, grabbed his hand again and placed it right back on her thigh. With a slap, she sought to assure him that his touch hadn't unnerved her. She was lying, but she couldn't let him have the upper hand so soon. "Compared to where I've been the past ten years? Dude, you're so out of your league."

IN RUSSIAN, Bas directed the driver to return them to the tarmac. He glanced at Micki sidelong, amused by the way she seemed to light up whenever she sensed she held the cards. Likely, she'd had very little of that rush over her short lifetime and he more than anyone else understood the inherent, addictive appeal. Addictive. Yes, the word perfectly described the depth of his need to be in control, in the driver's seat of every interaction, professional or personal. He did indeed have a personality driven to possess a rush. For his sister, the rush came from drugs. For him, it came from power.

In silence, they returned to the plane. Without a word, Michaela headed to her seat, smiling graciously when Victor brought her a fresh drink. Bas took a seat in the copilot's chair and restarted the preflight check. Soon, they'd be in the air. And soon after, he'd know precisely what kind of fantasy Michaela Carmichael wanted him to make real for her.

And, perhaps, she'd fulfill a few fantasies of his.

MICKI SWIVELED IN HER CHAIR, all too aware of the rasp of paper against her breast. The *Sexcapade* was tucked inside her bra for safekeeping. The minute she'd decided she could trust Sebastian Stone with her life, she'd leapt to the decision to trust him with her body as well. Unlike Jazz or any of the other men she'd slept with in the past, Sebastian couldn't possibly want anything from her that she wasn't already willing to give. What could a man like him want besides sexual freedom and pleasure? He had everything in the world—and what he didn't have, he could buy with one quick phone call.

Everything except love. She knew he craved it—she could feel his loneliness as if it were tangible and thick, like his butter-soft cashmere coat. And while Micki guessed other women might be scared away by this unacknowledged need of his, she wasn't. Love was easy to give. Long-lasting trust was harder. Devotion and commitment, those were impossible. She'd run away from home at fifteen to be independent, but only now, after ten years of struggling to stay clean, out of jail and alive, was she truly on the brink of being her own person, making her own way. She couldn't possibly commit to anyone else until she'd found her own place in this crazy, screwed-up world.

But could she love Bas, if that's what he truly desired? Yeah, she could. Why not? She couldn't deny that his caring ways with his sister had already endeared him. Unlike their parents, Bas never once tried to deny his sister's problems. He made no move to cover them up or excuse them. He simply accepted the situation and then used his money and prestige and influence to get Danielle the help she needed.

On the plane to Paris, Micki had wondered if he'd arranged for Danielle's care overseas as a means to keep the situation under wraps. But after the incident with the threat and the plane, she realized his notoriety spanned the globe. He hadn't requested her to keep quiet and had actually commended her for bullying his parents.

Bottom line, he seemed to have a good heart, although one he rarely had the opportunity to use for anything besides pumping his blood so he could make his billion-dollar deals. And truth be told, his strength and power turned her on. He could likely have anyone in the entire world, yet in the back of the limousine he'd admitted that he wanted her.

As soon as he'd said that, she'd decided which fantasy she wanted to make real. So many in the *Sexcapades* book tempted her, with themes ranging from a romantic interlude on the beach to the erotic use of sex toys. The one she'd ultimately picked had a little of both. The title had said it all.

"Yes, Master."

Before she'd dislodged the glue that kept the invitation sealed, she'd expected a takeoff on the whole *I Dream of Jeanie* scenario—a sexy little costume for her topped by a tiny fez, Bas posing as Major Nelson in a pilot's uniform. Now the idea made her laugh. "Yes, Master" turned out to be infinitely more intense than anything based on an old sitcom. No, this fantasy delved into the darker realms of real sexual role-playing.

And she couldn't wait.

She finished her vanilla Coke, then once the plane leveled off and Bas made a short announcement inviting her to walk around and explore, she headed for the bar and swiped more of those luscious pickled watermelon rinds. She could eat only one or two at a time because of the rich, sweet flavor, but she could get used to such a tasty treat. Maybe she'd have Bas feed her some later…along with grapes. Peeled, of course.

"I should have had Victor store something more substantial for the flight,'' Bas said once he emerged from the cockpit.

Micki twisted the top back on the hand-labeled jar and placed the pickles back in the fridge. ''There's cheese, bread, wine and fruit. Isn't that considered a full meal in France?''

''In any civilized nation, so far as I'm concerned.''

She nodded, then, on a whim, selected a bottle of red wine from the temperature-controlled compartment below the counter and presented it to him. ''How's this?''

Bas read the label and if she'd made an inappropriate selection, he made no expression of disapproval. Beginner's luck, she guessed. Or his impeccable manners. Or, more likely, the fact that he'd never dream of stocking a wine that would ever be inappropriate. She was going to be a bartender, not a wine steward, so her area of expertise was mixing drinks. But she doubted Sebastian Stone would appreciate the flavors of a Slippery Nipple or a Sex on the Beach.

Though she couldn't be sure about that, could she?

Bas grabbed the corkscrew from a drawer. ''There's a warmer for the bread just behind you. I think Victor placed a loaf inside before takeoff.''

In a few silent minutes, they'd assembled a truly decadent meal. Bas had uncorked and then poured the wine into a large-bowled glass for her, a club soda for him since he'd relieve Victor at the controls in a few hours. Micki had sliced three different cheeses and arranged them on three plates, along with some grapes and apples and some funny-looking fruit she thought would look pretty on the side. Bas pulled the bread from the warmer and tore them each crusty servings.

''Club soda for Vic, too?'' she asked.

He nodded and she poured, twisting a slice of lime on the rim.

"I'll take this to him," he said.

Micki slid the glass over. Funny how naturally Bas took to servitude, though she never would have guessed. Hoped, yes. Guessed, never. "Wait, let me. I'd like to see the cockpit."

Bas handed her the plate. "Be my guest."

Balancing the plate and drink, she squeezed through the door that separated the cockpit from the cabin.

"Brought you a snack," she announced.

Vic glanced over his shoulder. "Thanks, I'm starved."

"Sebastian thought you might be hungry."

Micki placed the plate and soda on the ledge Vic indicated with his hand. At his gesture, she sat in the copilot's chair, equally amazed by the view outside the window as by the blinking and bleeping instruments surrounding her. How could anyone possibly ever understand what they all meant?

"Bas knows I'm always hungry. How was the cola?"

"Delicious. Were you a soda jerk in another life?"

Vic laughed. "I've been lots of things in my other lives."

"I've never met a butler slash pilot slash bodyguard."

"Slash friend. Don't forget that part. I take care of Bas because I like him. That's the bottom line."

Micki tore her gaze away from the altimeter long enough to catch the clear warning lights twinkling in Vic's eyes. "Spit it out, Vic. I don't do well with innuendoes or hints."

"No hints from me, sister. I just didn't want you thinking that I was here just for the salary."

Micki watched him carefully. "What does it matter what I think?"

He snagged a slice of cheese. "I guess it doesn't. Thanks for the snack."

Micki knew she'd been dismissed, and she left the cockpit suddenly very confused. What had that all been about? Did Vic not like her? Was he warning her to watch her step around Bas, maybe suspecting she might have designs on his money? Or was the pilot only trying to allay any of her residual fears caused by the death threat, assuring her that his devotion to Bas's safety was more than part of his job description?

Shrugging, Micki decided she'd ponder that mystery later. After they were on the ground. After she'd had a chance to show Bas which *Sexcapade* she'd chosen. His desire was going to have to run damned deep for him to do what she was about to ask.

"How's Victor?" he asked.

"Fine, I think."

"Did he say something?"

"Nothing I can translate. I don't know, either he was trying to warn me about something or reassure me. Could have gone either way."

Bas smiled. "Don't mind Victor. Looking out for me is his calling in life, but he's likely experiencing great turmoil in regard to you."

"Me? Why?"

Bas reclined in his chair, crossing his ankles and looking more relaxed than she'd seen him since the moment they'd met.

"In general practice, Victor distrusts any and all women who spend time with me."

"Why?"

"He thinks they're all after my money."

"Aren't they?"

"I do have more to offer."

She snagged her wineglass and wiggled her eyebrows. "I'll bet you do. Actually, I'm counting on it."

She took a quick sip, instantly struck by the rich taste and intense scent, followed by a smooth but potent kick of warmth. *Wow.* So this was what fine wine tasted like. She lowered herself into her chair and took a second sip, more slowly this time, to savor the explosion of woodsy flavors. She tasted a hint of fruit, yet no sweetness.

"Am I doing this right?" she asked before taking a third sip.

"Doing what right?"

She lifted the glass toward him. "Drinking this."

He shook his head. "Don't be sucked into snobbery, Michaela. There is no right or wrong way to drink wine, so long as you enjoy it."

Until that moment when the muscles in her neck relaxed did Micki realize she'd been nervous. She tried to tell herself she was unimpressed and unaffected by wealth and luxury, but who was she kidding? Anyone who stepped out of their comfort zone into a foreign world—be it Mars or the playland of the filthy rich—was bound to feel off-kilter, out of place. Heck, even on the streets, Micki never felt like she'd fit in. Yes, at first she was angry and desperate like the other runaways and throwaways she'd met. But after about a year the anger had turned away from its initial target—her dead mother and her overprotective grandmother—toward herself for being so stupid and stubborn as to chuck a warm bed and an occasional fight over curfews for living hand-to-mouth and sleeping in doorways.

But she wouldn't sleep in a doorway tonight. This jet sported excellent sleeping accommodations—two private rooms, small but luxurious, in the rear of the plane. And with Victor busy with the controls, she and Bas might utilize one of those bedrooms to implement the torn-out page from *Sexcapades.*

She took another longer sip of wine and mulled the flavors while she considered his claim.

"I hope you apply that same philosophy to other areas of your life," she said.

"What philosophy?" he asked, as if the mere suggestion that he might subscribe to a collection of core values appalled him.

"That there is no right or wrong, so long as you enjoy yourself."

He nodded as he grinned. "Nothing objectionable in that statement."

"Good."

She slipped her hand beneath the hem of her shirt to retrieve the tear-out, but when she noted the quick darkening of his gaze, she slowed down. Her breasts tingled from the contact with her skin, and from the way he looked at her, as though no other thought existed in his mind except desire for her. How she would feel in his hands. How she would taste. How she would respond to his sensuous seduction.

She flicked the paper out of her bra and offered him the carefully folded square. Without expression, he put down his drink, reversed the folds and scanned the front. There, the title of the sexual fantasy streaked across the page in a swirling font, following by a teaser that revealed just enough of the content within to whet the appetite.

"An interesting choice, Michaela. Suited to you, so far as I can tell."

"Not so suited to you, though, is it?" she said, issuing the challenge that would right here, right now, make or break this deal.

She wanted Bas to be her love slave. She wanted to

control the controller, wield intimate power over the ultimate power-wielder. Instead of "Yes, Master," it would be "Yes, Mistress." She could think of nothing more erotic, more desirable and decadent than bringing a man like him to his knees.

With cool nonchalance, he tossed the paper onto the table, the inside unread. "That depends."

"On what?"

"On you."

Micki knew he'd just issued some sort of challenge—likely one that would somehow flip this fantasy to his advantage—but she wouldn't back down until she knew his game. Not even when she might have to forfeit her leading edge.

"What are you talking about?"

"A wager," he answered simply.

"What kind of wager?"

"The kind you can't lose."

She flattened her back against the recliner, watching the way his gaze remained steady, the way he moistened his lips before he took a sip from his drink.

She leaned forward, elbows on her knees. "There's no such thing as a wager you can't lose."

He mimicked her position, even scooted his backside on the edge of the chair so they were nearly nose to nose. "You've never played a game with me, Michaela. The secret to my winning is that I make my own rules. Now, are you up to the challenge of sporting with me, or should we play this the old-fashioned, predictable way?"

Micki bit her lip. No one had ever accused her of acting predictably—or of being a coward, his unspoken accusation. Sure, men like Bas didn't up the stakes unless they had a strong plan to win, but even if the odds were a million to one against her, Micki figured she'd always end up better off for playing than for taking the easy route to surrender.

"I'll take your challenge," she answered.

He smiled, but didn't move one muscle so that their lips remained just a half inch apart. The scent of his cologne teased her nostrils, mingling with the essences of the sweet fruit and crisp lime in the seltzer. She had to use all her control not to inhale deeply and lose herself in the dizzying effects.

He didn't move his face, but he did move his hand, flicking a button beside the table. An intercom.

"Change of flight plan, Victor."

His pilot answered with no sound of surprise for the sudden alteration. "Where to now, boss?"

When he licked his lips, he came a hairbreadth from swiping the moisture over her mouth as well. God, she wanted to kiss him.

"New Orleans."

At this, Victor sounded surprised. "We're going to the party?"

"Party?" Bas scrunched his brow, as perplexed by the question as she was. "Oh, that. Well, I suppose we should make an appearance. Make the arrangements. And while you're phoning in our RSVP, inform Reina that I will be purchasing that piece I admired in her catalogue."

Victor asked no more questions, so Bas disengaged the intercom and returned his attention to her.

"Just what have you got up your sleeve, Bas Stone?"

He placed his hands over her knees, then slid them up her thighs so that the sleeves of his coat pulled back, revealing the starched cuffs of his black shirt. "Well, that's for you to find out, isn't it?"

6

IN THE CORPORATE WORLD, Bas's patience was nothing short of legendary. But in his personal life, he'd become incredibly accustomed to getting what he wanted when he wanted it. Perhaps too accustomed. Seemed Micki Carmichael was going to put a stop to his complacency whether he wanted her to or not.

In his opinion, the qualities of virtue associated with delayed gratification were exaggerated at best. He wanted Micki. He craved her taste, her touch. To feel her skin, warm and slick against his was a goal in the forefront of his mind. Very soon, he intended to inhale her scent until the sweet combinations were imprinted on his memory forever. But using the *Sexcapade* tonight wouldn't be in his best interest—or hers. He had a clever idea as to how they'd determine who played the master and who played the slave—but until they arrived in New Orleans, he couldn't implement his plan. For tonight, he'd have to improvise.

Luckily, improvisation was one of his strongest talents.

"Are you still hungry?" he asked, noting that from such close range, he could see that her crystal blue irises had flecks of brighter blues and silver, creating eyes so enchanting, it almost hurt to stare into them.

"I'm starving," she answered, her tone breathy, hot. His hands still pressed against her thighs, and beneath the cool leather, she quivered.

"Then allow me to...alleviate that problem."

With one hand, Bas reached to the tray and snagged a slice of cheese, careful not to pull too far out of the tight, electric space they'd created. Her breath teased his mustache and, almost instantly, the creamy Camembert melted across his fingers.

"Looks like my body temperature has risen," he said. "Too hot for the cheese."

Her eyes sparkled with brazen pride. "I'll be the judge of that."

Boldly, she took his hand and guided his fingers to her mouth.

"I just love finger food, don't you?" she asked.

The minute her lips surrounded his finger, he didn't dare attempt an answer, not with the surge of lust shooting through him like wildfire. She suckled away the creamy cheese, her eyes fixed on his, anxious and lusty at the same time.

"Finger food is highly underrated," he finally managed to answer, evoking a smile from her and a second wave of need within him.

"Maybe you should try some then."

She reached for the tray, but before she could snag another slice of cheese, Bas grabbed her by the elbows and guided her off her chair to sit beside him on the larger love seat. He knew Victor would not interrupt them, and still Sebastian's instinct to protect the intimacy crackling between them forced him to excuse himself in order to dash to the cockpit for a word with his pilot. He shed his coat in the process, but the action brought no relief from the heat. Nothing would. Nothing but Michaela's firm body beneath his own.

When he returned, she'd removed her boots and her jacket. In her simple black button-down blouse and leather pants, combined with the midnight hue of her hair, she looked every inch the mysterious femme fatale. But Bas knew better. His instincts told him that Michaela's strong, controlled exterior had been carved by a past fraught with distrust and disappointment.

From the minute she'd shown him the page from the *Sexcapade* book, Bas had known why she'd chosen that particular fantasy over all the others. Taking the role of the master to his slave created a perfect scenario for her to grab a seductive power she'd never known before.

Lucky for her, Bas knew the inner workings of power and control better than most. He knew her plan had a fatal flaw—one that might leave the experience empty and cold. He'd already devised a way to work around the pitfalls. He would soon teach Michaela the true essence and advantages of real power. The payoffs and the prices. Once they reached Louisiana.

Until then, he intended to give her the pleasure they both deserved. With any of his other female acquaintances, that's all he ever would have wanted. He gave his lovers sexual gratification, and received a healthy dose of the same in return. With Michaela, he wanted more, though his motives, even to him, were unclear.

But, frankly, his motivations tonight didn't matter. Ultimately, the journey would bring this woman into his bed, where he would savor every sensual moment.

Once sure of their continued privacy, Bas settled in beside her, smiling when she slid the tray onto her lap, then crossed her legs over his. Her toenails sparkled bright crimson on surprisingly pale, delicate feet.

"What do you want to try first?" she asked.

Bas looked over the tray and nodded toward a fig.

She lifted it, eyeing it with her standard wariness. "Isn't this just some funky garnish?"

"A garnish? I suppose it could be used as one. But it's a fig. Have you ever had one?"

Her lips twisted in a grimace while she twirled the brownish-purple-skinned fruit in her hand. "Not unless it was inside a Newton."

Bas laughed. Fig Newtons had been a favorite cookie in his childhood, but the real fruit, freshly picked from a homegrown vine in Italy, bore little resemblance to the filling in the store-bought treat.

Just as he suspected of Michaela, the outside of the fruit was tough, misleading. But the inside…his mouth watered before he'd taken one bite.

Besides, a fig was an inherently sensual fruit. The fact that Michaela would taste her first at his hand thrilled him.

"Ah, well. There is no comparison. Poets have written odes to this sweet little morsel."

She pulled the brown fig closer, eyeing it from all sides. "This? The stuff of poetry?" she asked, doubtful. "Pomegranates must have been out of season."

Bas was impressed, knowing that while Michaela was by her own admission undereducated, she didn't by any means lack intelligence or wit. He, on the other hand, tipped the scales in terms of formal schooling—and yet if they were let loose separately in a room full of diplomats, world leaders and celebrities, he had no doubt who would be more popular.

Maybe that was why he wanted to feed her the fig, why he wanted to take her to New Orleans where he could watch her eyes soak in the sights, listen to her commentary, gauge her reactions. She'd been around the block, and yet so much remained new to her. He couldn't imagine how long ago he'd lost that kind of true wonder for life.

Likely, sometime back in college. And try as he might, even when he closed his eyes and concentrated, he couldn't remember as much as a full phrase of the poem he'd memorized in college about figs. Seemed a million years ago. He'd mainly studied macroeconomics and business theory, but he had taken a few literature classes to support his minor in humanities. He'd always possessed a hunger to broaden his knowledge base. Besides, lit classes had allowed him ample time to check out the bevy of female coeds with insatiable tastes for randy authors like D. H. Lawrence.

"Open it," he suggested.

She glanced around, but he hadn't supplied a knife. Bas took the fruit and tenderly tore it in half, preserving the natural pear shape. The brownish purple skin opened to reveal a fleshy center in a rainbow of pinks, from the lightest shade, nearly white, lining the outer rim, to the bright magenta deep in the core.

But what Bas turned to show Michaela was not just the colors, but the shapes, the textures. "See this deep slit slicing down the center? The folds of sweet flesh teasing from the sides? Look how moist it is. How wet. The juices glisten, promising a delicate flavor unlike any other."

Michaela looked as he instructed, and only a few seconds later she made the symbolic connection.

"Are you trying to be subtle?" she asked.

"Would you rather me be crude?"

She snagged her bottom lip, thought, then held out her palm to accept her half of the fruit. "I've had too much crude in my life. I'll take subtle, thanks."

He smiled. "Not too subtle, I hope. I wouldn't want us to suffer from any misunderstandings."

Her stare captured his, level and steady. "Good point. How about we try a little bit of both?"

"Starting with the fig?"

Her grin, a lesson in subtlety itself, was prelude to a soft shimmy of her bottom against the seat. "Why not? Is there a right way to eat this or is this one of those 'just enjoy' situations again?"

Bas forced a serious expression. "Oh, no. There is definitely a nuance to the eating of a fig. Some people ravish the fruit, devour the flesh and the juices in one ravenous bite."

"Fools," she commented, her voice a whisper.

"I agree." Bas drew the fruit to his lips, took a sweet, tentative lick over the soft pink flesh. "I prefer to savor the experience. Take a brief taste first, allow the flavors to mingle on my tongue."

She mimicked his action, licking the inside, her tongue stiff, sure. Her eyes dark and desirous. Her lips lustrous with the moisture from the fruit. She hummed her pleasure and, instantly, Bas's cock hardened. God, making love to this woman would be either his greatest adventure or his greatest failure.

And Sebastian Stone didn't fail. Ever.

"It's such a light flavor," she said. "Sweet, but not too sweet. And exotic. I've never tasted anything like it."

He grabbed his glass and took a sip to offset the sudden dryness in his throat. "A fig is like a woman in many ways. Unique. Complex. Take a bite, now. The textures are indescribable."

She took a dainty nibble first, then a more generous bite. He sampled the fruit at the same time, closing his eyes and enjoying all that he'd described, and all that words never could. The taste of the fig eased onto his tongue and, before he could contain himself, he groaned.

"Enjoying yourself?" she asked, her eyes glittering.

"Not nearly as much as I could be," he answered.

"Why's that?"

His stare locked with hers. The moment had come.

"Something's missing from the mix. The fig is exquisite, the wine perfect, and yet..."

She glanced at the tray. "You want more cheese?"

He chuckled. "No."

"A grape?"

"Hardly."

She hesitated, then almost unconsciously swiped the fig around her lips, spreading the sweetness over her mouth. "A kiss?"

"I've never wanted to kiss a woman more in my life."

She sat straighter, then shook her head. "Maybe I shouldn't let you kiss me, then. What if you're disappointed?"

He lured her toward him. "I'll live."

Disappointment never entered Bas's mind. Not much entered his mind at the moment his lips touched hers, the flavors of the wine and the figs and the kiss meshing into a concoction so delicious, he thought he might never set her free. Just like with the fruit, her tongue boldly sought her target, dueling with his without apprehension. And yet a coyness existed in the way she held her hands firmly on her lap, cradling the unfinished fig in her palms.

He tossed his aside, intent on feeling her under his hands, even through the fabric of her blouse. He encircled her waist, stretching his fingers up her back, branding her curves with his heat. He tugged her completely onto his lap, wincing when her thighs pressed hard over him. After a moment, he accepted the appetizing torture of wanting something he couldn't immediately have.

Or could he?

In a flash, she'd shifted, kicking one leg behind her and landing in a bold straddle. She speared her fingers into his hair and pressed closer so that her breasts crashed into his chest. She wanted him—and, just like him, Michaela took what she wanted at the very instant the need occurred. The tide of need and lust nearly swept him into the torrent her kiss caused, yet before he lost his ability to think, he broke the connection.

"Michaela," he said, careful to keep his tone neither demanding nor admonishing.

"What?"

"Slow down."

"Why?"

Micki searched his eyes, desperate to pinpoint the reason for his hesitation. She didn't know why she trusted Bas Stone—and she didn't care. She just knew that for the first time in years, her body raged with wild sexual need unhampered by the demons that had clouded her desire when she lived on the street. Alcohol. Desperation. Loneliness. That persistent suspicion that no matter how romantic, no matter how perfectly arranged the sexual liaison was—somehow, her lover was using her.

With Sebastian, none of those fears harangued her. She had to take this moment while it lasted.

"Good question," he finally answered.

She smiled and leaned back just enough to unbutton her shirt and peel the material away from her skin. "Don't think too hard, Bas. Moments like these don't come too often, at least, not for me. You know you were getting me all hot and bothered with the fig." She shifted, pressing her sex fully against his erection, feeding the flame he tried so valiantly to contain. "Time to put your mouth where your money is."

"I prefer to put my mouth on your breasts."

She reached around and unclipped her bra. "Be my guest."

Bas needed no more invitation and Micki, who thought she couldn't possibly experience a higher level of arousal, was proved oh-so-wrong. She'd intended to remove his shirt while he had his fill of her, but the minute his tongue connected with her nipple, she forgot everything except the desire to feel him suckle and flick her incredibly sensitive flesh. He took his time arousing her, buoying her breast with his hand, sampling her skin as if she were some rare delicacy, whispering descriptions of his pleasure in fine detail.

She almost couldn't take it. The words. The adoration. The complete and total arousal. She flew off his lap, panting, and slipped out of her pants and panties, her back to him. When she turned, he'd removed his shirt and unbuckled his slacks, but she knew from the tight expression on his face that he wouldn't go further.

Not yet. Deep within her chest, her heart emitted a soft cry. What was he waiting for? He was hard and hot and had a naked, willing woman flying with him over the Atlantic Ocean. She almost didn't look—almost didn't want to see—and yet, his dark gray gaze said it all.

He hesitated out of some concern for her. And that had never, ever happened. Never in her life. Not even her very first time, when she would have given anything for the guy to slow down.

The memory must have flashed in her eyes, because Bas was up with his arms around her in a flash. Yet, for some reason, instead of feeling gratitude for his sensitivity, she brimmed with sudden anger.

"Are you just playing with me?" she accused, unable to look him in the eye and hating herself for it.

He cupped her chin with his hand. "Not in the way that you think."

"You don't know what I'm thinking," she snapped.

"So tell me."

She tore her face away. "No."

"Then sit down. I'll be right back."

He gently propelled her toward the love seat, then strolled beyond a partition in the rear of the plane without so much as a backward glance. Micki grabbed her shirt from the heap on the floor, and punched her fists into the arms. Why had he stopped? What had she done?

When he returned, he carried a plush dark red chenille blanket. Without glancing her way, he stepped to a control panel on the wall and pressed a button. She nearly shrieked when the love seat flattened, converting to a small bed. Then, he dimmed the lights to a soft amber glow. He removed satin-covered pillows from a hidden bin above them and tossed them to her, followed by the blanket. Confused but curious, she arranged the pillows and floated the blanket over her, removing her shirt again. Maybe doing it on the couch half-undressed wasn't his idea of romantic. Frankly, it wasn't her idea of romantic, either.

Thing was, Micki never let herself admit how much *romantic* meant to her. And either Bas somehow guessed, or his tastes ran along the same lines as hers—even if she didn't really know what her tastes were.

Her tiny smile of gratitude seemed all he needed to pick up where they had left off. Ever so slowly, he slipped his unbuckled belt from around his waist, coiling it in a loose circle before he placed it silently on the table. He sat in the chair across from her, his gaze locked with hers, as he took off his shoes, then his socks. And with unabashed pride, he stood, removed his slacks and boxers.

He didn't parade for her, but gave her a mere moment to drink in the sight of him. Micki knew she'd never seen such an impressively sculpted man. His tanned muscles rippled with each step he took. His upper chest had very little hair, but what was there enhanced the utter masculinity of his body. Slim hips and a tight ass were the perfect backdrop for his sex. Her mouth dried as she anticipated feeling him inside her, hard and thick.

He joined her in the makeshift bed, tossing the blanket aside so he could stretch fully against her.

"I'm sorry I snapped," she said, relaxing the moment his warmth enveloped her.

"Don't apologize. We have a long flight, Michaela. Why rush?"

She shrugged. "I don't know. Wild, hot, unthinking sex isn't so bad, is it?"

He shook his head. "Not if that's what you like."

"I like it," she answered quickly.

He didn't respond, but his penetrating gaze compelled her to reconsider.

"Okay, wild, hot, unthinking sex is pretty much all I've ever had."

He nodded. He'd obviously suspected as much. But he didn't say another word about it, preferring to toy with the fringe on the blanket. He twisted the yarn, then feathered the soft edges over her flesh like tiny fingertips, dusting light sensations on her shoulder, then down her breasts and over her nipples.

Micki closed her eyes, her awareness captured by his light movements.

"How does this feel?" he asked.

"You're touching me, but…"

"…not touching you. Your breasts are so beautiful, so sensitive."

With her eyes squeezed shut, she didn't know he'd bent to take her in his mouth again until his warm, moist lips encircled her, his tongue flicking lightly while he drew the blanket down and teased the flesh over her ribs, her navel, her hips. When his fingers slipped into the curls between her legs, his touch was as light, as feathery, as the edges of the blanket. The soft pads of his fingers skimmed over her mons, eliciting a fluttering sensation she'd never before known. He touched, yet he didn't touch. He aroused her, teased her. His concentration remained on her. When she reached over to touch him, he blocked her artfully, applying just a tad more pressure with his fingers between her thighs so she could think of nothing but taking what he so skillfully offered.

A trickle of moisture beaded from within her, and Bas captured the creaminess and spread it generously over her sensitive flesh. Micki held her breath, amazed at his languid pace—and wondering how much longer she could endure the sweet torture. His fingers skimmed and explored, but never probed, never dipped to satisfy the throbbing deep inside her.

Yet the minute she thought she'd go insane with wanting, a sound ripped from her throat. Pleading, yet pleasured. As if he'd been waiting for her, he took her moan as the invitation it was and explored her deeply.

She nearly bucked out of her skin. Colors flashed behind her eyelids, psychedelic swirls of sensation that blinded her with need. Before she could think, she begged him to finish what he'd started in the crudest words she knew.

"No," he admonished, his voice a sultry whisper. "But I will make love to you. And when I do, you'll never think of that word again."

7

For an instant he was gone, but he returned quickly. He'd donned a condom, and in the seconds it took for her to register that he'd done so, he climbed over her. She opened her legs wide, knowing nothing except that she couldn't go another moment without feeling him inside her.

He pressed inside slowly, hissing his pleasure at the tightness. The snug fit surprised her, enthralled her. He pulled out, then thrust deeper, making sure every fired nerve ending experienced the fullness of his sex joined with hers.

"Oh, Bas," she murmured.

He took her hands, curling them inside his even as he trapped them above her head. The effect was gently possessive. She felt cherished, yet claimed in the most elemental sense. The back of her throat burned and even the dim lights of the cabin flashed too brightly in her eyes.

God, why didn't he hurry? What was he waiting for? She couldn't bear another minute on the precipice like this, trying to hold her balance, trying to contain the fullness of her need.

"Michaela," he said.

She opened her eyes.

"Relax."

She swallowed, confused. Wasn't she the most relaxed woman in the western hemisphere?

"Take a deep breath," he commanded.

To humor him, she complied. Only after she felt the tension flowing from her muscles did she realize how she'd tightened up, almost as a defensive move against the pleasure he could bring.

He rewarded her by sliding deeper within her. "That's better," he urged, moving slowly, but with a rhythm that increased incrementally with each measure of her surrender. "Isn't that better?"

"Yes," she answered. "Yes."

He moved faster. "Feel how well we fit?"

"Yes." She closed her eyes, losing herself in the sensations.

He shifted, then drove deeper, and this time she cried out. The sound of her pleasure spurred him on, until the tempo bordered on frenzied. Wild. Micki tried to hold on, tried to waylay her climax, but she couldn't. Colors light and dark and sparkling exploded. Her muscles clenched. Her breathing and heartbeat seemed to stop, then kicked in with a rush and gasp.

Only then did she feel him tense. A slight sound spilled from his lips, something close to "Michaela," but not quite.

And then, she didn't know what to do. He didn't collapse atop her or immediately climb off her and disappear into another room. Instead, he shifted his body so they could lie side by side, entwined. Connected so intimately, the marvel of such closeness nearly tore her in two.

When he lifted his face to hers, she noticed a bead of sweat just along his temple. The glistening drop fascinated her, made her realize something actually existed that the man couldn't completely control. She smoothed the moisture off his face, losing her fingers in his temples, which she suddenly noticed held a touch of gray.

"You're an amazing lover, Sebastian Stone," she said,

knowing she had to say something, even something incredibly stupid. Or in this case, obvious.

"I can say the same about you," he replied.

"But will you?"

He grinned. "Do I look dissatisfied?"

She shrugged. "So you had an orgasm. Most men can manage that without even having a woman around."

"True," he teased, punctuating his blasé comment with a kiss to her nose. "But the event wouldn't be half as glorious as what just happened here."

She wanted to ask him what had just happened, but settled for common sense. He'd made love to her and she'd enjoyed herself immensely. And, apparently, he hadn't had such a bad time, either. And yet, she knew if she dissected the event, she'd figure out what had made it so special.

But she wasn't in the mood to dissect or theorize. She snuggled into his arms, and closed her eyes, content for now to allow the glorious sensations lull her to a dreamy sleep.

SHE AWOKE ALONE, but once she'd disappeared into the bathroom to clean up and dress, she heard someone moving in the main cabin. She half expected Vic to be righting the cushions and pillows, but she opened the door to find Sebastian tending to the details. She smiled, relieved. Vic must have known what they were doing in the cabin while he flew the plane, but for some reason, she actually minded someone other than she and Bas knowing the details.

He disappeared into the cockpit to relieve Vic for a few hours, and Micki entertained herself with a movie while Bas's right-hand man rested in a back room. Just as the credits rolled, Victor emerged and took over for the remainder of the flight. Bas joined her again, and though she spied a hungry look in his eyes every so often, he kept his hands to himself.

If another man had acted like this, she would have suspected he was done with her already. But, with Bas, Micki knew better. He was biding his time. Forming a plan. He refused to discuss the details, but instead entertained her with engaging conversation.

By the time they landed in New Orleans, Micki had a greater understanding of how a venture capitalist made his money. She also now understood his odd, if not emotionally bankrupt, relationship with his parents.

She'd never expected Bas to be so forthcoming about his family, but once again he'd surprised her. Apparently, having children had never been in the great Stone plan. William and Dorothy had married young, both from relatively wealthy families, but with much higher aspirations than what their respective trust funds could offer them. When Bas came into the world, they immediately decided that he would be the ticket to their expanded wealth. Much to their delight, he'd turned out to have a genius IQ and a remarkable talent for reading people. But with those skills, it hadn't taken young Bastian long to realize that his mother and father would never love him for him, just for what he could give them.

Bas insisted he'd come to terms with this at an early age, but when his sister came into the world—again, unexpectedly, nearly twenty years later—he'd worried for her emotional well-being. With regret, he'd explained how whenever he went home for visits during college, Danielle had been starved for affection and attention. In hindsight, he guessed he should have used his increasing capital and power to improve her care, but he'd been young then—focused on his wealth and his standing in the business world. By the time he'd finally reached a plateau, he'd been assured by his parents and his sister that all was well.

And he'd believed them. His biggest mistake. And one he wouldn't repeat.

Micki had been much less forthcoming in the tale of her childhood, telling Bas about Katherine, her teenage mother, who'd been the proverbial bad seed from birth. She'd run with a rough crowd, defied the strict rules her widowed mother forced on her, then had eventually run away and gotten pregnant with twins. Three weeks after giving birth, she'd abandoned Michaela and Aurora to their grandmother. Soon after, she'd died of an overdose. She'd been just another nameless junkie lured to the streets with promises of independence and freedom. Micki now knew firsthand about those gilded lies.

Surprisingly, Bas didn't ask her many questions about her life on the streets. Instead, he listened with such rapt attention that soon Micki's self-consciousness overrode her big mouth and she decided to stop. She blamed fatigue, and in minutes Bas had taken over for Victor in the cockpit again so the butler could arrange for Micki's comfort in a small, private bedroom near the tail of the plane, away from the main cabin. By the time she'd awakened, they'd landed in New Orleans. Bas had disappeared on some "secret mission" Victor wouldn't give her one clue about. Meanwhile, Micki was whisked away to a cozy house in the French Quarter so she could shower and change before Vic spirited her off to shop for clothes.

By the time they reached The Camellia Grill to make good on Bas's promise to provide her with a heart-stopping, mouthwatering, all-American hamburger, Micki decided she was as close to overwhelmed as she'd ever allow herself to get. Even the restaurant surprised her. A neighborhood joint directly across the street from the St. Charles streetcar line, the Greek Revival-style house looked like a small plantation home. Families and tourists and locals crowded the diner-style lunch counters and tables. Waiters in crisp white shirts and black bow ties worked the crowd with a combination of efficient experience and slow southern charm. By the time she'd ordered a hamburger platter with fries smothered in chili, she'd decided she liked New Orleans. A lot.

The feeling ricocheted into near nirvana once she took her first bite. She was so entranced by the marvelous flavors, she barely noticed when Bas joined her at the table and Victor ever so subtly disappeared.

"Couldn't miss this, could you?" she asked, still munching on her food.

She expected him to cut his burger, maybe even eat the grilled-onion-laden monstrosity with a knife and fork, but she was wrong. Just like her, he lifted the entire delicacy to his lips and took a generous bite. Unlike her, he didn't spill one drop of ketchup or grease onto his plate.

He did, of course, wait until after he'd chewed and swallowed before he replied. "I never miss lunch at The Camellia Grill."

"You almost did. You've been gone for a while," she said, dabbing some chili off her lips with her white linen napkin.

"Missed me?" he asked.

She shrugged one shoulder, but he didn't buy her nonchalance. Why should he? She *had* missed him. Victor had been great company and the best shopping buddy a girl could have—a man who could assess the fit and flattery of clothes with honesty *and* who had an unlimited balance on his credit card—but he wasn't the best conversationalist. Micki still felt unnerved by his strange comments at the beginning of their flight, but when she'd asked him about them point-blank while they'd perused strappy sandals, he'd declined to answer and begged her not to ask again.

Not that she would honor that request. She sensed that Victor liked her a great deal, so it would only be a matter of time and persistence before she cracked the wall he hid behind.

"Yeah, I missed you," she admitted. "Surprised?"

"I assumed a shopping spree would sufficiently entertain you. Did you get everything you needed?"

"And then some. You're very generous."

"It's just money. I want you to enjoy yourself."

"Then you should have come with me."

"Wasn't Victor a sufficient companion?"

"Sufficient, yes. Fun even, every once in a while. But I think I would have liked to see your expression when I tried on some of the nighties. We could have had a real Julia Roberts/Richard Gere moment."

He narrowed his gaze. "Who?"

She rolled her eyes. The man was helplessly out of touch when it came to popular culture. "Never mind. In fact, it's better if you don't know." While she adored *Pretty Woman,* the film detailing the unlikely love story between a prostitute and a rich guy, she didn't like the implied parallel. "What's next on the agenda?"

Bas took a sip from the cola Vic had ordered for him, cleaned his hands with a napkin and pulled a slip of paper from his billfold.

The *Sexcapade.*

She'd thought he'd forgotten about that. Apparently, her initiation last night into the mile-high club had not been the end of their liaison.

"Time to get down to business, don't you think?"

She tried to match his sudden serious demeanor, though she had trouble keeping a straight face. Sebastian Stone thrived on the art of the deal, and if she didn't want to find herself on the losing side of this proposition—no matter how win-win he claimed the proposal would be—she needed to pay attention.

"Business?" she asked.

"Serious business," he assured her, though she was nearly certain she spied a teasing glint in his eyes. "We need to set the ground rules before we go forward with our wager and this fantasy."

"Rules?"

"Every mutual agreement must have provisions."

"Uh-huh." She wasn't convinced, but decided to play along. For as long as she could remember, Micki had a hate-hate relationship with any and all rules.

"You first," he said.

She glanced around, wondering why the crowd suddenly seemed to be listening when she knew they weren't. The din from the noisy diners, staff, china and even the sizzle from the grill overrode any semblance of intimacy. Maybe that's why he'd chosen this place to discuss their proposed foray into sexual territory she'd never imagined she'd explore. The sex they'd had last night had been unique beyond her wildest dreams—slow, sensual, gentle. But with the *Sexcapade* she'd chosen, she knew all her preconceived notions about sex would be blown off their hinges.

She leaned forward. "Do we have to discuss this here?"

He smiled. "Discretion? I like that in a woman."

She frowned. "Okay, that'll be my rule, then. No one will ever know about our…arrangement."

"Do you care if anyone knows?"

She didn't want Danielle to know. Otherwise she didn't care. Funny how she could share just about every other private thing about her life with her friend, but this topic seemed completely off-limits.

"No, but you do," she answered.

"Not for the reasons you think, I'll wager."

She snagged another French fry from beneath the pile of chili on her plate. "Doesn't matter why. I just think that keeping this private will be, I don't know...better."

"Like a secret," he said, nodding. "One only we share."

She plopped the spicy fried potato in her mouth and grinned. Yeah, she liked that.

"Your turn."

He took a deep breath. "I'm not certain I like including this provision, but, with your agreement, I propose we limit our time together to this week. It ends when you return to Chicago."

She sat up a little straighter. She figured any other woman would have been offended by a time limit, but for Micki the rule worked perfectly. "Makes sense to me. I'm due back in six days and I'll bet you have some corporation to buy and revitalize. Yeah, this works. Knowing there will be an end will keep us from...getting too wrapped up in the fantasy."

He nodded, but she spied a quick flash of something in his eyes that told her there was more to this story. Well, this was one secret she would delve deeper into. Later.

"Your turn again," he pointed out.

She picked up the *Sexcapade,* unfolding the paper and rereading the teaser page. "Oh, yeah. I want to be the master."

He shook his head. "Not negotiable."

"Excuse me? This is my fantasy, Mister."

"Yes, but the execution of this fantasy was wisely put in my hands. If we established the master and slave dynamic ahead of time—and permanently—what mystery would there be?"

"I don't know," she snapped. "I think how you'd react to being my slave is fairly uncertain."

He cleared his throat. "Yes, but I propose we find a mutually equitable way to determine the leadership role."

She sat back, another chili fry in her hand. "You're bumming me out here, Bas. I mean, all this negotiation crap is taking away the fun."

He leaned forward, his eyes level with hers. Before she knew it, he'd snagged her fry. He popped it in his mouth, his smile way too smug for her liking. "Tonight I'll demonstrate my proposed method of determining who is the master and who is the slave. We'll each have a fair chance at the dominant role, each and every time we make love."

She thought he was way too confident, way too arrogant—and way too sexy. After last night, she knew he had the capacity to put her pleasure ahead of his. Whether he would again was another matter. But he wouldn't mislead her. He promised her an equal shot at being the master—an offer more than fair.

"All right. We'll..." she searched for the right word, certain it existed somewhere in her brain, "defer that decision until tonight. What else?"

He sat back, relaxed. "Nothing else on the agenda. You've shopped sufficiently for tonight?"

"Victor assures me I have. Where are we going again?"

"An art gallery showing."

She pressed her lips together, nodding with a decided lack of enthusiasm. "Sounds like a real kick."

"Oh, it will be. The artist is Reina Price."

The name meant nothing to her and she could tell he was disappointed.

"The erotic jewelry artist?" he added.

"Erotic jewelry?"

Bas grinned. "She's the hottest thing in jewelry design right now. And she's an old friend."

A shiver raced up Micki's spine. An old friend? Why did she think there was more to that than he said? Was it the wistful sound in his voice? The way his eyes suddenly dilated from gray-green to smoky pewter?

"An old friend or an old lover?" she asked, crossing her arms before she realized how childishly jealous she looked.

He had the good grace not to snicker. "Does it matter?"

She wouldn't lie. "Yes."

"She's a former lover," he replied honestly. "But, truth be told, she became bored with me rather quickly. She's married now to a man who apparently has inspired her greatest work. We've remained friends, however. I won't pretend otherwise, not even for you."

Micki smiled, doffing her embarrassment over her flash of jealousy and impressed by his sense of loyalty. If Reina Price had become bored with Bas, either he wasn't at his best or the erotic jewelry artist was an impossible woman to please. "You value your friendships."

"A man who doesn't have many friendships learns to value them a great deal."

She picked up her hamburger and he did the same, and they finished their lunch in silence. She never imagined the billionaire venture capitalist and a runaway like her could have so much in common. For the first time, Micki wondered if she could fulfill the promise she'd made to Danielle to get to know Bas better. Because the more she learned, the more she feared that a week wouldn't be nearly enough.

8

REINA PRICE'S GALLERY oozed sex, from the thick, curved handle on the glass door entrance to the lush, sculpted chairs placed strategically through the refurbished warehouse space. With the lights dim and saxophones crooning from speakers hidden somewhere in the recesses of the two-story-high ceiling, The Price Gallery sought to seduce from the minute Sebastian and Micki strolled past the doorman. They immediately received flutes of champagne from a waitress dressed all in diaphanous white. As her first excursion into an art gallery, Micki decided this one was right up her alley.

Inside dozens of internally lit, cube-shaped display cases, Reina Price's newest collection drew Micki's attention as soon as Bas escorted her through the door. Enthralled by the pins, rings, chains and pendants, shaped provocatively and inspiring all sorts of naughty possibilities, she hardly noticed when Bas left her side. He returned a few moments later with a slick brochure that detailed the history and use of each piece of jewelry.

Micki flipped through the pages, wishing she'd had time to read this before she arrived. She didn't want to say anything stupid when she met Reina Price. She didn't want to say anything stupid, period. She resented that she was worried about her conversation skills in the company of the movers and shakers who attended such events as this, but she tamped down that annoyance. She knew she looked incredibly hot in the gown Bas had bought her. A sparkling confection hand-painted with a spectrum of blues, and hand-sewn with beads, the dress draped her curves perfectly. And with so much cleavage spilling over the tight bodice, no one would be the least interested in anything coming out of her mouth.

"Now this is interesting," Micki said, her voice a whisper in case the information she'd decided to share was common knowledge to everyone mingling around them. "This collection was inspired by an illicit love affair between Reina's ancestor, a man known as *il Gioielliere,* which means 'the jeweler,' and his mistress. Reina recently inherited the schematics for the collection and reproduced them, some with the original gems. Each piece has dual purposes—aesthetic, as jewelry, and erotic, as a tool to enhance sexual pleasure."

Micki glanced at the cubed display case in front of her. Attached to a sculpted nude of a woman's torso were two tiny, jeweled clamps clinging to the nipples. A chain dangled from each then disappeared into the space between the statue's thighs. Micki's eyes widened.

"The third clamp is attached to the woman's clitoris," Bas informed her.

"Really," she responded, trying to contain the tingle that shimmied through her. Oh, the possibilities. "Interesting."

Bas chuckled. "Quite. *Il Gioielliere* had too much time on his hands, if you ask me."

She glanced up at him, then traded the brochure for her champagne. "Against the use of sex toys, Bas?"

He dipped his head, so his lips were barely an inch from the shell of her ear. "Personally, I've never had a need to purchase artificial enhancements. However, I'm not against anything that will bring you more pleasure. Why do you think we're here?"

She glanced up into those dreamy eyes of his, entertaining a dozen possibilities. ''To get me all hot and bothered?''

His hand slid to the small of her back, and he turned his shoulders slightly so no one could see how low his fingers dipped, smoothing down the light material of the dress over her buttocks. ''Is it working?''

She bit her lip, bewitched by his sinful, secret touch. The silk fabric of the dress clung to her skin, so she'd chosen thong panties to ensure nothing showed through. The feel of his hot hand on her nearly bare backside caused an instantaneous tightening of her nipples. Unfortunately, she also wasn't wearing a bra. She curved her shoulders, hoping no one noticed—no one but Bas.

''You'll just have to wait and find out,'' she said.

He tipped his champagne glass, his gaze locked with hers through the bubbly liquid. She matched his gesture, stifling a giggle when the champagne tickled her nose and teased her palate with light, crispy flavors she didn't expect. She'd never had champagne before. She'd never attended a gallery opening before. She'd never worn a dress that cost more than a month's rent or spiky shoes that defied the basic laws of physics. What an adventure this was turning out to be!

Silently, she toasted Danielle, then sipped again.

Bas gently cupped her elbow, directing her around the room so they could see the entire collection. He introduced her to his acquaintances, deflecting attempts to discuss business with uncharacteristic charm. Micki listened politely and smiled, but she couldn't help scanning the room for any sign of this Reina Price woman. She shouldn't feel jealous, but she couldn't help herself. For this fantasy week, she wanted to live under the illusion that she was Bas's only lover. As far as she was concerned, he was her only lover.

Yes, she'd had sex with other guys, but after last night on the plane, she knew without a doubt that she'd just had her first experience truly making love. After they'd returned to the house earlier, she'd realized that everything with Bas was a form of seduction—from the food he fed her to the clothes he asked her to purchase. He'd even sent a manicurist to her room after her bath, to prime and paint and buff and shine her fingers and toes. Afterward, as she'd reclined on the bed, her nails too tacky for her to attempt anything but relaxation, she'd realized that some women scheduled this luxury weekly, and it probably meant no more to them than a trip to the grocery store. Well, even a trip to the grocery store was an indulgence to Micki. And she vowed right then and there never to forget how special this time with Bas made her feel.

Reina Price entered the gallery from an upstairs office, arresting the attention of everyone in the crowd. All conversation halted and champagne glasses were juggled or abandoned so the audience could applaud.

Micki, on the other hand, nearly dropped her drink. She'd expected Reina to be gorgeous, but the woman's sensuality vibrated through the room like ripples from sonar. Her dress was a brilliant geometric collection of black and white triangles, with a strategically placed slit that showcased her long, shapely legs. She wore her glossy black hair swept away from her slim neck and shoulders and her smile, confident and just a tad cocky, told everyone in the room that she appreciated their adoration, but at the same time, she wasn't the least bit surprised. In the minute it took her to cross the room, Micki studied her stunning, but subtle confidence—though she did steal a glance or twelve at the gorgeous man holding Reina's arm possessively every step of the way.

Reluctantly, Micki looked at Bas, not really wanting to witness the adoration she guessed he felt. Though Bas applauded politely with the rest of the crowd, his dark gray gaze hadn't strayed from Micki. In fact, the look in his eyes sapped the moisture from her mouth and caused a flutter deep in her belly. She finished the rest of her champagne in one lingering sip.

"You must be Michaela," Reina said, surprising Micki so she almost choked on her drink. Close up, Reina Price was even more beautiful. Her voice held a cultured European cadence, and her dark eyes reflected keen intelligence. Gorgeous, mannered and smart, too? If not for the genuine welcome in her eyes, Micki might have had to hate her.

"I am." She extended her hand, which Reina warmly took in her own. "I'm very honored to meet you."

"Not as honored as I am to meet you. Thanks to Michaela," Reina said, explaining to her husband, "Bas made the first purchase of the evening."

Micki glanced over her shoulder at Bas, whose grin was enigmatic. Had he made the buy to please her, or Reina?

"I hope he spent a bundle," she said, curious as all getout about what he'd bought. She remembered now that he'd instructed Victor to arrange the purchase even before they arrived in New Orleans, but at that time, she hadn't known the nature of Reina's designs. Just what did he have in store for her?

Bas took another sip of his champagne. "Nothing less than a bundle will do for you, Michaela."

Reina's brow rose over her dark, exotic eyes. They may have been lovers in the past, but Sebastian's attitude evoked a look of shock from his former paramour. Micki grinned like an idiot before she caught herself and hammered the triumphant feeling down to size. It wasn't classy to be unkind.

Reina introduced her husband, and Micki couldn't fault the woman for her taste in men. Grey Masterson, like Sebastian, was cultured and mannered and incredibly hot. Man, Micki needed to reassess the crowds she ran with. She could get used to keeping company with women who knew how to capture the interests of such incredibly sexy guys while earning a living legally.

"May I show you around, Michaela?" Reina asked, taking her empty glass and handing it to Grey. "If this is your first gallery showing, I want to make sure you have a high standard by which to judge the next one."

Micki grinned. "Chances are this will be my first and only, but what the hell. I can't pass up a chance to chat with the artist herself."

Reina's laugh, despite the cultivated sound, contained just the right amount of warmth to put Micki at ease. She allowed Reina to steer her to cube after cube, entertaining Micki with the sordid history of each piece, and inferring, more than once, that she and her husband could personally vouch for the effectiveness of the sensual design.

"So which one did Bas buy?"

Reina frowned. "I promised I wouldn't tell. It was an unusual choice, but I'm intrigued he bought anything at all."

"Really? Why?"

Reina took Micki by the elbow and casually maneuvered her to a quiet corner. "You must understand that Sebastian is a dear friend of mine."

"And a former sex buddy," Micki said, not wanting any misunderstandings here. "Bas told me."

One eyebrow lifted at Micki's choice of words, but otherwise Reina didn't falter. "Honesty is very important to him. When we were involved, I knew exactly what to expect and what not to expect.''

''Same here. You're not going to warn me off or anything, are you? Because I'm not after his money and I don't even remotely believe in happily ever afters.''

Reina's tiny pout was likely as close to a frown as she could get. ''That's sad, but I can relate. Until I met Grey, I didn't believe in happily ever afters, either. But don't misunderstand. I would never presume to anticipate your motives with Sebastian. That's between the two of you and, frankly, he can take care of himself.''

''So can I,'' she insisted.

''I don't doubt that, either. Sebastian isn't attracted to weak women.''

Micki sighed. ''No, I guess he isn't. So what did he buy?''

Reina's laugh was light and conspiratorial. ''I can't tell you, but I suppose I can drop a hint.''

''Hints are good. Is it smaller than a bread box?''

''Most definitely.''

''Does it have more than one use?''

This question caused Reina to think. Her brows tilted inward and her red-tipped fingernail tapped her equally crimson lips. ''An infinite number, I believe.''

Micki's eyes widened. ''Should I be afraid?''

At this, Reina's chuckle was secretive and weighty with possible meanings. ''Afraid? With Sebastian?'' She stopped for a minute and considered her answer seriously. The pause made Micki shift from foot to foot, suddenly aware of her precarious balance on her shoes, not to mention the dangerous equilibrium of her emotions. She wanted only a fantasy, and yet, with Sebastian, she anticipated receiving so much more.

''Never be afraid with Sebastian,'' Reina concluded.

"Not so long as you've both been honest with each other. I've never seen him so interested in a woman before, so devoted to her enjoyment. You must be very special."

Micki glanced down, humbled by this woman's assessment. "Let's not jump to conclusions. Sebastian and I are just together for the kicks."

Reina shrugged with utter grace. "Believe me, Michaela. Sebastian Stone doesn't do anything just for kicks."

"Maybe he should," Micki answered.

Reina swept her hand toward a display they hadn't yet explored, her smile wide and deep. "I've never heard a truer statement in my entire life."

THEY REMAINED AT the gallery for an hour more, and by the time they left, Sebastian knew Michaela had thoroughly charmed everyone she'd spoken with. Not that he cared. The bottom line was that she charmed him more and more each moment. She didn't shy away from the provocative discussions Reina's artwork inspired, and yet she injected the conversations with humor and wit. If the sexual nature of the collection made her the least uncomfortable, she never let on. To any casual observer, she was totally at ease with her surroundings. And as she lifted the hem of her skirt to slide artfully into the back seat of the limousine he'd rented, Bas realized Micki would likely be comfortable anywhere. The most effective survival tactics he knew included the ability to meld into any situation with ease.

He hoped her confidence held steady, because tonight she'd need her courage to meet the challenge he planned.

Victor pulled the car from the curb. Michaela watched the buildings streak by outside the window, her gaze lost in the mirrored glass.

"I hope you enjoyed yourself tonight," he said.

She turned and rewarded his attempt at small talk with

a relieved grin. "I did. I thought I'd feel out of place, but between you and Reina, I fit right in. Thank you."

Bas nodded, silently perplexed as to why her simple words of gratitude touched him so deeply. "Reina is a remarkable artist."

"She's more than that. She obviously comes from your world, not mine, and yet she really went out of her way to make me feel at ease. She's very warm, friendly."

Bas toned his amusement down to a chuckle. "She is now. Marriage and true love agree with her. Not so long ago, she was exactly like me. Bored with the world."

"Bored?" She mulled this over, her hands smoothing the material of her skirt, drawing his attention to the slim shape of her legs underneath. He had a hard time concentrating on the turn of their conversation, knowing he wanted nothing more than to lift that skirt and make love to her right there in the car.

"Bored, unaffected, or at least acting that way," he admitted, moving an inch or two closer to her so their thighs touched. He wouldn't attempt a liaison here. Not when he had something so delicious planned for when they reached their destination. "When I first started traveling for business, I always included a day or two for sightseeing and exploring. But that didn't last. I found it more efficient to concentrate on the deal. Soon after, I'd been everywhere at least once. Besides, it's quite fashionable to appear as if the world holds no interest for you."

"Fashionable? In my world, acting like the world bored you was a matter of survival. If you showed interest in anything, some jerk would find a way to take it away."

"Is that what happened with Danielle?"

Michaela nodded her head. "Sometimes, yeah. Mainly, people tried to push me out of Danielle's picture so they could get their greedy hands on her money."

"This fascinates me, you know. How you seem so uninterested in financial stability."

"Uninterested in financial stability?" she asked, clearly shocked. "You've got to be kidding me. I can't wait to have money of my own."

"But you wouldn't take money from me."

"Back up. Listen to what I said. Money of my own. I took care of your sister and she took care of me, that was mutual. And with my sister, I don't mind so much her giving me a place to stay or food or helping me find a job, because that's what sisters do and I know that at some point I'll repay her."

"But you don't feel that way with me?"

Conflict flashed in her eyes. She desperately didn't want to insult him, but he counted on her honesty.

"How could I? I mean, other than sex, what can I give you that you don't already have? And if I think about the sex as anything less than mutual, then I'm no better than a prostitute, trading my body for fancy clothes and expensive travel."

"I understand."

The conversation ended there, as Bas didn't know what else to say and Michaela's gaze instantly sought out the window again, as if she were determined to leave what she'd said as her last word on the subject. He considered confessing how her mere presence in his life over the past two days had changed his outlook. Watching her at the gallery had been fascinating and even he, practiced at quelling his emotions, hadn't been able to squelch the enthusiasm over the art that had rubbed off from her. The champagne tasted fresher, the caviar richer. In fact, he couldn't remember the last time he'd eaten caviar and registered the taste at all. He ate it because it was expected. Tonight, he indulged because he cherished the bursting effects of the saltiness on his tongue—and he credited this change to Michaela.

And even if the variation was temporary, he would forever be grateful to Michaela Carmichael for giving him someone to care about other than himself.

They circled around onto Bourbon Street, avoiding the traffic from the bars and clubs that lined the street closer to Canal. And still, an eerie silence loomed. Vic pulled up in front of the house Bas had leased, but instead of killing the engine, he rolled down the partition.

The hair on the back of Bas's neck prickled to attention.

"Boss, I should check things out before you go in. Hang tight a minute."

Bas hated to allow his friend to venture out alone when they both sensed trouble, but if he tried to leave Michaela behind, she'd likely find a way to follow. Besides, protecting Bas was Victor's job and Victor would be insulted if Bas denied him the chance to earn his keep.

"Should we double back?" Bas asked.

Vic considered the suggestion, quickly and furtively following Bas's gaze when he glanced at Micki, who sat forward and listened to their exchange with rapt attention.

"Good idea, boss."

Vic turned and shifted the car into drive. They were no more than twenty feet away when an explosion rocked the street, rattling the windows of the car and sending Bas to cover Michaela with his body.

9

In what seemed like seconds after the blast, sirens pierced the night. Micki tensed. Her instinct was to run. But for once she hadn't done anything wrong. Someone had tried to hurt them. An explosion, likely from behind the house. If not for Victor's premonition of danger, they could have been inside when the blast occurred. Had the attack been aimed at them, or had they just been in the wrong place at the wrong time?

"Are you all right?" Sebastian asked, his arms and chest locking her into a curled position in the back seat. She heard the driver's door slam shut, heard the scuffle of footfalls outside the car. Not just Victor's, either. There were others all around them.

Maybe Victor hadn't had a premonition at all. Maybe he'd had extra eyes and ears—as in the security team Bas had promised, though she'd seen nothing of them up until this moment. Good. That was good.

"I'm fine," she insisted, desperate to see what was happening outside. "Let me up."

"Not until the police arrive."

Even in the evening gown, Micki knew how to move quickly. In two twists and a turn, she managed to free herself from Sebastian's protective hold. She threw herself against the seat and grinned triumphantly. The look in his eyes was as close to livid as she'd ever seen, and she further antagonized him by patting his cheek.

''You're reckless,'' he said, his words hissing through his teeth.

''No, I'm a big girl who knows the danger is over already.''

She glanced out the passenger window, her view blocked by the dark suit of a man she didn't recognize. Similarly dressed men blocked each of the four doors of the car. Behind them, another guard stood dead center of the trunk. Victor's commanding voice broke through the silence of the car.

Her gaze turned to Bas, her hand indicating the men outside. ''More security?''

''Victor arranged for a contingent of bodyguards when we arrived in New Orleans. An old army buddy of his runs a personal protection firm here. They've been guarding the premises since we arrived this morning, and we've had a tail all night. With any luck, we'll soon know who set off that explosion.''

By the time the police arrived and commandeered the crime scene, Sebastian learned that Victor's men were in hot pursuit of the perpetrator. The damage to the house had been contained mostly to the garden in the back. It amounted to several destroyed statues, shattered windows and a hole the size of a small crater where there had once been marble tile. A fire smoldered beneath the cracked floor, but nothing that would threaten the overall structure of the house. Still, had she or Sebastian been in the garden or in any of the back rooms, they might have been hurt.

And yet Micki couldn't help but suspect this wasn't so much an attempt to harm as it was another effort to scare. Distract them, maybe. But from what?

When an all-clear signal arrived from Vic, Sebastian and Micki exited the car. In addition to the fire truck, several squad cars had arrived, as well as a collection of neighbors wrapped in robes and pajamas. A contingent of patrons from the nearby Blacksmith Shoppe bar wandered down the block to watch the excitement. Luckily the night was warm. And yet Micki couldn't help but shiver while listening to a tall, handsome bodyguard named Brandon Chance run down the details of the attack with the bomb squad detective who'd just arrived.

Brandon stroked his hand through his thick dark hair, reminding her of Bas, who listened as intently as she did, but no emotion dared crack his serious, concentrated expression.

"I had a bodyguard positioned in the upstairs bedroom of a neighboring house," Brandon explained. "He watched a man wearing a dirty jacket approach through a back alley, poking in the trash bins. He reported the guy to my central contact, but the operative in command assumed he was a local hunting for recyclable bottles and cans."

"Was he there long?" Micki asked.

"Yeah, even climbed onto an overturned oil drum to peer over the stone wall."

Micki groaned, amazed how little the professionals knew about people who lived on the street. "That should have tipped you off. He wasn't from the street or he would have moved on quick. You don't loiter around ritzy houses unless you want to get arrested, harassed or worse."

Brandon nodded, and she figured that tidbit would be repeated to his contingent. "After the limousine came around the corner at Dauphine and Esplanade, my guard saw a flash of flame from under the man's coat. The explosion gave him just enough time to flee to a car parked in the alley—one we assumed belonged to a homeowner. Two of my guys are in pursuit. We hope to intercept him soon."

The detective stopped Brandon there and demanded a

description of the man and the car, which he instantly relayed to dispatch. He ordered Brandon to see to it that his bodyguards remained at a safe distance until patrol cars could intercept. No one seemed happy with this turn of events, particularly Bas and Brandon Chance, but the cops had muscled in and they had no choice but to follow their orders.

Less than an hour later, the bomb squad detective identified the explosive as common dynamite, just a quarter stick. He'd sent the remnants to the lab, hoping to identify the origin of the explosive and the make of the fuse, which might allow them to trace who had procured the dynamite. And though the house remained mostly undamaged with the exception of some broken windows, Bas sent Vic in to fetch Micki's stuff.

The simple request sent the guards from No Chances Protection into a swirl of activity. Vic emerged moments later, a scowl deepening the scars and lines on his face.

"What?" Micki asked, her heart pounding. She gazed up at the window that would have led to her room. A sinking weight dropped in her stomach.

He shook his head. "It's all ruined."

"From the explosion? How is that possible?" Micki heard her voice crack, which only made her wonder when she'd become so attached to things she'd owned for less than a week. Bas slipped his hand silently onto her shoulder.

"Not the explosion," Vic insisted. "Someone got in. Everything's destroyed." Her bag and borrowed bedroom had been ransacked, her new purchases torn to shreds. The packet of papers Bas had assembled to allow her easy access to Danielle had been ripped into tiny pieces.

"This isn't about you," Bas assured her once Victor excused himself to lead a team of police investigators upstairs to chronicle the damage. Bas stalked away silently. Though he didn't allow more than a few feet to separate them, Micki couldn't hear a word of what he said to Brandon.

When he returned, anger simmered beneath his level-toned voice. His eyes betrayed his rage. Rage not for himself, but for her. "Brandon's men had the inside of the house under surveillance, but in the melee, they weren't monitoring closely enough. A uniformed officer entered through a side door moments after the blast. They just replayed the tape. The cop had quite a good time destroying your things."

Micki shook her head. That made no sense. "How did a cop get here so fast? And why would a cop go through my stuff?"

Bas stared at her, silently verifying the only logical explanation. No cops had been called on the scene yet. The intruder had been a fake, obviously an accomplice of the man in the alley. "At the time, the bodyguards guessed the cop had wandered down from the Blacksmith Shoppe. If it gives you any solace, their erroneous assumption just got them fired."

Micki scowled. She hadn't had her new stuff for long, but she loved every pair of underwear, every blouse. And the lotions and bath salts, the makeup and shoes. Oh, the shoes! She'd lucked out on a pair of purple suede ankle boots that would have looked so slick with the new jeans embroidered with violet threads. And the *Sexcapades* book! She'd bet that son of a bitch had had one hell of a time ripping that to shreds.

"Are they sure it was a man?" she asked.

Her question must have surprised him, because his eyes widened. "Why do you ask?"

"Why would another guy care about my stuff? More and more, this sounds like the aftermath of a jealous rage."

Bas shrugged. "Brandon says they didn't get a clear enough shot of the phony police officer. He mentioned it could have been a woman. But I personally don't believe that."

"I hope those bodyguards on your payroll catch them first," she growled, but she could tell by the twinkle of amusement in Bas's eyes that he understood her anger. She wanted the perpetrator caught by men under Bas's control so she could have five, maybe ten, minutes alone with them.

"I believe the police have already usurped the pursuit. This man should be in custody soon."

"Know any prison guards...preferably ones named Snake or Brutus?" Micki quipped.

Bas quirked an eyebrow. "No, do you?"

Micki huffed, then walked back to the limousine, her shoulders curved from frustration and exhaustion. Bas was no more than a step behind her, his palm hovering just beneath her elbow, just in case she faltered from the emotional depletion seeping into her bones. She tried to ignore the intimacy of the gesture, tried to stir up her indignation that she could take care of herself, thank you very much.

But she couldn't. For once, she wanted someone else to handle the trouble. She just wanted to escape back into the fantasy of what she and Bas should have been sharing upstairs, right now, in the bedroom on the third floor, rather than deal with the fact that Bas's once faceless, nameless, purposeless stalker had become very real. And had multiplied.

"Michaela, everything lost can be replaced. I'm sure Victor will have the situation remedied by morning."

She nodded. "At least you know that whomever you thought *might* be after you, now most definitely is."

"I preferred living in the dark."

Startled, Micki turned and caught the honesty in his expression. The minute the tone and inflection of his confession caught up with the content, Micki realized that he'd said much more than he'd planned. His comment could be construed as an innocuous remark along the lines of ignorance is bliss. Yet Micki sensed that he was talking about more than the threats. He was talking about his philosophy of life.

Did wealthy, powerful Sebastian Stone truly know the depths of real darkness? Didn't the darkness he had grown accustomed to possess gilded lamps that could be switched on at will? Micki tried to contain her growing connection to Bas by belittling his loneliness, thinking that his couldn't possibly compare to the hungry despair she'd survived over these past ten years.

But the indignation wouldn't hold. They'd each experienced darkness in various scenarios and to various degrees. Their spirits were kindred. Alike. Matched and yet incomplete. At least, for now.

Micki grinned, knowing exactly what Bas needed to clear the clouds from those hypnotic pewter eyes of his—and, luckily, she needed the same tonic to steady the quiver that still resonated through her bones. Violence. Threats. Near escapes. For too long, those tight scrapes had been her daily routine. And while the threat on the plane and the explosion tonight had marred her time with Sebastian, she wouldn't allow the ugliness to color what, so far, had been the most remarkable time in her life.

"The dark has advantages," she said. "So many things two people can share without being seen, without being discovered."

The hand lingering below her arm finally made contact. The warmth of his flesh seeped through her skin, injecting her with a fire not unlike the one still smoldering in the garden behind the house. Spawned by something incendiary, flashing with the potential to consume.

The fire reflected in the centers of his irises, burning straight through her. "You amaze me, Michaela Carmichael."

"Why, because I want you? Because I'd settle for the back seat of that limousine right now rather than wait for you to sweep me off to someplace luxurious and decadent?"

He drew her closer so his breath bathed her ear in opulent heat. "No, because you make me say things, think things, I'd never admit aloud to anyone else."

She tried to shrug away the swell of pride his words inspired. She couldn't. Although she could barely admit the idea to herself, she wanted to be special to Bas. Special enough so he'd never forget her, even after their designated time together ended.

"It's easy to be honest when you know I'll be gone in a few days," she commented.

He snaked his arm around her waist and gently guided her toward the car. Only after he opened the car door and helped her inside did she realize that his gallant actions had masked his reaction to her reminder of their time limit.

He slid in the seat beside her, then waved to Vic before closing the door. "There's nothing easy about you, Michaela. Nothing at all."

THEY ARRIVED at the Windsor Court Hotel in less than fifteen minutes. The hotel manager, dogged by Vic, who remained in constant contact with Brandon Chance via cellular phone, spirited them to a sprawling suite on the twenty-second floor. While the bodyguard and the manager inspected the rooms from top to bottom, Sebastian never released Micki's arm, his hold wavering partway between protective and possessive. They stood in the corner of the foyer, their eyes locked, their skin flushed, the plans for the rest of the evening crystal clear.

Once the others left, they'd burn away the terror spawned by the bomb and the threats. Micki and Bas were two of a kind—adept at blocking out the darkness that existed around them and lived inside them. But when the pressure built to near-combustible levels, both of them sought release. Escape. Even for a brief moment. This is how they'd survived, how they'd flourished against the odds and despite the emotional desert that was their lives.

Two days ago, Micki would never have guessed she and Bas had anything in common. Now, she knew better. Like her, Bas protected himself from the world at the same time he sought to conquer it. Like him, she forced distance, even with the people she allowed close. Even Danielle didn't know her most intimate fantasies. Yet, for tonight, she entertained the romantic notion that Sebastian Stone was actually her other half, split apart from her by class and distance.

After Victor did a thorough check of the terrace, Micki drew Bas toward the open door. A soft breeze fluttered the sheers so that they swept against the polished black surface of a grand piano. Scents assailed her, exotic essences of flowers blooming just beyond, mingling with the rich scents of soil and earth. The penthouse overlooked the city, with the kaleidoscopic lights of Harrah's Casino glimmering to her right, the sultry waters of the Mississippi raging just beyond. If she closed her eyes, if she blocked out the sounds of the automobiles and cable cars trekking on the roads below them, she could have easily imagined that Bas had swept her off to a hidden paradise. A safe, secluded hideaway where, at least for tonight, no one would disturb them. No one would hurt them. No one would intrude on the fantasy they'd share just as soon as she heard the door click.

Tentatively, she explored the steps that led to a clearer view of the city. Bas allowed their contact to break while she scanned the skyline, amazed by the romantic allure of the city even from over twenty stories above. Behind her, she heard Bas and Victor whispering, planning. She pressed her lips together, closed her eyes, trying to control the rush of anticipation surging through her bloodstream.

Just before they'd left Reina's gallery and long before the explosion at the house in the Quarter, she'd witnessed a quiet exchange between Victor and Sebastian, who'd slipped a velvet pouch into his pocket. No doubt, his secret purchase from Reina's collection was inside. What had he bought? With any other man, Micki would never have entertained the idea of introducing a sex toy into their lovemaking, even something as lovingly handcrafted as the pieces Reina produced. But Bas wasn't just any man. Whatever Sebastian planned for them, she knew without reservation that she'd wake up tomorrow morning one satisfied woman.

The only worry niggling at her consciousness was the part of their deal they hadn't yet settled—who would be the master in the *Sexcapade* scenario they would explore. She'd counted on taking the lead, holding the reins to what might be her last shot at a full-fledged fantasy. At lunch, she hadn't even considered telling him about her past, about the scarring effects of her affair with Jazz, about what specifically had driven her to distrust nearly every man who entered her life since. God, she'd tried to put that black episode of her life behind her. The despair, the shame, would otherwise haunt her, disable her, stop her forward momentum.

After Jazz had beat the last of his frustrations out on her, she'd pulled herself back together and cleaned up her act. She tried to cling to that end result, but ultimately she couldn't deny her past. She'd hit rock bottom before she'd bounced back. She'd decided that as long as she lived on the streets, she couldn't depend on anyone but herself to watch her back. Taking Danielle into her life had been risky enough, but that one act of kindness had led her here, to a luxurious suite overlooking the seductive city of New Orleans with a man she knew would never hurt her.

Meeting his former lover tonight had only deepened Micki's trust of Sebastian Stone. Reina Price wasn't just a successful businesswoman and inventive artist—she was a smart, warmhearted woman who respected Sebastian, even after the end of their affair. Micki hadn't had that many lovers in her lifetime, but once she ditched one, he was history. No friendships, no mutual respect. In her world, there had been no reason for either. But once she'd seen Reina and Sebastian interact, and enjoyed Reina's personal hospitality, Micki understood once more just how different her life on the streets had been from the rest of the world.

If she ended up on the losing end of tonight's proposition, she wouldn't run, wouldn't hide—wouldn't surrender to the fear she thought she'd overcome so long ago. She'd work through this. In Bas's hands, she could find a pleasure to last a lifetime, if she gave herself the chance.

She emerged from her thoughts to realize Victor had disappeared. Bas joined her on the terrace, quietly climbing the stairs and standing behind her so his body heat touched her even before his hands encircled her waist.

"Anything new on the lady in the alley?" she asked.

Bas clucked his tongue. The sound sent a shiver racing down her spine and she instinctively curved her neck so he could put that tongue of his to better use.

He placed a soft kiss just below her ear before he answered. "When he started driving recklessly on the freeway, the police called off the chase. Victor and Brandon intend to investigate further. They're returning to the house now to retrace the steps, try to pick up a second trail."

"Who's watching our backs tonight?"

Bas grinned. "The hotel is alert to the situation and the manager is remaining on duty all night to ensure that nothing and no one disturbs us. And Brandon Chance has several men positioned around the hotel. We have nothing to worry about inside this suite."

She twisted around in his arms, enjoying the feel of the scented night air on her skin while Bas embraced her with his heat. "Must be nice to have so much money people are tripping over their feet to take care of you."

He pursed his lips, nodded. "It doesn't suck."

She laughed. "That phrase so doesn't fit you."

His eyes twinkled. "Really? What sort of words fit me?"

"Why don't you try on 'Yes, Mistress' for size?"

With humor in his scowl, he dipped his hand into his jacket. "How about we flip for it?"

He pulled out the velvet pouch, untied the cord and after grabbing her hand and positioning her palm flat, he poured out the contents. Cool metal kissed her skin. When she glanced closer, she realized he'd given her a coin.

"We're going to flip a coin?"

He toyed with the coin still cupped in her palm, his fingers stroking the sensitive skin inside her hand. "A quaint custom. Inherently fair, if you consult the law of averages."

Micki tilted the coin toward her fingers, then pinched it between her thumb and forefinger. In the dim light, she couldn't make out the images stamped into the metal. But if the piece had been part of Reina Price's erotic collection, she could only imagine how heads and tails were represented.

Bas held out his hand, inviting her back indoors. She complied, and instantly sought a lamp. She wasn't so far off the mark. On one side, the image of a man's hand caressing a woman's bottom was etched into the gold. On the other, an erect penis just about to press into a woman's mons.

"Just what is the history of this coin?" she asked, knowing each and every piece in the collection they'd seen had a sensual purpose. A notch in the top told her the coin could be worn on a chain.

He slid up behind her, his hands smoothing over her hips before he cupped his palm beneath her hand. "According to the brochure, the jeweler attached this coin to a chain his mistress wore around her stomach. They'd often flip the coin to decide the direction of their lovemaking. Would he take her from behind, with his hands free to arouse her from all angles," he asked, stepping closer so Micki could feel his full erection against her backside, "or would he slip inside from the front and use his mouth to stimulate her breasts and neck and shoulders?"

He punctuated the possibility with a warm, wet kiss at the sensitive curve of her neck, then suckled a sweet path to her ear. She could barely concentrate on the coin with Bas arousing her so easily, so thoroughly.

"For our purposes, I propose we first flip the coin to decide who plays the slave in our scenario tonight. I call heads, for obvious reasons."

Micki swallowed deeply, then spun around, knowing that holding on to her determination required she act quickly and with as little thought as possible.

"You're on."

10

AS THE COIN FLIPPED in the air, Sebastian heard Michaela catch her breath. He stepped back, allowing the gold disc to drop to the carpeted floor. It bounced. Twice. The light from the nearby lamp glistened off the surface. He dropped to one knee to examine the result.

"It's heads," he announced.

Even in the dim light, he didn't miss the subtle fade of color from her skin. Before he could decide if her lips truly quivered or if it was a trick of the uncertain light, she pressed her mouth closed with tight determination.

He recognized the reaction—she hated to be afraid. But fighting the natural reaction to danger had likely saved her life on several occasions. *No fear* would be the most appropriate motto to describe the Michaela Carmichael the world at large saw when she walked into a room. But in a short span of time, Sebastian had learned to see past the image she projected, beyond the persona she clung to like a lifesaver in a storm. He'd seen the look of fear in her clear sapphire eyes before—too many times over the past forty-eight hours. He never intended for fear to be the most prevalent emotion between them. Desire, yes. Passion, absolutely. But not fear.

And yet, between the threat to his airplane, the bomb tossed into the garden of their rented house and his brilliant idea to turn the tables on her *Sexcapade* fantasy by denying her absolute control, fear had become too familiar for his comfort—or hers. And he hadn't even told her the latest news Vic had delivered just before his departure. The bomber had not only ransacked Michaela's bedroom at the French Quarter house, the culprit had left a calling card. They'd found a sweetly scripted letter stabbed into Michaela's pillow with an ice pick lifted from the kitchen. He didn't know the specific verbiage. He didn't need to. All he knew was that he'd move heaven and earth to make sure nothing bad happened to Michaela—especially at his hands.

"We can dissolve our agreement right now, Michaela, if you aren't comfortable."

He watched the possibility play in her eyes. The brief consideration slowly dimmed the underlying anxiety, but after a few seconds, she shook her head.

"No. We have a deal."

Bas pocketed the coin and rose. "What we share shouldn't be about deals."

A half grin lifted the side of her mouth. "What about mergers?"

He closed the scant distance between them. Her resilience amazed him, and when coupled with her beauty and her innate sensuality, he knew he didn't stand a chance at denying her anything she asked for, even if he knew she feared the ultimate outcome. When he touched her hand, his suspicions were verified. She was shaking, no matter how ramrod straight she held her spine to keep the quiver from knocking her off her feet.

"I propose we drop this *Sexcapade* proposal and move on to a merger that isn't so binding," he suggested.

She quirked one eyebrow. "Binding? What, were you planning on tying me up?"

"The possibility occurred to me," he answered, though in truth he'd never attempt anything so constricting with Michaela. Not yet. And if things didn't progress over the next few days, perhaps not ever. She was skittish, yet secretive. He realized that while he'd divulged a great deal about his sexual past, she'd remained relatively silent on the matter. He'd respected her privacy, content to ignore whatever she didn't want to share. But right now he reconsidered the wisdom of that strategy.

"I'm game," she said, every aspect of her expression and body language exuding bold, brazen confidence.

She was good at putting on a show. Even if only for herself.

But if he called her on it, where would that get him? Or her? He had to look outward—toward the end result. He wanted to make love to her, but he wanted her to do so without any doubt. Bas knew that uncertainty and conjecture could be powerful aphrodisiacs, when administered in palatable doses. *When will he kiss me? When will he touch me? If he licks me again, I'll come, but if he doesn't, I'll go insane.* These were the only concerns Michaela should entertain tonight.

"I'm sure you are. If that's how you feel, then let the fantasy begin.... But I suggest we keep tonight simple. Okay, slave?"

Her smile wavered, but she recovered in the split second it took for him to take both her hands in his and lead her toward the bedroom. In the distance between the music room and the master suite, he altered and arranged his tactics. Yes, tonight Michaela Carmichael would become his love slave. He'd direct her, order her, test her. He'd push beyond the unspoken limits stamped into Michaela's psyche, perhaps her very soul.

Yet, at the same time, he'd ensure that she experienced her ultimate, hidden power—that undeniable domination a sensual, uninhibited woman would forever hold over a man like him.

MICKI TRAILED BEHIND Bas, her fingers locked in his, her eyes focused on the slight undulation of his shoulders beneath his tailored jacket. Even crossing a room, he exuded power. She doubted there was anything she could say, anything she could do, that would break down the steel foundation of his control. Even last night on the plane, when they'd tumbled through the air in sexual bliss, she suspected he could have pulled back at any moment, if he'd wanted to. Luckily for both of them, pulling back hadn't once entered either of their thoughts.

But tonight was different. The closer they got to the bedroom, the more Micki wondered if she could go through with the fantasy scenario now that she wasn't in charge. For the first time, she acknowledged—to herself—that she was scared.

Not because she thought for one minute that Sebastian Stone would wield his power to humiliate her. Over the past two days, she'd come to know that he respected women, revered them even. He wasn't Jazz. He wouldn't trick her or charm her into believing she was the most special woman in his life just to turn on her later, try to degrade her in the worst way possible.

The memory slammed her in the gut, stopping her from crossing the threshold with Bas.

He turned, his eyes brimming with questions, concern. "Michaela?"

She pressed her lips together, but quickly decided that silence wasn't serving her the way it had in the past. She couldn't run from the memories anymore. So long as she continued to confront her sensual self, the recollections would haunt her. And now that she'd tasted sexual pleasure again, she couldn't imagine denying herself any longer. But if Bas heard the truth about her affair with Jazz, if he understood the depths she'd sunk to...what? She didn't want

Bas to save her. She could save herself. And yet, she wanted him to know.

"I once had a lover named Jazz Jericho," she said, her words rushing out, breathless, urgent.

He turned and took both of her hands in his. "You don't need to tell me about your past, Michaela. Your former lovers don't matter to me."

"They matter to me. Well," she said, rolling her eyes as she formulated an amendment, "my *past* matters, because it effects what happens here, between us."

"No," he insisted, reeling her closer. He encircled her with his arms, then drew his hands up her back so his fingers could toy with the thin straps of her dress. He didn't slip them over her shoulders or attempt to undress her. He just played with the material, making her wonder if or when he'd bare her breasts to his hungry gaze.

"You don't have to confront your past now if you don't want to. This time we have can be about fantasy, dreams—the perfect love affair. You can forget everything else and lose yourself in the illusions I'll create for you."

Her mouth dried, and a tiny ache twisted in her chest. What he offered sounded so tempting, as alluring as the wondrous lovemaking she knew she'd experience with him, no matter who took the role of the master or the slave.

And yet Micki had spent so much of the past ten years running away from her life. From her childhood difficulties with her grandmother, to her mother's abandonment of her, to her decision to run way from home and, ultimately, to her life on the streets, Micki had become infinitely adept at casting the ugliness of her reality to the back of her mind. The talent had served her well in some cases—allowing her to hold tight to hope when she had little reason to believe—but it also set her up for her disaster and disillusionment, thanks to Jazz.

She didn't want those emotions with Bas. Yes, she wanted the fantasy—but, dammit, she wanted the reality, too. If only for this brief time.

"You sure know how to make a girl an offer that's tough to refuse," she confessed.

He placed his hands on her cheeks. "But you will refuse," he guessed.

And, of course, he was right.

"I want to tell you," she said, glancing over his shoulder at the dark bedroom. "Before we go in. Before I indulge the fantasy, I want to lay the reality to rest."

Though she watched his jaw quake slightly, a tiny smile tilted the corners of his mouth and lit his eyes to glossy silver. He dropped to his knees, leaned his back against the doorjamb, and guided her down to the carpet beside him. The act was so casual, so unexpected—so unguarded and real—she thought she might cry.

"Tell me," he said, his voice deep with assurance, "but know that nothing you say will change what I've decided about you."

"Which is?" she asked, curling her legs beneath her and snuggling close. Only a couple of days ago, she wouldn't have given a damn what Sebastian Stone thought about her, as long as he made the arrangements to help his sister. Now, she cared very much. More than she wanted to admit.

"Michaela Carmichael," he said, his voice appropriately wistful, "a woman with an irrepressible sense of fun and love for life. More intelligent than she gives herself credit for, and yet if she gave herself any more credit, she'd be annoyingly cocky. Her beauty runs deep, to her soul, and even though I'm neglecting all my business to make this week special for her, I consider every moment worth it. Whoever this Jazz Jericho person was to you, doesn't matter to me in the least."

She didn't doubt his sincerity, but knew he was working with limited information. How could he make that type of assessment before he knew the whole story? "What if I told you I murdered him?"

He cracked another smile. "I'd say he deserved it."

She rolled her eyes. "You didn't even know him."

Bas cleared his throat. "Anyone named Jazz Jericho is highly suspect in my book."

She laughed, despite the serious confession she was about to undertake. "I'm fairly certain that wasn't his real name."

"All the more reason to knock the guy off." The utter and complete seriousness of his expression and declaration stunned her. He was cracking another joke, in his irrepressibly dry, Sebastian Stone way.

She slapped him on the shoulder. "Would you stop that?"

He had the audacity to adopt an innocent expression. "Stop what?"

"Humoring me!" she said.

Bas shook his head disapprovingly. "You're ordering me. Remember who won the coin toss?"

"We're not in the bedroom. Yet," she replied.

"We set no perimeters regarding location."

She pressed her lips together. "True. You're not going to try and distract me from telling my tale, are you?"

His eyes lit with endless possibilities. "How devious do you think I am?"

"I think you invented the word *devious,*" she answered.

"I plead the Fifth."

She nodded, but his ruse worked, and instantly she second-guessed her decision to tell him about her past before they made love again. God, the appeal of shedding her inhibitions and walking into that bedroom with nothing more than her focus on pleasure and Sebastian's devious mind to guide her was truly tempting. His fingers snaking sensually around her ankle didn't help. With concentrated interest, he manipulated the tiny buckle on the strap of her shoe with his strong, yet elegant fingers, then oh-so-skillfully guided her foot into his lap.

"Bas," she said, her voice fraught with warning.

"Yes?"

Again, the innocence. As if he didn't know that his smooth and steady touch, tracing the sensitive skin along her arch, would soon drive her insane.

"You're distracting me. Again."

He continued his fascinated exploration of her foot for nearly a full minute before meeting her stare. "Am I? Seems to me if I can distract you this easily, the confession you seem so intent on making can wait a few minutes more. Maybe even hours."

Dare she? Micki stared into the unlit bedroom again, her eyes searching for some reassurance, some promise, that she'd be able to go through with the scenario she'd chosen from the *Sexcapade* book without chickening out, without allowing the hideousness of her past to overshadow the beauty that could be in her future. Confession might have been good for her soul, but perhaps facing the fears head-on would produce an even more rewarding result. She believed Bas when he claimed nothing she said about her past would change what they'd shared so far. If he hadn't judged her harshly from the minute they'd met—her in her piss-poor clothes and trash-talking mouth, he wouldn't judge her because of a mistake she'd made once in the name of misdirected love.

Though her concern hadn't been Bas's opinion of her—it was taking orders from a man, truly and honestly allowing him to direct their lovemaking.

She gathered her silk skirt and pulled her knees under her, preparing to stand. Bas moved quicker, on his feet and helping her up gallantly before she could change her mind.

"You're right. My story can wait."

His smile reached his eyes, and she knew then he would have been happy with whichever choice she made. Sex first, discussion later—okay by him. Discussion first, sex in the aftermath—that was fine, too. As long as they made love again, they'd both find satisfaction.

"You're ready to submit to me, then?" he asked.

She took a deep breath. God, if any other man had asked her that question, she would have turned tail and run so fast, he might have gotten windburn. Or else, she might have socked him in the gut. Or maybe, she might have suffered through the challenge he presented, surrendering to his will only because of her pride, because she'd made a deal and she'd be damned if she'd show any weakness by backing out now.

But none of those scenarios applied here. She would take on the role of Bas's love slave willingly, for two reasons. One, to prove to herself that Jazz Jericho no longer held any power over her. And two, because Sebastian Stone was incredibly adept at taking control. She could only imagine what delights his mastery would bring her.

"Yes, Master. I'm ready."

NEVER IN HIS LIFE had Bas admired a woman's courage more than he did Michaela's at this moment. A concentrated desire surged in his blood, rushing to his head, knocking his equilibrium for a loop.

Whoever this Jazz Jericho character was, Bas would see to it he suffered greatly for whatever unnamed trouble he'd caused Michaela. But he pocketed his thoughts of justice and revenge to be explored another time.

Tonight was about Michaela.

She placed her fingers gently in his palm, and he led her into the darkness of the bedroom. He'd had no time to set the stage ahead of time as he'd planned at the leased house in the French Quarter. Again, he'd have to improvise. He knew only that Victor had supplied two toiletry bags salvaged from the ransacked bedrooms, along with a fresh box of condoms his bodyguard had purchased in the gift shop downstairs.

Tiny pinpoints of moonlight streaked into the room from around the edges of the drawn curtains. Bas's eyes quickly adjusted and his mind worked overtime creating the best scenario. Yes, he was the master tonight, but that didn't mean she wouldn't enjoy the subjugation he had planned. The slave must follow the master's every command. Tonight, the only command he really had was that Michaela forget the bad memories that had almost waylaid this fantasy.

When he and Michaela reached the center of the room, inches from the footboard of the bed, he dropped her hand and ordered her to remain still.

The lamp from the other room beamed on her, sending shards of light sparkling off the beads on her blue dress. Her skin shimmered, gleaming from the glittery lotion she'd smoothed over her skin after showering. It smelled like lavendar and violet—sweet, floral, fresh. He spied a tall cushioned stool in a corner, retrieved it, then set it down beside her.

He kicked off his shoes, discarded his socks. He took off his jacket, knowing he didn't have to order Michaela to watch because never once did her gaze stray from him. She didn't hide her admiration, her desire, or coyly look away. She stared with brazen boldness, even licking her lips expectantly when he unwound his tie and tossed it to the floor.

He popped the top button of his shirt. After fluffing the pillows high on the headboard, he reclined on the mattress and folded his arms behind his head so he could see her clearly when he issued his first command.

''Undress for me, Michaela.''

The request was so simple, even she smiled.

''A striptease?'' she asked.

''Something along those lines. Too predictable for you?''

She shook her head, her gaze locked with his. ''I've never stripped for anyone before.'' She pulled one strap down off her shoulder, then traced the thin line with her finger as it curved on her arm. ''You'll have to tell me exactly what to do.''

His blood pressure spiked—he could feel the rush through his veins. Bas closed his eyes briefly, chastised. And turned on. He should have known Michaela would find a way to match his authority and set him on the edge of his comfort zone. Yes, he wanted to direct her—but when she laid down her demand, so cleverly masked behind innocent words, the stakes shot through the roof.

She'd put herself on equal footing, and likely had no clue.

''How specific do you want me to be?'' he asked.

Her chin lifted, her sapphire eyes wide. ''You're the master. I'm just the slave. You tell me what you want, and I'll perform for you.''

Pushing back against the cushions, he raised his body higher, ensuring he could see nearly every inch of her. ''Hmm, I've never asked a woman to strip for me before. Where shall I begin?''

She shrugged her shoulders, which further dislodged the bodice of her gown. Her luscious, round breasts were nearly unveiled, yet cast in dark shadow, thanks to the light glimmering behind her.

He rolled over, clicked on the bedside lamp. Micki flinched, which caused one breast to bare for just a flash until she covered herself quickly. She'd promised him a striptease, and apparently she would stick to her word.

"Your dress is so snug around your rib cage and waist. Turn around."

She obeyed.

"Reach behind you and open your zipper."

Again she complied, glancing over her shoulder with erotic interest, biting her bottom lip as if the unlatching of each metal tooth in the zipper revealed something as arousing to her as to him. Smooth flesh, pale and creamy. A spine curved by her comfortable stance. A slim waist, flared hips, buttocks round and full. When the zipper reached the bottom, the dress pooled to the ground like a sparkling blue cloud.

She didn't move.

"You're so lovely," he said, intrigued by the *T*-shape of her thong panties, curving around her derriere in glimmering white. White panties. He'd expected black, even dark blue, perhaps. Aquamarine to match the dress, her eyes.

But white?

Bas acknowledged long ago his appreciation for all things sensual. Gourmet food, fine wine, rare art and casual sex. That he noted the color of her panties didn't surprise him, nor did he connect any symbolic meaning. It's just that he never realized how flattering the stark glossiness of the white silk could be.

"Face me," he ordered, "but cover your breasts."

He didn't wish to be distracted. And he wanted his revelations doled out slowly, so he could aptly appreciate each and every one.

The tiny triangle of white between her legs barely covered the dark curls beneath. His mouth dried, anticipating the sensation of those tight coils against his trimmed mustache and beard. Last time, on the plane, he'd had no time to taste her. Yes, he'd intended for their encounter to be slow and thorough, but, in retrospect, he realized how much he'd missed.

He'd miss nothing tonight.

And neither would she.

11

AS MICKI TURNED, the light from the lamp bathed her body in lustrous gold. Sebastian's expectant eyes inflamed her flesh from the inside out, and yet she couldn't imagine a more glorious heat. Her mind flashed back to their liaison on the plane. Foremost in her mind about that night—second only to the glorious release of their joining—was the slow pace Bas had set. At the time, she'd guessed that he preferred his sexual encounters this way—with a lazy pace that allowed for maximum pleasure. Completely the opposite of her former affairs, which were more along the lines of *wham-bam, thank you, ma'am.*

Now, she wondered. At his current pace, she wouldn't feel him inside her until dawn. And no matter what deal they had made, she didn't think she could wait—even though he adored her with his eyes, his words. Even though he made her feel like the most amazing creature ever to walk the earth.

The brightness of his teeth contrasted with his tanned skin. His thick brows tilted over his glossy gray eyes, his expression wavering between reverently worshipful and devilishly determined. Either way, her body tingled. Her nipples, cupped beneath her own hands, pebbled and tightened. She was nearly tempted to pinch the edge off her own throbbing need, but she didn't dare.

"White looks lovely against your skin."

She glanced down at the tiny triangle of her panties. "I'm not wearing much," she said.

"A little goes a long way. When I make love to you, I want you to keep your panties on. And you'll be on top. I'll use my finger to hook aside the sliver of material between your legs. How does that sound?"

Like sweet torture.

"Whatever you wish, Master."

This time, she couldn't hide the sardonic sound in her voice. And by the way his brow arched, he'd heard it, too.

He clucked his tongue. "Michaela. You sound as if you aren't taking our bargain very seriously."

She licked her lips, but didn't reply. He had no clue how seriously she took him. She was seriously hot for him, seriously enthralled by the sensations, the pace, the ultimate outcome. He'd just told her she'd be on top. He'd described how he would make love to her with her panties still on. The possibility appealed to her on wickedly intimate levels.

"Well?"

Oh, he wanted an answer.

She swallowed. "I'm having trouble concentrating on our little game."

"Really? Not interesting enough? Maybe too tame?"

She glanced aside. Yeah, so far, things had been on the mild side, but she definitely wouldn't classify her slow, sensual striptease as uninteresting.

She shook her head, unwilling to form an answer.

"You expect me to degrade you, don't you?"

Her tongue thickened. No, she didn't expect it. Not from him. But wasn't there an edge of subjugation in a sex slave fantasy?

"I'm not going to degrade you, Michaela. You've been degraded. I'm not going to force you to do anything you don't want to do—I imagine that's old hat to you as well."

She nodded slightly. She hadn't told him anything about Jazz yet. Nothing specific. Did he know?

"What I'm going to do, Michaela," he said, his voice brimming with sensual promise, "is pleasure you. In ways you've never imagined."

He let his vow linger in the air. The moment she understood what he said, it must have shown on her face, because he sat back, grinned, and issued his first order.

"Sit on the stool," he commanded, his voice a little rougher this time, though still deep and fluid like warm, spiced honey.

She did as he asked, cocking one side of her buttocks onto the plush cushion.

"Sit completely on the cushion. Hook your feet over the side rungs."

She complied, spreading her knees to accommodate his request. The material of her panties parted, and the cool air kissed the warmth pooling between her thighs.

"Uncover your breasts."

She did, but he stopped her when she dropped her arms to her sides.

"No, cup them, for me. Such a lovely, female shape."

Her flesh felt heavy in her hands, swollen with the rush of hot blood surging through her. For the first time, Bas moved closer, inching across the bed on his hands and knees, like a sleek, mighty cat stalking toward his prey. So raw, powerful. He stopped at the footboard, his hands gripping the wood.

"When I taste you, Michaela, you'll soar, I promise."

She closed her eyes.

"Don't you believe me?"

She could tell from his tone that he toyed with her.

"Yes."

"Open your eyes, then."

She did.

"Let's see how it will feel, when I flick your nipples with my tongue. Wet your fingers."

Her stare shot to his gaze and the intense heat nearly forced her to turn away.

"What?"

"Take your fingers in your mouth, your thumb and forefinger. Wet them. Then show me exactly how you want me to arouse you."

"You know how," she insisted, not sure where this could lead, though she had a strong idea.

He arched a disapproving brow. She was arguing with him. Love slaves didn't argue.

Her fingers tasted salty. She imagined her breasts would, too. The sultry night air blew through the suite, bathing her skin in a thin sheen of perspiration. Every glance from Bas, every utterance from his mouth, and her body heat intensified. Before the night was through, she figured she'd be no more than a pool of satisfied gelatin snuggled in the satin sheets on the bed.

If she ever got to the bed.

The sooner she complied with his commands, the sooner she'd receive her reward. And yet applying her own moisture to her breasts seemed over the top, even for her.

"You're hesitating."

She grinned, caught.

"I've never pleasured myself before."

"Never?" His disbelief rang clear.

"Not with someone watching," she amended. She talked a good game, but for the most part Micki had ignored her sexuality. On the streets, sex was something done for kicks, something to release the tension. It was fast and physical, lacking any of the emotional and sensual depth Bas had introduced into the mix. When she'd first torn the *Sexca-*

pade page out of the book, she'd imagined one raucous evening telling Mr. Sebastian Stone how she wanted her toes licked. But he'd turned the tables on her, so much so they still spun.

He swung his legs over the bed, leaning forward on his elbows. With two quick flicks, he detached his cuff links and sent them clattering to the ground. He turned back his cuffs and released another button on his shirt.

Yes, he was as hot as she was.

"Wet your fingers again, then show me what you like."

This time, Micki quickly moistened her fingers and without stopping to think, she pressed the wetness directly against her nipple in a slow but steady squeeze. She licked her other hand, so she could experience the explosion of pleasure in both breasts concurrently. Her chin dropped to her chest. Her hair dangled around her face, veiling her expression from him—and vice versa. The pressure built, then ebbed as she traced the dark ring around her nipples, massaging and arousing, amazed at the change in the length and color of her flesh.

"You want me to pleasure your breasts?" he asked.

"Yes," she answered.

"For how long?"

"Not too long."

"Other parts of you need me, as well. Where? Show me."

Without direction, her hand seemed to slide down her slick body, toward the triangle of silk and curls quivering with need. She caught herself for a moment, diverting to the other areas of her body she knew deserved and desired his attention.

She splayed her hand across her belly, then up to her neck. She stabbed both of her hands through her hair, lifting the glossy strands off her damp neck, so he could see how she wanted him to run his tongue from her shoulder to her earlobe as he had the night before. Soon, she was touching her breasts again, kneading and massaging, wishing her hands were his.

"You're driving me wild," he claimed, tearing off his shirt, but remaining perched on the edge of the bed. A foot away and drinking in her every writhing movement, Bas concentrated on her as if he'd never watched a woman work herself into a lusty frenzy before.

She stopped, focused all her attention on him—her hands still, her gaze locked with his.

He looked wild. Wide-eyed, nostrils flaring, mouth slightly open in a hungry pant. All because of her?

The thought was stupendously liberating. She'd already done more with Bas, for Bas, than she had with any other man. And while she'd feared that being his love slave would somehow counter the independence and self-reliance she was determined to carve for herself, she knew now that wasn't the case.

Not with Bas. Because, so far, all of his orders had centered on her pleasure, not his.

"What next, Master?"

His eyes flashed, as if he suddenly remembered the game they played.

"More of the same, love."

Her heart skipped a beat. She knew what he wanted her to do, but could she? With him watching?

"I can't," she said, a deep flush suffusing through her body.

He clucked his tongue. "Where's fearless Micki Carmichael? Certainly you aren't afraid to show me how to get you hot."

"I'm not afraid of you," she said, half defiant, half surprised.

"There's no need to be, because when I use this knowledge against you, it will only be for your sexual pleasure. Go on, Micki, show me."

With an athletic leap, he pushed himself off the bed and stood, barefooted, bare-chested and magnificent, not twelve inches away from her. Her skin, still thrumming, tingled. He circled her, hunting, admiring, inhaling the essences of her perfume, her lotion, her natural musk. He dipped his head once to pass his nose along the slope of her shoulder, setting all her nerve endings on alert. God, she wanted him.

At last, he positioned himself in front of her.

"Do it."

She closed her eyes tightly and slipped her hand lower. Her flesh instantaneously reacted, throbbing wildly, creaming with sweet moisture. She slipped one finger inside, and the shock stole her breath.

"More," he demanded. "One slim finger will hardly prepare you for me, now will it?"

Her eyes flashed open wide and she swallowed, slightly calmed by the feral look in his eyes, dangerous but captivating. He leaned back against the footboard, content to watch. She did as he asked and the minute she made contact with her clit, she sucked in a ragged breath.

"Yes, that's it. Build it. Touch your breasts with your other hand. Take the pleasure, Michaela. Make it yours."

Seduced by the sensations, she followed his commands. She pressed deeper, harder. Her body skittered on the edge of climax, just another few seconds away.... Then he commanded her to stop.

"What?" she asked, dazed.

"You don't think I'm going to allow you to have all the fun, do you? Catch your breath. Then remove my slacks."

The first order all night that resembled anything close to a real command and Micki couldn't wait to comply.

What she'd discovered about herself, about her body, was worth the price of his gentle slavery. She calmed the quiver in her hand and forced herself to undo his belt slowly, eking the leather strap out of the tight loops without rush, watching his eyes the entire time, trying to recognize one glimpse of impatience, one spark of unchecked eagerness.

All she saw was desire. Desire for her. And the desire to do whatever it took to have her, no matter how much time passed. Her own body pulsed with a sweet, persistent ache—because of him and his seductive manipulations.

For an instant, after she dropped the belt to the floor and pressed her fingers to the button on top of his waistband, she thought she spied a glimpse of wildness again. But even when she released the zipper, her hands pressing against his stiff erection, he held his gaze steady, even if his pupils had dilated to nearly black.

With a tug, his pants whooshed to the ground. He stepped out of the dark tailored slacks and kicked them aside. Only then did he grab her by the hips and press her close, nearly swallowing her with a long, hungry kiss. His tongue mastered hers in moments, and caught up so completely in the sensations, she nearly forgot to kiss him back.

But when she remembered, she unleashed all she had. She pressed her hands on his chest, explored the tight sinews of his pecs and abs, then found his nipples and plied the magic she'd learned on her own body to pleasuring his. A groan, torn from so deep within him she almost didn't register the sound, spurred her to push harder. She dropped one hand to his waist, grasped at his firm buttocks and, in the same instant, reached for his sex with her other palm.

He countered by lifting her off her feet. His cock teased her, taunted her, but remained out of reach, even after he laid her on the bed, then turned toward the bedstand. She heard a rustle. He was going for the condom. And damn, she wanted to be the one to put it on.

"Let me," she said anxiously, scooting toward him.

"Lie back," he ordered.

She frowned. And yet before she could push her lust aside long enough to form words to express her disappointment, he joined her on the bed, pressing her hard into the soft mattress.

His mouth thoroughly explored hers. With tongue and lips and teeth, he awakened every nerve ending in her mouth, cheeks, chin, neck, ears and lower. He bathed and tasted and tweaked every inch of her skin, finally descending to her breasts.

"You wanted the pinch first, yes?" he asked, then nipped her so she cried out in surprise and delight.

"Then something hard, but not so hard as before."

He suckled her then, sending her body into sensitivity overdrive. Her eyes flew open wide, then shut tight. Her hands grasped at his back, neck and hair. His mustache teased her sensitive flesh, his thin beard taunted as his chin brushed against her. She moaned his name over and over.

He stopped, eyeing her through long, dark lashes.

"But you wanted me to pleasure both breasts at once. How will I do that?"

Wickedly, he licked one breast thoroughly, then used his fingers to manipulate the moisture while he attended the other breast with his mouth. Micki's body flamed with need, and he wished he'd move lower and sate the relentless tremble deep inside her. She didn't have to speak her yearning—practically a split second after the thought dashed through her mind, Bas descended the length of her body.

Micki closed her eyes, filled with anticipation of his mouth exploring her most intimate flesh. He didn't disappoint her. After slipping his arms beneath her knees and gently tilting her hips, he dipped his tongue tentatively into her moist, dark curls.

Her breath deserted her. Her heart slammed against her chest, beats echoing in her ears. His tongue stroked, explored, aroused her to the point that she lost her place in time and space. The room swirled when he probed deeper, and by the time he reached her center, she knew she was lost.

She soared over the edge, propelled by a cascade of sensations that rocked her to the core. He eased her to calm with soft kisses and whispered words. When her mind was clear enough to listen, she committed each and every promise to memory.

She licked her lips, her mouth dry, her throat hoarse. Had she screamed that loudly? ''I thought I was supposed to be the slave. The one giving you pleasure.''

His deep, low chuckle shot heat straight through to her marrow. ''Don't I look like I'm enjoying myself?''

Surprisingly, he did. But while each moment with Sebastian led to another discovery regarding her limited experience with real men—men who didn't need to own or control a woman—she couldn't ignore the basics.

He'd touched *her. He'd* pleasured *her.* He knew every private part of her, but he'd yet to allow her the same exploration.

''Please, Sebastian.''

He slid back up her body, kissing and stroking as he traveled, but didn't speak until his mouth could brush against hers. ''I'll tell you what,'' he said, brushing her legs apart with his knees and pressing the firm head of his cock against her. ''When you win the coin toss, you can do whatever you like. Right now, the master wants to slip inside his slave. And I want to hear your pleasure, do you understand?''

He captured her hands in his, held them with mock-roughness above her head. ''Loud and clear, now, Michaela.''

Micki felt her body melt into the mattress, curving into the softness in compliant anticipation of their joining, then realized he was changing the rules. He'd promised she would be on top. As master, he had that prerogative. But she wasn't any ordinary love slave. She was one determined to make this man lose control.

''Oh, I'll scream for you, Bas, if that's what turns you on. But you promised I could be on top, remember?''

He quirked one eyebrow, a half grin denoting that he had indeed forgotten, and that by reminding him, she'd won some serious points.

''Never let it be said that I renege on my promises.''

Micki acted quickly, pushing him over onto his back before he had a chance to flip her. Still wet from her orgasm, still pulsing from release, Micki slid her moistness over him. He'd chosen a ribbed condom this time, and the tiny purls of latex fired her quickly. When he tilted his head and laved her nipple yet again, she knew she couldn't wait.

She drew her knees beside his hips, used her hand to hold him as straight as his thick, naturally curved penis would allow. She'd promised to voice her pleasure, so as she eased him inside, she groaned aloud. Sitting up so straight, his sex reached straight through to her core. God, she was going to come again, and she hadn't even moved.

His smile was incorrigible. His eyes flashed with satisfaction and delight. He grabbed her hips, held her still, then shifted beneath her so slightly, the room started spinning again and she cried out, dizzy.

"Take my hands, Michaela."

She did as he asked, needing his strength to remain upright amid the draining affects of the slow, torturous orgasm he'd given her. After several deep breaths, she regained her equilibrium and recognized the power of her position. She started to move, undulating, lifting, milking the pleasure he offered and giving the same to him. She arched her back, her hair teasing her skin, her breasts thrust forward, nearly losing herself in the added sensation, not realizing she'd tempted him beyond reason.

He sat up, held her hands steady and devoured her breasts while she stroked him with her body. Time stopped, swirled, exploded. A keen cry tore from her throat but was drowned out by the powerful sound of his pleasure.

The instant her body was spent, Bas caught her in his arms, rolled her beside him and pulled the comforter over her. She waited for him to leave her and, again, he didn't. They snuggled together in the warmth of their lovemaking, until Micki was just seconds away from sleep.

"Did I please you, Master?" she asked, yawning.

His voice soothed her into her dreams, so she didn't have the energy to untangle his response.

"More than I can afford, Michaela. More than I'll ever be able to repay."

12

THE AIR CONDITIONER finally kicked on. Michaela knew this when the cool breeze from the vent chased over her skin, waking her from a deep, dreamless sleep. Halfway conscious, she distinctly remembered Bas covering her with the comforter just after they'd made love. Oh, and how glorious that lovemaking had been. Why she'd entertained a moment's worry over becoming Bas's love slave was beyond her. She should have known a man with such absolute power as him didn't need to lord cruelly over some woman to get his kicks. She'd never met anyone like him. Sensual and strong, and surprisingly funny in his own dry, unexpected way. A girl could fall hard for a guy like him. *If* she didn't know better, which Micki most definitely did.

Didn't mean she couldn't enjoy him while their affair lasted. For approximately four more days.

She reached out to touch him, but found nothing but bare mattress. Peeking one eye open, she realized she'd not only kicked off the covers, but Bas was no longer in bed beside her.

She glanced around, not surprised that the open doors leading to the terrace revealed a dark night sky. She felt sated, rested, but still groggy. Between international travel and remarkable sex, Micki was one tired pup.

And yet as tempted as she was to roll over on the heavenly mattress and drift back to sleep, she couldn't help wondering where Bas had disappeared to. The bathroom behind her was dark and no sound came from any other area of the suite. Then it dawned on her that the doors leading from the master bedroom to the terrace hadn't been open when they'd made love. Bas had escaped into the night instead of sleeping beside her.

Why?

For an instant, her mind flashed with nefarious possibilities before she brushed them aside. No way had some weirdo with access to dynamite made it past the cache of guards she knew must be posted around the hotel. This wasn't exactly the Dime Time Motel. The Windsor Court reeked of discretion and class, and likely catered to a celebrity crowd every night.

She wondered if his reason for defection wasn't more personal, but then chastised herself for allowing such a thought. Bas didn't have anything to worry about. Nothing to keep him up at nights. It wasn't like he was brooding on the terrace, silently questioning the wisdom of limiting their relationship to seven days. She didn't doubt she'd made a strong impression on the man—he'd admitted as much. But enough of an impression to rearrange his plans? To stay put in Chicago, content to see her on the nights she wasn't working at the club?

She was crazy. Certifiable. Worthy of the "What the Hell Are You Thinking?" Hall of Fame. If she roped Bas into a serious relationship, she wouldn't have to work the graveyard shift at some noisy club, slinging booze to the dating desperados. Only, Micki had spent the greater part of the last five years wanting little more than a steady job and a place to call her own. She wouldn't give it all up for a man, no matter how amazing he was. Besides, she had nothing to give up. Bottom line—he hadn't asked her for anything more than the week long fling. If nothing else, she'd make sure they both had the times of their lives.

Micki sighed, crawled across the bed and stumbled into the bathroom. Man, hot sex sure did a number on her muscles. She was either woefully out of shape or twenty-five years doubled automatically when you traveled across the ocean, drove your body over sexual limits, then deprived it of sleep. Once certain she didn't look too scary despite the circles under her eyes, she grabbed a complimentary hotel robe from the hook on the door and went in search of Sebastian Stone, the man who'd set her world upside down.

"Bas, you out here?"

She found him near the ledge, his hands gripping a brick planter, his gaze lost in the glow that was New Orleans at night. Tall office buildings shot into the sky all around them. The lights and sounds of Harrah's Casino glimmered and sparkled against the night. And yet the cast of his gaze told her he could have been anywhere in the world when she'd intruded on his thoughts.

"I'm sorry," he said, "I didn't mean to wake you."

She smirked. "You didn't. Well, you did, sort of. I couldn't sleep when you weren't there beside me." She yawned, careful to cover her mouth with her hand. "Aren't you exhausted?"

He smiled. "I don't require much sleep."

"What are you, a vampire?"

"Only the social variety. Usually, I'd just be finishing dinner about now."

"Usually, you'd be up in your plane, soaring from one city to the next, making the next deal, pocketing the next million." She crossed her arms over her chest, contradicting his claim. Maybe, in his past, he'd been a playboy to the rich set, but she knew that was no longer true. There was a lot she didn't know though, and she wanted to learn more about him. They had just four days left together. She wanted to know everything she could before they parted so their time together wouldn't feel so incredibly short.

"When's the last time you actually stopped in New Orleans for more than a few hours?"

He chuckled, his gaze still lost in the neon glimmer of the city. "I think Jean Lafitte still ran the place then. Can't remember exactly."

"Ha, ha. What do you say we get some sleep, then tour the city tomorrow?" she suggested, only half joking. "I mean, really tour, like tourists. I'll even buy you a Big Johnson T-shirt on Bourbon Street and you can wear shorts with dark socks and carry a big camera."

"Sounds appealing," he replied, his sarcasm clear. But after a minute of silence, he turned. "Actually, we are in no rush. We could spend the day in the city, if you'd like."

"Riding around in your limousine or surrounded by an army of bodyguards?" she asked. "Not that tooling around in a big long car isn't fun, but if you want to see a city, you have to get out on the streets. And not with an entourage."

"The streets of New Orleans can be rough."

She covered her mouth to contain a painful snort. "Compared to the streets of Chicago? Come on. This is the frickin' south. They might rip you off, but I'll bet they say thank-you when they're through."

He laughed, which is what she'd intended. She had no doubt that the criminal element of this city was like any other, but she'd desperately wanted to see him smile. It wasn't so much that Bas didn't smile often, just that the happiness didn't last, didn't take root. Like their affair, the glee existed in the now, with no nod to the past and no plans to recur in the future.

Which summed up the man entirely. Even with jokes, he didn't lose control. Didn't laugh too hard or too long, didn't chuckle inexplicably ten minutes later because his brain got caught in a humor loop so that he heard the joke over again in his head. Micki couldn't shake disappointment over the fact that in the two times she and Bas had made love, he'd never let go of his temperate persona. Yes, he'd been wild with wanting. Yes, he'd been passionate and honest and real. But damn it, just once, she wanted him to cross that line into crazy, blind lust. She figured he'd only make that leap once in his lifetime. More than anything, she wanted to be the woman who brought him there.

Before she could formulate a strategy for achieving that goal, he turned away from the view, captured her hand, kissed her knuckles so gently she sighed, then led her indoors.

"Are you hungry?" he asked.

She sniffed, loathe to admit that she was ravenous. "I could snack," she answered, hoping he didn't hear the understatement in her voice.

"Call room service. Order whatever you like. I want to check in with Victor. But please don't answer the door until I'm through."

She nodded, then did as he asked, wondering about the progress in the investigation of the stalker. If she and Bas were going to explore the city tomorrow—and they were, if she had anything to say about it—she wanted to do so without a cache of bodyguards.

He was off the phone before she was. After she finished ordering two rather decadent desserts, he commandeered the phone and made a few additions of his own. He hadn't even had time to fill her in on the update on the search when the knock sounded at the door.

Micki watched from the dining room as Bas answered. A large man stood beside the hotel manager, who had delivered the cart himself. He wheeled the tray into the foyer only. Bas took over, dismissing them both politely.

Dressed in nothing but a silk robe and his tuxedo pants, Bas pushed the cart toward her looking every inch as delectable as she knew the sweets hiding beneath the silver hoods would be. A bottle of cognac and two snifters glimmered under the lights. Bas poured a finger of liquor into a glass, but before he poured the other, he looked at her with all seriousness.

"Do you like cognac?"

Micki pressed her lips together, a pang from her past dampening her curiosity. "I've never had it."

"Do you drink? You had wine on the plane, but I didn't think to ask..."

She waved her hand. "I think that wine was the first I've had in a long time."

He put down the bottle. "I don't have to have this, if it offends you. If you're in recovery yourself..."

She smiled, touched at the self-recrimination clear in his voice. "I'm not an alcoholic," she answered, not the least offended by his concern. The question only attested to the man's sensitivity. His sister was an addict. She was his sister's best friend. It only made sense to at least broach the topic. "But thanks for asking. I did have a little trouble with drinking too much when I first hit the streets. Cheap booze was easy to get and, what the hell, there wasn't anything else to do with your nights, especially when it was cold. But after a while, hangovers lost their appeal. I just quit."

He filled the other glass and placed it in front of her. "I should have asked last night."

"No problem."

He uncovered the plates she'd ordered, his eyebrows lifting at her choices. One order of crème brûlée with raspberries and one order of New Orleans-style bread pudding with bourbon sauce.

"Fine choices," he complimented, placing both plates on the linen-covered table.

"Hey, a girl's gotta know her desserts," she said, uncertain about which one to dig into first.

He handed her silverware wrapped in a napkin, and proceeded to sit down, only his snifter in hand.

She waved her spoon at him. "There's a bundle of silverware for you, too."

He opened his mouth to argue, but she silenced him with her steeliest glare. Not that she was embarrassed to indulge alone while he watched. She didn't give a damn if she gained a few pounds this week. More than likely, they'd find some interesting ways to burn off the calories. But she sincerely believed that Sebastian Stone needed at least one late-night sugar high as part of his life experiences.

He unfurled his napkin with flair. "Which one is mine?"

"Neither." She grinned. "Both. We're going to share."

SHARE. There was an interesting word, Bas thought. As an only child for the first ten years of his life, Bas had been ostracized from most children his age thanks to his overbearing parents. As such, he had never developed much of a talent for dividing his belongings with others. His life had been about accumulation. Of knowledge, of wealth. Perhaps, even of women and the pleasure they brought temporarily into his life. But once he had them, the wanting waned. He'd been relatively lucky so far, never having toyed with a woman who wanted more from the game than he offered. Even Michaela, he was quite certain, could walk away at the end of the week, content that they'd shared something unique and special. On the surface, he'd tend to agree. With any other woman, he wouldn't have taken this much time away from his business just to explore hedonistic pleasures. He wouldn't have focused all his attention on making her life the stuff of fairy tales, no matter what kindness she'd shown his sister. But beyond that, Bas knew this relationship possessed no more depth than any of the many he'd had before. Not because Michaela Carmichael wasn't worthy in some way—but because Bas didn't know how to dive through that barrier he'd constructed around his heart.

Of course, no other woman ever made him think of that before. So in a way, he'd stumbled into something outside his experience, and damned if he knew what to do about it.

Micki situated the desserts between them, then considered seriously which one she wanted to try first. Her wide eyes, bright and blue despite her lack of sleep, alternately flashed between the ceramic ramekin holding a creamy, vanilla-scented custard with a burnt sugar crust, and the other heaped with a soft, buttery bread pudding smothered in fragrant sauce. She deliberated intently until he cleared his throat.

She went for the crème brûlée.

"Wait," Bas insisted, crossing her spoon with his like a master swordsman. "Allow me."

She deferred instantly. Obviously, the only thing that could possibly top indulging in rich desserts in the middle of the night after a round of incredible sex was having her handsome lover feed her himself.

Another first for Bas.

He cracked the hard sugar crust with the tip of the spoon, then scooped out a generous helping. The golden custard, glossy and firm, glimmered under the light from the chandelier. He imagined that her mouth, the same mouth he'd spent a glorious amount of time kissing, now watered in sweet anticipation. As he drew the spoon nearer, she closed her eyes and he slid the spoonful between her parted lips.

He watched her mouth undulate as she chewed, watched the subtle slackening in her jaw as the flavors spread. She groaned, and when her tongue darted to catch any last taste, he almost echoed the sound.

''Delicious,'' she said finally. ''I love the crunch of the sugar.''

She filled her spoon and offered it to him. He leaned forward, but she stopped midway to his mouth.

''What were you thinking about on the terrace?''

He blinked twice. ''Excuse me?''

She retracted the spoon an inch. She wasn't exactly holding the most valuable bargaining chip in her arsenal, but she apparently thought the delicious dessert was a fair trade for the truth.

''When you left the bed and went to the terrace, you were deep in thought. About what?''

His glance slid to the uneaten custard, then his eyebrows arched as he weighed his options. He could tell her he'd been thinking about the dynamite-throwing stalker. But that would be a lie. He trusted Victor to do his job, and other than concern for his friend's safety, he hadn't given the situation in the French Quarter a second thought. He could say he'd been worrying about any number of things, including his sister, but he'd never been good at lying. The truth, however, wasn't something he could readily admit. At least, not totally.

''I was thinking about you.''

She inched the spoon closer. ''What about me?''

''How I've never met anyone like you.''

She snorted, rolled her eyes. ''That doesn't surprise me.''

''It should, Michaela,'' he said, pushing himself to admit more than he wanted to. She deserved to know everything—how she'd touched him, how she'd pushed him beyond boundaries he'd lived behind all his life. Of course, he couldn't admit that much—not when he still couldn't explain how or why she'd accomplished this feat. But she still deserved to know her value. To him. To the world.

"I've traveled the entire globe several times and contrary to popular belief, I encounter men and women from all walks of life, all financial and social backgrounds. And yet I've never met anyone remotely like you."

She shoved the spoon forward, desperate for a break from his honest interpretation. He swallowed the spoonful with ravenous delight.

"I'm just a girl who made some stupid choices and turned out okay anyway."

"And yet, you don't consider yourself stupid."

"Should I?"

He dug another helping of custard out of the oval ramekin, this time topping the sweet offering with a tart raspberry dusted with confectioner's sugar. "On the contrary, that's one of the reasons why you're so unique. You don't bathe yourself in self-pity or whip yourself with recriminations."

She held up her hand to delay her next taste, preferring to laugh at his remark without spewing crème brûlée all over him. "Not that I don't adore that you have this idealized impression of me, but, believe me, self-pity and I are well acquainted. And no less than two hours ago, I almost let my usual litany of recriminations keep me from experiencing some fairly amazing sex."

His mouth quirked in disbelief and he offered the custard again, which she took. "I assume you're referring to this Jazz Jericho person again."

He hoped the name rolled off his tongue without hinting at the disgust that caused his stomach to churn. He knew nothing about this former boyfriend, and hadn't been happy that the name hadn't popped up in the quickly drawn dossier he'd ordered before he'd met her. No matter what Bas had said before, he did want to know what this man had done to Micki that had caused long-lasting damage. And he wasn't sure he should ask. But since the topic had reared its ugly head again, he couldn't stop himself from prying further.

She took her turn scooping the custard, but, this time, instead of feeding Sebastian his share, she swallowed the helping herself. She didn't even realize her faux pas until the sweet pudding had found a nice home in her stomach. One thought of Jazz Jericho, and she apparently forgot about sharing.

"Sorry."

"No apologies, Michaela. He obviously flusters you, even after all this time. And I'm only assuming a great deal of time has passed."

"Almost six years, five since we parted ways. I was still involved with him when I first met Danielle, but it was just about over. Your sister saw me through some rough shit. After I recovered, I returned the favor."

His pewter gaze narrowed and he took a spoonful of pudding for himself, then abandoned his silverware and pulled his crystal snifter closer. A tightness formed in his chest and a strange, bitter taste shot up his esophagus, requiring a quick sip of cognac to quell it. Every instinct, every sense, sprang to alert, flashing red light warnings in his brain.

He shouldn't push her further. He shouldn't want to know. Six years was a long time, and whatever crime this man committed against Michaela, she'd undoubtedly put the bulk of the pain to rest. Delving into her past, compelling her to reveal secrets she'd struggled for so long to keep, denoted that he cared more than he should. More than he ever had in the past, for anyone, including himself, maybe even his own sister. Without a doubt, whatever heartbreak this Jazz Jericho had caused, Sebastian wanted to fix it, perhaps even erase the tiny lines that formed along the corner of her eyes while she entertained the memories.

He shouldn't ask. This was none of his business, outside his concern. And yet…

"Tell me about him."

13

"NOW YOU WANT TO KNOW?" she asked, wondering what had changed. She'd wanted to tell him before, but he'd discouraged her from divulging her past, assuring her that the details made no difference. Despite the shift in his request, she still trusted that his opinions of her wouldn't change. Not that she should care but, the truth was, she did.

He calmly sipped his cognac, revealing nothing about his motives in those cool, gray eyes. "Before, my options were between hearing about your past, which you've obviously overcome, or making love to you. I mean, was there really ever a choice?"

She grinned. "Not exactly equal picks," she admitted, knowing she would have gone for the making love part, too, had the choice been hers.

She slid the crème brûlée closer, sensing he didn't want any more dessert, just the truth. And she knew she could give him that. Now. After all this time.

"Normally, Jazz Jericho was the kind of guy I would have avoided like the plague." She tapped the spoon on the crusty custard topping, creating weblike cracks in the sugar. "Charming. Sly. A real player. He ran all kinds of scams, but he didn't mess around with drugs or hookers, so he wasn't a total pariah to me. We chatted off and on. He got me jobs when I needed them. *Never* offered me a handout. He seemed to 'get' me and never came on too strong."

She silenced the wistful sound in her voice with another small helping of custard. Who she'd thought Jazz was and who he turned out to be was a paradox she'd never understand. "And, I should add, he was absolutely slurpy."

"Slurpy?"

Micki smiled, not expecting a guy like Bas to have that word in his vocabulary. "Slurpy, as in gorgeous enough to slurp through a straw so you don't miss one drop."

His eyebrows rose. "A fascinating word, and one I'm not likely to ever put in a sentence."

She chuckled quietly, her mind working a dozen hilarious scenarios where Bas tried, unsuccessfully, to employ the word in his everyday interactions. "Definitely not a word you ever need to say. Though, for the record, you qualify."

"Thank you." He sipped his cognac, one eyebrow adorably quirked. "I think."

"You're welcome."

Now was not the time for her to start thinking about how truly slurpy Sebastian Stone was, or she'd never finish her story. With both of them relaxed and acclimated to the late-night hour, she figured it wouldn't take much to entice the man back into the bedroom for another round of sensual delights to work off the culinary ones she was polishing off.

Besides, now that she'd started telling the tale of her past, she needed to see this through. "One night, he invited me out for a beer, which, amazingly, led to a real dinner in a real restaurant. This led to dancing at this club where he knew the bouncer. Bottom line, he seriously swept me off my feet. Before I knew it, things got intense. I moved in with him."

"You said this was before Danielle?"

"Yeah. About a year before she hit the streets. I was

getting tired of the life. I was nineteen, ready to pick up the pieces and move on. Jazz had a place to live, a car. Money of his own. He understood that I had to pull my own weight, so he hooked me up doing deliveries for this pizza joint he had a stake in, and even lent me his old truck to drive around. I drank a little then, but otherwise life was looking up.''

Micki shook her head, wondering now how such a setup could have resulted in such unrelenting optimism. She'd known better than to believe in fairy tales and happy endings. To this day, she wondered how she could have slowly dropped her guard, allowing the routine of a job, a roof over her head and regular sex blind her to the reality of who Jazz really was.

If Bas sensed her regrets, he didn't show it. His face remained a mask of simple interest. ''And then?''

''And then,'' she said, raising her voice to enhance the ironic drama, ''the sex started getting a little raunchy. He asked me to try new positions, wear little costumes. I might not have grown up shopping on Michigan Avenue, but I know where Jerry Springer tapes his shows.''

She glanced up. He hadn't cracked so much as a half grin, so her joke died right there on the dining room table. Maybe humor wasn't her best tactic here. ''I really thought this was normal. A couple of consenting adults, trying to spice up their love life, you know? So, I did what he asked.''

Again, not an ounce of judgment crossed his eyes.

''You didn't enjoy the...experimentation?''

He sounded surprised. She smirked, completely understanding the foundation of his doubt. She didn't exactly come across as a prude, now did she? Last night on the plane, she hadn't exhibited the least reluctance to experience the full breadth of sexual pleasure. Hell, she'd handed the *Sexcapade* to him herself, and just a few hours ago, had helped him bring the scenario to life, even if she hadn't been the master as she'd planned.

Yet when that coin had flipped and landed, and from down on his knee Bas had informed her that she'd lost the toss, Micki had instantly wanted to lose herself in an ideal fantasy.

He had seen, though, that her wounded past had almost waylaid her.

But thanks to Bas and his sensitive, clever lovemaking, she could put the regrets of the past firmly in perspective. And she could tell him the truth without self-recrimination.

"At first, it was okay. But soon, my instincts were telling me something was wrong. I was so desperate for a normal life—or what passed for one—that I blamed my prudish upbringing for my fears. My mom was a real slut and my grandmother never let me forget it."

Bas tilted his head, his expression questioning. Her words were harsh. And, perhaps, oversimplified.

"Look," she emphasized, "my mom ran around with a rough crowd, got herself knocked up with me and my twin, gave birth, dumped us with Nanna and took off and overdosed before our first birthday."

"And your grandmother resented taking on two children?"

She shook her head. Resentment wasn't the right word. "No, Nanna just overcompensated. I mean, she always had to know where we were, always had to check out our friends, interview their families. She was obsessed with rules and regulations and restrictions."

"Oh, she was cruel then," he prompted, and it took Micki a minute to realize he was baiting her, luring her toward a truth she hadn't wanted to accept.

"Nanna just didn't want us to turn out like her daughter had. But she went too far."

"But obviously she had reason to fear for you. You ran, just like your mother did."

She paused. She'd had this same conversation with Rory after their reunion. But, at the time, she'd been too overwhelmed with anger to listen. Anger at her grandmother for creating a home environment that had stifled her. Anger at her twin for making the best of an unbearable situation. Anger at herself for not being able to deal with her reality, instead running off to find some nonexistent neverland of unlimited freedom.

"Yeah. She was strict as hell, and I couldn't take it."

"So you ran away, and eventually fell in with a man who made you question, at the deepest level, if you weren't exactly like your mother in other ways as well?"

She swirled the spoon along the bottom of the ceramic dish, scooping up the last of the creamy dessert. He was hitting way too close to home. "Damn. You should have been a psychiatrist instead of a venture capitalist. You could cure the whole frickin' world."

He laughed, apparently not stung by her words. "Doesn't take a professional to figure you out, Michaela. Not now that you've laid all your cards down. What surprises me is that you haven't truly accepted the differences between you and your mother. You had instincts telling you something was wrong. Apparently, she didn't."

"Or she did, and, like me, she taught herself to ignore them, because if she dealt with them, she'd have to admit she was afraid."

"And that's a sign of weakness."

"Or so I thought."

"But you don't anymore?"

"No."

"Why not?"

She swallowed, sure she wanted to admit this but not wanting to sound corny. Still, she couldn't go on behaving as though the past two days with Sebastian hadn't affected her. She'd learned about herself in ways that stretched beyond the physical, the sexual. She'd learned from him, *about* him. And the lessons would last her a lifetime. They'd have to. Because by her count, she had just over four days left.

"Tonight, when that bomb went off, you were afraid. For me. For Vic. For yourself, I'll bet. No one wants to get blown up. You probably don't experience fear very often, but when you do, you don't hide it. I can see it in your eyes. I saw it when Danielle and I first walked into the hotel lobby in Paris, and you witnessed how shaky she was when she walked, how thin and pale. I realized that you do feel fear sometimes, and yet it doesn't stop you from being the strongest man I've ever met."

"No," he said. "Fear doesn't stop me. Fear is an emotion that can keep you alive."

She shook her head. She knew that—self-preservation and she were old friends. This was something more. "You make me want to face my fears, overcome them. You make me want to be more than I am, and yet you do that without asking, without judging."

"I'm in no position to judge anyone. And you have nothing to fear from me, Michaela. You do know that?"

"My head does. My heart, too, I guess. But I just wanted to get this in the open—about Jazz. So if I hesitate again, when we're making love," she said, glancing with longing toward the bedroom, "you'll understand it isn't your fault."

Bas's grin was nothing short of arrogant. "I don't think that would have occurred to me."

She grinned, captured her snifter from the center of the table and pulled the drink closer. She took a tiny sip, amazed at the smooth warmth of the cognac—and the potent kick.

"You're a cocky bastard, you know that?" she said.

"I've been told. So what exactly did this Jazz person do to you?" he asked matter-of-factly. "Beyond the sexual requests. I don't mean to be forward, but I'd like to know before I send Vic to break both his legs."

She choked on her next sip of brandy. "That's so sweet! No one's offered to break someone's legs for me before. At least, no one who could really get the job done."

He saluted her with his glass. "You've been hanging out with the wrong people."

"Established fact," she concluded. "But don't sweat Jazz. Last I heard, he's at Joliet serving twenty-five to life. After he knocked the crap out of me, he developed a taste for knocking women around. He killed one, got caught red-handed. The stupid governor commuted his death sentence, but he's in until the day he dies. For a player like him, that has to be pure torture."

Bas shook his head, his mouth a firm, intimidating line. She was moved by the intensity of the anger she could see he was repressing. He took a deep breath and said, "You're satisfied, then."

Micki thought back on the nights Jazz hung out on the street or on the fire escape, loathe to remain trapped inside for more than an hour at a time. Nothing drove him crazier with cabin fever than the dead cold of winter in their tenement apartment on the south side of town. If prison hadn't sapped the cockiness out of him yet, it would eventually.

"Yeah. Now I am. Now that I'm here, living the good life…or even once I'm back in Chicago with my sister, with my new job and new place. I don't give a shit what happens to him anymore."

So caught up in her nonchalance, Micki almost didn't catch the signs of Bas's continued rage. His eyes sought a distant focal point over her head. His jaw tightened. A vein in his temple throbbed. His hands clenched the snifter so hard she thought the crystal might shatter in his hands. Compelled to calm him, she scooted her chair closer and laid her hand gently on his thigh.

"It was a long time ago, Bas. He can't hurt me anymore."

Slowly, his dark gaze slid toward her. "But he did hurt you. He hit you."

"Hit is an understatement," she whispered. She considered stopping there, not telling Bas the scope of Jazz's violence, but why should she protect the scumbag? Besides, she'd never really told anyone the whole story. Not even Danielle.

"He'd never hit you before?" he asked.

"No. I guess I never pissed him off like that before. Not that I'm blaming myself—I'm not. Seems Jazz had decided to branch out into the porno trade. His sex games with me had been…how did he put it…training?" Her mouth was thick with disgust and she had to swallow a resurgence of anger and wash it down with more booze. "One night, I found a hidden camera in our bedroom. To say I went ballistic would be an understatement. I destroyed the tape, right in front of him. In return, he tried to destroy me."

Bas reached out and took her hand. She was proud she wasn't shaking. Not with leftover fear. Not with bitterness. Yes, she was still furious that she'd allowed herself to care for the creep in the first place, but now she accepted her rage as a badge of courage. So long as she could live without old bitterness seeping into her psyche, she'd wear it proudly.

At least, to a degree. Some parts of the story she'd never feel proud of.

"There's more," Bas deduced, quickly.

She sighed. "You're too sharp."

"Tell me."

She glanced into the custard plate, bummed that she'd finished it off when she could use another spoonful to help ease this part of the story down. She eyed her cognac, but her brain was already feeling the effects of the concentrated alcohol. With no other option, she reached for the bread pudding, though her appetite did a quick retreat as the most hurtful moment from her past rammed forward into her present.

She had just signed herself out from the hospital, and with a cash handout from the chaplain, had bought herself a cab ride from the city to Berwyn. It had been, after all, her twenty-first birthday. She'd wanted to finally share the day with her twin, her family—what was left of it. But the drugs she'd been given to manage the pain from her two broken ribs, bruised jaw and fractured shoulder muddled the memory even now.

"After I got out of the hospital, I decided it was time to go home. To my grandmother, my great-aunt, my sister. It was our twenty-first birthday," she announced, shocked that tears welled in her eyes now, after all this time. She shoved another helping of bread pudding into her mouth, chewed the raisins more than she needed to and swallowed what felt like a pillow-sized lump of cotton down her throat. The dessert was delicious. The regrets steamed with bitterness. She pushed the plate away.

"You must have still been in a lot of pain, physically," he noted.

"Actually, I was flying high, thanks to the meds. I don't really remember any details, except that my grandmother was so sad to see me. And then angry." Her voice shrank with each word, so Micki pushed away from the table and grabbed one of the glasses of iced water still sitting on the room service cart. She took a long swallow, concentrating on the slushy feel of the water streaking down her throat.

"So you went back to the streets," he concluded.

"Yeah, well. Home apparently wasn't an option. Or I thought it wasn't. Now that I look back, now that I know all the details thanks to my sister, I realize how I screwed up. I'd been missing for six years, then I show up on my grandmother's doorstep on my precious twin's birthday, high as a kite, sporting cuts and bruises, and saying who knows what. I'm sure whatever anger she tossed at me, I threw back ten times stronger." Micki wandered back to the table with the water and sat on the chair with one leg tucked beneath her. "Ends up Nanna had been diagnosed with cancer just a few days before I popped back into her life unannounced." She shrugged. "So I guess in a way I've been blaming Jazz for my prolonged estrangement from my family. And that's not right. I screwed up. I should take the heat for that."

Bas polished off the last of his cognac. "Have you reunited with your grandmother since?"

She laughed, but the sound echoed with hollow emptiness. "What? And cancel out all these productive years of blind hate and cold rage? Who am I to upset the balance of our topsy-turvy universe?"

"You're a woman who wants to make peace with her past."

"I am at peace," she insisted, though she knew it wasn't true.

"You just said you weren't afraid to be afraid anymore, Michaela."

She sniffed, rubbed her nose and swiped away the moisture clinging to her eyelashes. "I'm not afraid of fear. I'm afraid of not being angry anymore. What will I have then?"

"Love," he answered.

"Love sucks," she countered.

Bas inhaled, then twisted his lips while he considered her declaration. "Wasn't that a song?"

A chuckle shook her chest, and he smiled in triumph. "That was 'Love Stinks,' and it was before my time."

"Mine, too," he said.

She did the math in her head, vaguely recalling that the song came out sometime in the early eighties. By the time she was ready to contradict him, she noticed he'd cleared the table of their late-night snack and rolled the cart toward the door.

"That's not right. That song is right during your time," she insisted, following when Bas strode confidently toward the bedroom. She had to walk twice as fast to match his purposeful stride. Then he caught her unaware when he swung around and lifted her into his arms.

"Can't be," he said. "I haven't *had* my time. Yet."

She curled her cheek against his shoulder, loving the feel of her skin against his warmth, not to mention his strong arms beneath her thighs. This man existed in more dimensions than she ever thought possible. On the surface, he was all power and control, money and fine possessions. But beneath the thousand-dollar suits was a body built for sinful delights. And not far under that layer, she found a heart and mind concerned with her well-being. And not just because of what she'd done for her sister. That gratitude had long been rewarded. He cared about her for no other reason than because he found her worthy of his consideration. He liked her. He respected her. If she allowed herself a moment's self-indulgence, she'd admit he admired her for the aspects of herself she often questioned. Her stubborn streak. Her smart mouth. Her inability to blindly forgive and forget.

Bas Stone was a remarkable man. And she had only a few days left in his company. Suddenly, all thoughts of sleep fled her brain.

"Haven't had your time yet? Really. You still have that coin?"

His gray eyes glinted with interest. "For what I paid, I'll have that coin for a long, long time."

"Unless you want to give it to me," she suggested.

"Why?"

"I was thinking I wanted another shot at being the master."

He marched them through the threshold to the bedroom. "You're on."

14

By nine o'clock the next morning, Bas had returned the coin to its velvet pouch and slipped it inside his jacket pocket, grinning as he patted the slight bulge. Michaela, still snuggled amid sheets, comforters and pillows, snored gently. He knew the noise was a result of her exhaustion—they hadn't concluded their lovemaking session until a few hours ago. Besides, he was starting to make a habit of watching her sleep, and he knew her behavior. How she fanned her thick hair over the pillow to keep the heat off her neck. How she often turned onto her side, and drew her legs close to her stomach. Amazingly, he'd become fascinated with cataloguing her actions and reactions. Couldn't imagine ever losing interest in the details of Michaela's daily life.

But he also knew that if he remained in the bedroom any longer, he'd doff the clothing he'd put on after his shower and snuggle back into bed with her. As much as the thought tempted him, he had business to attend to. His clothes had survived the attack on the house. Hers had not. So by nine-fifteen, he'd arranged to have clothes in Michaela's size delivered from a nearby boutique, one which happened to be owned by Reina Price's sister-in-law, Toni Masterson.

Unfortunately for Bas, Reina insisted on delivering the clothing herself. He wasn't pleased. His friend had a certain lilt to her voice that prickled the hairs along the back of his neck. She was coming to the hotel herself because she wanted to discuss something personal with him. He had a pretty good idea what she wanted to talk about. And as fond as he was of Reina, he didn't want to have his love life dissected by a woman still floating on the cloud of matrimonial bliss.

She arrived at ten, only a minute or two after Michaela had stepped into the shower. She assured him she needed a long, hot soak, so he knew he'd have no respite from Reina's interference for at least a half hour.

With the practiced ennui only a woman of her stature and breeding could accomplish, Reina entered the hotel room and swung the hot pink, glossy shopping bags imprinted with the logo for The Feminine Touch boutique onto the nearest couch, then turned on him with her searing obsidian gaze.

"Tell me about the dynamite," she said first.

Bas nodded, not surprised she'd be privy to what must be the talk of the French Quarter. Wild and unexpected things happened in the Quarter every night, but rarely did anything explode.

"I don't have much to tell. The police are looking for a rather shabbily dressed man who was seen in the alley moments before detonation. A team of bodyguards had this person in pursuit, but deferred to the police, who promptly lost him."

Reina eased herself into a nearby chair. Bas watched her intently, still amazed at her natural grace. The peaceful calm she surrounded herself with might have looked to others like boredom or superiority. But to Bas, she was just Reina, a woman so like him they should have been soul mates. He should have loved her forever. But love had never occurred to either of them. As it was, she held the distinct title as one of his few and trusted friends.

Last night at the opening, she appeared every ounce the

woman he'd once known. Sophisticated, intelligent, beautiful beyond words, completely in command of the social circle she swirled around like dark, smoky incense. But today, dressed in slim black jeans and boots, topped with a simple white tank top and a white, silk artist's smock, she looked as close to casual as he'd ever seen her. And completely comfortable in her skin.

"High speed chases don't appeal to the southern sensibility," she joked. "Grey told me the police called off the chase after the suspect sideswiped two cars. The general public was being put at risk over someone who really did nothing but make a great deal of noise and cause minor damage to an old building."

"Your husband has connections with the police?" Bas asked. He'd been impressed with Grey Masterson from the first moment they'd met, even if the man had shaken his hand a little too tightly to be civilized. Bas grinned at the memory. If he'd married a stunning woman like Reina, he might be a little territorial as well.

"Grey has many connections, as the editor of the local newspaper would. He doesn't know anything new, if that's what you're asking. The New Orleans police don't like outsiders coming into their town and bringing trouble with them. They have enough trouble from the locals."

"Duly noted. I'm prepared to take matters into my own hands."

Reina shook her head. "That won't exactly engender gratitude from the local police, either."

"I don't require their gratitude, but a bit of competent police work would be appreciated."

With a doubtful shrug, Reina conveyed no confidence in the New Orleans's police department's ability to help him. Bas remembered that just about a year ago to the day, Reina had been suffering through a string of thefts at her art gallery. Thefts the police had been unable to solve. When she'd called just a few months later to announce her engagement to the newspaperman, she'd told Bas about how Grey had helped her sort out the mystery. And if Masterson could ignore the intimate past between his wife and Sebastian, the man might provide some useful information.

"Grey promised to let me know if he heard anything he didn't think you'd be privy to. But you've done what you can. You hired Brandon Chance. He and my husband are old friends. He's the best in the business."

Bas nodded, wishing he could agree, but Bas had been isolated for far too long to trust anyone beyond his inner circle. If he could call two men a circle. "Victor trusts him. For now, that's good enough for me."

"Security is tight in the lobby, if that eases your mind. Luckily for me, Brandon's sister-in-law and partner was just coming on duty. We know each other, so she let me up."

"Is there anyone you don't know?" he asked.

"As many people as come through this city on a daily basis, it's really still a very small place. But now that you mention it, I don't know Michaela Carmichael. At least, not as well as I'd like to."

At this, he sat. "Why?"

She shrugged her shoulders with subtle rhythm. "I'm fascinated, that's all. She has you tied up in knots, as much as Sebastian Stone can be knotted. I can't help but wonder exactly how she's pulled off such a feat."

"You're imagining things," he said with a smirk.

"Am I? You forget who I am," she said. She leaned forward, her dark hair spilling over her shoulders. "You forget what I know about you."

"You are an old friend, who, as I recall, was never concerned with other people's private lives before now. And what you *should* know about me is that I don't share the details of my private life with anyone."

She laughed. "What private life? All you have is downtime between international flights."

"I never heard you complain," he remarked.

She speared him with a cold glance. "That's because, at the time, layovers between international flights worked perfectly for my lifestyle."

"Clearly not the case any longer."

She glanced down at her left hand, where a generous collection of exquisite blue diamonds sparkled on a curved band. "Clearly. Marriage actually agrees with me. Would you ever have guessed?"

Bas answered honestly. "Not in a million years."

"There might be hope for you," she ventured.

He chuckled, then leaned forward to pour coffee from the tray he'd ordered earlier. "Is that why you came here today? To impart the joys of matrimony on me?"

"I came to see if Micki wanted a personal tour of the Quarter. I also have an appointment at the spa this afternoon and thought she might want to join me."

"Why such an interest in Michaela?"

"I could ask you the same thing."

"I asked first."

Reina accepted the cup of coffee Bas had poured for her before serving his own. "I'm curious."

"I don't suppose it occurred to you that my private life is none of your business," he pointed out civilly.

"Of course the thought occurred to me. Obviously, I ignored it."

"Are you intending to find wives for all of your former lovers?"

She laughed out loud. "That project wouldn't leave me much time for my own husband, would it? But you're not just a former lover, Bas. You're a friend. A friend who has some serious issues in his life right now.'' She lowered her voice. ''I heard about your sister.''

He sniffed. Gossip traveled quickly, not that he cared. ''She'll be fine.''

Reina nodded and wisely dropped the subject. ''Then there is this bomber...stalker...whatever you wish to call him.''

''Criminal works for me. Though we might be dealing with a her. Unclear at this time.''

''Yes, well, the police's favorite theory is that the threat left in the house was aimed at Micki, not you.''

Bas scoffed, but didn't like knowing that such a detail had been leaked to the press. He made a mental note to keep Michaela away from any newspapers. He saw no reason to upset her, particularly since he believed that scaring Michaela had been the reason for the note altogether.

''A ruse, I'm certain.''

Reina set her coffee and saucer down gently on the table. ''Is that what your instincts tell you?''

''They haven't failed me yet. This criminal is seizing the opportunity to use Michaela against me, but not necessarily to harm her. The whole scenario is quite odd.''

''Maybe you're right. Maybe whoever is behind all this doesn't want to hurt Micki, just wants to scare her away.''

Bas chuckled. ''They chose the wrong woman. She doesn't scare easily.''

''I gathered that or she would have been long gone by now. Which is part of the reason she fascinates me, makes me think you've finally met a woman worthy of you. What's your next move?''

Bas sipped his drink and frowned, not certain of the right course of action. He didn't like the idea of waiting for the stalker to move first, nor did he relish the thought of exposing Michaela to danger again. Still, depositing her back in Chicago before the end of their prearranged week didn't sit well, and not just because of his personal desire to enjoy as much as they could of their remaining time together. This matter needed to be settled before they parted. Who was to say she wouldn't be pursued there? Harmed or used against him when he wasn't close by to protect her?

He could arrange more security, but Micki was smart enough to catch on. And slippery enough to ditch anyone he paid to watch her. Which he knew she would, given her independent nature. His best bet would be to catch the criminal before the end of the week.

The news from Victor last night hadn't been entirely disheartening. He and Brandon had found a trail to follow for the accomplice who'd ransacked the house. Both men considered the find too easy for comfort, so they promised caution in their pursuit. Bas glanced at his watch. Hours had passed and he hadn't yet heard a word.

"I will keep Michaela very close."

Reina's mouth turned down with doubt. "Is that safe?"

"She won't be harmed while she's with me."

"I wasn't asking about her safety, Bas. I was asking about yours. I have a feeling your world is very slowly turning inside out, all because of Michaela Carmichael."

Bas grumbled and finished his coffee in silence, ignoring the omniscient gleam in Reina's gaze. The woman could be insufferably arrogant at times—especially when she was right.

MICKI SIGHED with relief when she heard Bas escort Reina to the door, refusing one last time her offer of a guided tour through the French Quarter. Micki liked the woman, she truly did, and the clothes she'd purchased from her sister-in-law's boutique had been the perfect reflection of

Micki's personal tastes, but she wanted to spend the day with Bas, alone. Last night, after she'd poured her heart out about her past, they'd returned to the bedroom and flipped the coin again. And again, she'd lost.

Relatively speaking.

Once again, Bas had turned the master-slave scenario into a languid, sensual pleasurefest. Yes, he'd commanded her beyond a few more of her personal boundaries, directing her to lie belly down on the bed while he explored, massaged and aroused every inch of her body. Yes, he'd tested the limits afterward by instructing her to turn over and ask him for everything he'd do next.

Master, please lick my breasts.

Master, please kiss my clit.

Master, please make me come.

But again, all of the actions had focused on her sexual delight. He'd forbidden her to turn her requests to his pleasure, as much as she'd wanted to. He'd forced her to focus on herself yet again, and she'd enjoyed every delectable second.

Before last night, she'd never asked for anything of anyone, especially not in the bedroom. And while she was in no place to complain, his game only increased her desire to turn the tables on this master lover of hers. She wanted another shot at that wily gold disc.

But she didn't want to be cooped up in this hotel room for the rest of the day, either. She was certain there were innumerable places they could flip the coin in the city.

Once again, she rifled through the bags that Bas had deposited in the bedroom of the suite while she'd still been in the shower. Then she dressed quickly, choosing a slim pair of hip-hugging jeans, a fire engine-red tank top with flirty silk ruffles around the low-cut V-shaped neckline, and matching red sandals with low heels, ideal for walking.

She'd washed and dried her hair and applied a bit of makeup from what Vic had salvaged from the house. Dark crimson lipstick. Blue eyeliner. The natural glow of sexual satisfaction.

When she checked herself out in the mirror, her confidence surged. She looked young, fresh. All dolled up. For Sebastian though, she wasn't sure he'd appreciate the trendy look. Too bad, because she thought it rocked. She shot into the main room of the suite, ready to knock his socks off.

She stopped dead when she caught sight of him pressing the end key on his cell phone. His face had drained of color. One hand was fisted tightly at his side.

Before he noticed that she'd entered the room, she listened to a string of curses spout from his mouth, made nonetheless foul with his cultured voice.

"Bas, what's wrong?"

Several long seconds passed before his eyes finally focused on her. He blushed red and apologized for his language.

"I didn't mean for you to hear that."

"Is Danielle all right?" she asked, dashing across the room to his side.

"What? Oh," he hesitated, as if the thought of his sister threw him. "I must assume she's fine. It's Vic."

"Vic?" Micki repeated, shocked.

"He's missing."

"What? I thought he went searching for the accomplice to the guy who threw the bomb."

Bas nodded, but Micki could see that his mind reeled from whatever news he'd just received on the phone. She took his arm gently and led him to a nearby love seat, pulling him down beside her.

"Start from the beginning," she instructed. "Who just called?"

A rush of adrenaline finally seemed to shoot through him and in an instant he was standing, his color returned, his eyes narrow and sharp. "Brandon Chance. He and Vic followed a few leads last night, but lost the trail around five o'clock this morning. They went back to Brandon's house in the French Quarter and caught a few hours of sleep before getting back to work around eight."

"He told you that last night," Micki guessed, knowing Bas had contacted Vic somewhere around three or four o'clock, before their second round in the bedroom. At the time, Bas hadn't shown the least concern or worry. His trust in Vic was immeasurable. Apparently, so was his concern for his friend.

"They got some good information this morning and followed the tip to an old run-down neighborhood not far from the Superdome. Brandon went into the building, figuring that as a native he'd sound more convincing trying to get information out of the locals. Vic was supposed to watch from the car, as well as listen with a device Brandon wore. But when Brandon went back to the car, Vic was gone."

"The car, too?"

"No, that's the oddest part. The car was still there, engine running, keys in the ignition. Brandon wasn't gone long. If he had been, he figured someone would have stolen the car and we'd have no clues to Vic's whereabouts."

"We have clues?"

"Potential clues. Brandon is checking over the car now. He'll let me know immediately if he finds anything."

Micki shook her head, disbelieving. Vic wasn't exactly the kind of guy who could easily be kidnapped. He was big, tough. Retired military and in excellent shape. He wouldn't go without a struggle. And the struggle would be very physical, very loud and very noticeable to anyone who might be near.

"So Vic's missing and no one saw anything."

"No one is talking. Brandon isn't convinced no one witnessed what happened. But this is two slipups under Brandon Chance's watch. First, the fake cop slipping into the house and now this."

Micki shook her head. She'd been impressed by Brandon when they'd met last night, and the fact that Vic had trusted his old army buddy enough to hire him to provide additional security for Bas convinced her the man had to be the best in his field. "You can't blame Brandon. Sometimes, shit happens. Who would have guessed Victor would become a target? And, frankly, I can't imagine Vic going willingly with anyone, unless they somehow convinced him that you were in danger."

Bas shoved his cell phone in his pocket. "Vic isn't easily fooled. And even if someone came at him with a gun, I don't think he'd cooperate."

Micki's mind whirled with a million possibilities, each one uglier or more terrifying than the next. Vic was a man, after all. He could be incapacitated. He could be killed. But if there'd been evidence of physical violence, Brandon would have called the police.

"Did you try Vic's cell phone?" she asked, even though she knew he would have.

"Three times. No answer."

"What do we do?"

"Meet Brandon. He gave me the address and has contacted his partner, who will meet us downstairs in the lobby."

Micki listened as Bas's voice flattened, the inflections in his normal speech patterns nearly imperceptible. His gaze narrowed, focused on nothing, yet brimmed with anger.

"You don't trust Brandon," she guessed.

"I don't trust anyone."

"Vic trusted him."

"Yes, that's why I'm going to give him an opportunity to redeem himself, though you're right in that I can't blame him for this turn of events. What I don't understand is why no one has contacted me. If they have Vic, they have his cell phone. So they also now have my private number."

Her mind racing, Micki tried to push her emotions aside and come up with a logical scenario. She didn't understand why anyone would go after Victor, except as a means to draw Bas out. But then, just recently *she'd* been the target of threats. Only her room had been trashed at the house. Only her stuff had been destroyed.

None of this made sense.

"Maybe they're waiting to get to a safe place before they call. How much time has passed since Vic went missing?"

"Not long. Brandon guessed fifteen minutes."

Micki stood, wiped her sweaty hands on her thighs. Her heart drummed in her chest, tight with fear for Vic and dread for Sebastian. If anything happened to his friend, Bas would never forgive himself. "Let's go meet Brandon. Maybe we can help. Maybe they just want you out in the open."

"Or you," he offered.

She knocked him in the shoulder confidently. "Don't try and trip me up now, Bas. You said last night you didn't think this was about me at all. You can't use that line to scare me into staying behind."

His grin was pure unrepentant guilt. "I had to try. But I prefer to keep you where I can watch out for you myself."

She decided a little humor at a time like this could only help, not hurt. "Then look your fill, lover boy," she said, taking a sassy twirl so that the silk around her neckline fluttered. "Once this is all cleared up and Vic is safe, you may be begging for another chance to flip that coin."

Bas took her hand and patted the pocket on his chest, where he'd apparently stashed the coin. "I'm prepared, Michaela. Rest assured I'm completely prepared."

15

AT BAS'S REQUEST, they'd ditched the limousine in favor of traveling in the back seat of Samantha LaRocca's dark blue Jeep Cherokee. Brandon Chance's partner, a petite blonde with an athletic build and quick, assessing eyes, directed them quickly out of the hotel. Tinted windows and perceptive driving kept their departure from being noticed. A former stuntwoman, Samantha impressed Bas quickly, seeming more than competent in the field of personal protection. He only hoped she and her boss had enough experience in private investigation to help him locate his missing friend.

Samantha's backup, stationed in cars hanging back in traffic, verified that they were not being followed. While Samantha maneuvered through traffic with ease, Bas willed his cell phone to ring. He couldn't bargain for Vic's release if the kidnapper didn't make the first move, and he didn't want to think about the outcome for Vic if negotiation wasn't an option.

Hurting Vic would hurt Sebastian. Deeply. But who wanted to hurt him? And why? Whatever this was about, Bas felt sure the antagonism hadn't stemmed from his business dealings. The men and women he tangled with understood and appreciated the rules of the game. Sometimes you won. Sometimes you lost. But whatever the outcome, you moved on to the next proposal, the next project, the next game. Grudges were held and revenge often spawned boardroom brawls, but people in Bas's circle didn't initiate personal attacks. He simply didn't associate with those types of "businessmen."

He made another quick call, this one to France to check on Danielle. Convinced that all was quiet in the Parisian countryside, he shocked himself by contacting his parents next. He advised them to remain at home if they could, until he was certain they wouldn't also become targets. He gave them very few details, which suited them just fine. They didn't even bother to ask about his sister. With a disappointed grunt, Bas disconnected the call, not entirely certain he'd call back. Ever.

Michaela took his hand, squeezing gently, touching a vulnerable part of him he hadn't realized he'd exposed.

"Miracle you turned out so great, you know?" she said.

"I could say the same about you."

She nodded, her assurance increasing with each bob of her head. "We aren't always a product of our genetics."

"Maybe we are, maybe we're not. What matters is who we allow ourselves to become, in spite of who raised us. Or didn't raise us, as the case may be."

She speared him with a look so intense, Bas felt a chill along the back of his spine. "Do you like who you've become?"

He turned his stare toward the front windshield, watching as the neighborhood shifted from corporate buildings glimmering with glass and marble to run-down, single-family houses haphazardly painted in rainbow colors from electric purple to shocking pink. "Lately, yes."

She tried to tamp down a presumptuous smile, but couldn't quite manage. "Have I had anything to do with that?"

He flashed her an incredulous grin. "Do you have to ask?"

She settled quietly into her seat, and didn't say another word until Samantha pulled the SUV beside the sedan where Vic had disappeared. Brandon crouched beside the driver's side door, dusting for fingerprints.

Bas exited the car with Micki right behind him. He glanced at Samantha, who nodded knowingly. She'd keep an eye on Micki while Bas concentrated on questioning Brandon.

"Find anything?"

Brandon brushed the gunmetal gray dust over the tan paint near the door handle. Several prints came into immediate view. "Nothing solid. I wipe my car down for prints regularly as a precaution, but even if I find anything unusual, we need time to process the information."

"Time Victor may not have."

"Anybody call?"

"No."

"Weird," Brandon said, leaning his large body against the hood. "You're gonna have to fill me in, man. Because from what Vic told me, none of the threats you've received over all this time have ever acknowledged Vic. And I know as well as you do that Vic wouldn't go anywhere with anyone without a fight."

Bas nodded, wishing he had access to the file they kept on the threats. It was likely back on the airplane, in the locked file cabinet stored beneath the deck. Just a day ago, he would have simply ordered Vic to retrieve the file, and in less than an hour, it would have appeared. He was a valued employee and an even more valued friend. Bas wouldn't rest until he solved this mystery.

He glanced across the street, then down the block. Two clusters of people, one of teenagers, one of older men, huddled together, seemingly unaffected by the outsiders in their midst. Cars whizzed past. The traffic light was a good block away, lessening the chance that someone idling at a red light could have seen anything.

Micki and Samantha stood by the car, leaning their heads together conspiratorially. Bas experienced another chill and he stepped toward the car, but was stopped by Brandon.

"Don't worry about her. Samantha's my best. Let's back up, talk this through. When did the threats first start?"

Bas realized he had to have this conversation with Brandon Chance if he wanted to retrieve his friend. He had to trust Samantha to keep an eye on Micki and for Micki to stay close by. He began recounting the history of the threats as he remembered them until a cacophony of catcalls and whistles pierced the air.

Micki dashed through the traffic and approached the strangers on the other side alone. Bas cut off his recollections midsentence and turned to sprint across the street, but Samantha, for all her petite size, waylaid him.

"Let her go," she ordered.

Bas bristled, yanking his arm out of the blonde's surprisingly iron grip. "Excuse me?"

Samantha unceremoniously rolled her eyes and smirked. "Slow down, Romeo. The lady might get those guys to tell us what they saw this morning."

Brandon joined them, his gaze locked on Micki as she beelined for the group of old men rather than the teens. "Good choice. Sex appeal might work with that crowd," he offered.

Samantha slapped her brother-in-law on the upper arm, reminding Bas of Micki's frequent punches to his shoulder.

"Sex appeal, my ass," Samantha said. "The girl knows the streets. She knows how to talk to those guys, get them to spill. Give her a chance. It's not like we're not right here watching."

Bas pressed his lips together, realizing that, in this case,

Micki did have the advantage of her life experiences. He didn't have to like her venturing outside the sphere of his protection, but from the easy way the men on the corner seemed to talk with her, he figured he'd better rein in his protective instincts and let her work her magic.

After about ten minutes, she waved Bas over. Samantha and Brandon followed, but maintained a safe distance.

"This, gentlemen, is the man with the money," Micki said by way of introduction.

"He don't look so rich," one old-timer wheezed, his front tooth capped with gold. Gray shot through his curly dark hair and from the way the others nodded and kow-towed to his assessment, Bas figured he was their unofficial leader.

Micki shrugged her shoulders and shook her head, hooking her thumbs in the loops of her jeans and lowering the material ever so slightly.

Bas nearly had to mop drool off his Ferragamo loafers.

"You don't have to believe me," she said, "but you already told me what you saw. If you've been straight with me, this man can get you some serious coin for your trouble."

The five men exchanged not-so-furtive glances. Bas wondered exactly why Micki had called him over, since she didn't once make eye contact. He figured he and his designer clothes were simply a visual aid, so he remained silent.

"You want to tell me anything else?" Micki asked.

A short, stringy-haired man in an overcoat spoke up. "Yeah, the chick drove a rental."

A woman? Again?

"What company?" Micki asked.

The men grumbled, denying they could tell which company had rented the car just from a brief glance, but Micki leaned her weight onto one hip and eyed them in disbelief. "Must not want what we're offering. Bas, could you spare a couple of tens?"

"Tens?" the leader protested.

Micki fairly flattened him with her level stare. He'd get no more from her until he told her everything. Bas eyed her, impressed.

The leader named the company, then gave a better description of the van. Brandon caught Bas's eye as he motioned to Samantha to return across the street. She went straight back to her SUV and punched numbers into her cell phone, likely to mobilize their team.

Bas made a move to join Chance, but Micki stopped him. "Wait, babe. I know you're trying to pinch your pennies, but these guys know something more."

"They do?" he asked.

"We do?" the men questioned.

Micki strode closer to the leader, then glanced with pure cocky attitude at the other four, nearly surrounding her. "Yeah. I don't know about the chick, but her muscle was local. You know them, or one of them. You give us a name and you've just bought yourself winning lottery tickets."

Bas knew what to do without Micki asking. From his pocket he pulled his money clip, thick with large bills. The tension in the air crackled and Bas tightened his grip on his money. In a moment, they'd either come clean with the information, or they'd grab his stash and run.

"We call him Johnny," the older man said.

"We call everybody Johnny," the stringy-haired man said.

The old man spit, nearly landing a chunk of brown saliva on the other man's knee. Bas contained his revulsion. Micki had wrung more useful information out of these men than he'd ever thought possible. She used her instincts, trusted them. And her lack of fear drove them closer and closer toward finding Vic.

"Yeah, well, this Johnny lives on South Robertson Street. House with rusted shutters and gravel in front. If you pass the condemned lot with the pink mailbox, you gone too far."

Micki smiled, then shook each of the men's hands. She directed Bas to give them each a twenty, which he did without hesitation. Thanks to Michaela and these men, they had a description of a woman involved in the abduction and the location of the local muscle she'd hired to help her. A fine place to start with time so short.

"If we get our friend back, we'll come back with more," Bas promised.

The men nodded, eyeing him suddenly with increased respect. Anyone else might have thought he'd won them over with his cash, but Bas knew they looked at him with envy because Micki hooked her arm in his before they departed with Brandon close behind.

When they reached the car, Micki relayed all the information she'd gathered before Bas was in earshot.

"A woman, in her thirties, slim build, dark skin and hair, probably Middle Eastern. She wore white. Pants and a long tunic. No veil," she added, as Brandon took notes. "She approached the car and Vic didn't seem alarmed, but surprised. Kind of excited. He immediately got out of the car to talk to her."

"Did they hug?" Brandon asked.

Micki shook her head. "No, but the guys said it looked friendly enough. The woman started walking away, but the conversation continued, as if she was going to get something. Then a van drove by and the next thing they knew, Vic was gone. One of the men in the van is a local." Then she relayed the directions to the house on South Robertson.

Bas concentrated on the information Micki had so skillfully and resourcefully gained. A Middle Eastern woman, one Vic knew, one Vic trusted enough to let down his guard. One with enough money to employ local muscle, which required cash or connections. Bas was positive that if Vic knew her, it wasn't from New Orleans. Their trips here were too infrequent, too short. Except for Reina, whom Bas knew from when she lived in Europe, he didn't know anyone in Louisiana. Even Brandon had known Vic from the army, not from New Orleans.

Micki then recounted the information she'd gotten on the rental car. Despite attempts by the rental car companies to make their cars unidentifiable by removing logos from the bumpers and using standard license plates rather than the old rental variety, people who lived on the streets learned to spot leased vehicles by make and model. A brief glimpse inside often gave away the company, as customers often left maps and rental agreements on the front seat. Rentals were prime targets for car thieves.

The group across the street had theorized which company owned the car they'd seen. They'd also given a fairly detailed description of the older model van, likely stolen, that had torn off with Vic inside.

By the time she finished, Samantha returned. "The rental company won't release any information without a court order. Brandon, I think we should call in the cops. They might be able to trace the van."

Together, Brandon and Bas winced. They might have had more to go on if the police hadn't lost the dynamite thrower last night. As far as Bas knew, the police still hadn't recovered the stolen car the criminal had used the night before for his getaway.

"I hate to say this, Mr. Stone," Brandon said, "but I think Sam might be right. A few minutes ago, all we had was an adult who'd been missing for less than an hour. Contacting the cops would have been a waste of time. Now we have eyewitnesses to a kidnapping."

Bas glanced at Micki. "We paid the witnesses. Won't that taint the police's belief in their veracity?"

"Not if their tip pans out," Brandon said.

"Those guys aren't gonna tell that we paid them," Micki assured him. "Then they won't get more."

"Think they'll talk to cops?"

Micki shook her head. "If I asked them nicely, maybe. But how long until the cops get here? We've got directions to a house. We should at least check that out."

Brandon pulled out the business card of the lead detective from last night's explosion and handed it to Samantha. "Give us fifteen minutes, then call this number and fill the detective in on what's going on. Maybe we'll have time to handle this ourselves."

Bas agreed, trusting Brandon more now that he realized he was willing to put himself on the line for Vic. As Brandon and Samantha ran through the details, Bas separated from the group, wandering back to the sedan where Vic had last been seen. He opened the driver's door, sat in the seat, trying to imagine what Vic might have been thinking, and who could possibly have lured him away so easily when he was watching Brandon's back.

Only a friend could have done that. Someone close.

But who?

Micki joined him. "You're wondering about the woman?"

Bas glanced up, amazed at her intuitive powers. "We've been to the Middle East hundreds of times. And we meet women of all nationalities all over the world. She could have been anyone."

"No, she has to be someone Victor would trust. Someone he would be surprised, but not disturbed, to see again. Maybe even pleased."

Bas cursed, frustrated by his inability to piece this puzzle together. "Victor does have a personal life beyond taking care of me. He could have known any number of women that I've never met."

"But this one would have to have had money, the means to track your travel, hire local thugs."

"We're assuming she's responsible for all the threats I've received over the years. That may not be the case." Bas scowled. "Besides, anyone with contacts in the business world could easily find out where I might be from time to time. A legal assistant to one of my attorneys. A secretary to one of my regular business associates. Many of the threats came through my intermediaries. My location didn't matter."

"But she somehow knew you were coming to New Orleans, at least a little while before we arrived."

"We filed a revised flight plan. Standard procedure."

Micki leaned on the inside of the car door, careful not to disturb the fingerprint dust. "Still, I think it's safe to assume she's somehow connected to your business."

"Not necessarily." His face went slack with thought for a moment. "Wait!"

Bas shot out of the car, pulled Micki out of the way and slammed the door. "There was a woman, someone Vic knew before he came to work for me."

"Who?"

Bas shook his head, trying to remember. He'd met Vic during negotiations of a deal in Saudi Arabia. They'd immediately connected and Bas had made Vic a lucrative offer that had lured him away from the Saudi sheik he'd worked for at the time. Vaguely, Bas remembered that Vic had had to sever some ties that had been more difficult to break than others. At the time, he hadn't offered details, but over time as their friendship formed they'd exchanged stories.

Vic had mentioned a Saudi sheik's sister. Tahrah. The eldest of the sheik's female siblings and one who possessed some financial power. What had been the name? God, it had been so long ago. He'd worked with many Saudis over the years, in their country and in others. Damn, what was the sheik's name?

Bas quieted his thoughts, concentrated. Slowly, the deal itself crept back into his mind. Not oil. He didn't dabble in oil or refineries as a rule. This had been one of his first multimillion-dollar arrangements. Textiles, if he remembered. A favorite of his. Yes! Bin Yarin. Malik bin Yarin bin Sa'ud Al-Hijazi. And the sister—Tahrah bint Yarin bint Sa'ud Al-Hijazi. He's seen her once, maybe twice. But while he could not remember what she looked like, he imagined the description Micki had elicited would fit. It was a long shot, but it was all they had.

16

HE GRABBED MICKI'S HAND, tugged her behind him as they searched for Brandon.

"We found the house," Brandon told him the minute they broke through the circle of bodyguards. "A woman is inside. The men left, likely to dump the van and rental, then steal something for the getaway. My guys are on their tail, and this time they won't lose them. I've got someone else watching the place."

Bas nodded, impressed. Vic had been right to trust Brandon. "I think I know who is behind this. I need to make a phone call to verify it, then we'll know how to proceed."

"Do we alert the police?" Brandon asked.

"Not yet."

Bas repeated Tahrah's name to Brandon, who ordered Samantha to run a quick check for a possible photograph on the computer linked to her car. Bas joined her, and before she punched in Tahrah's information, requested she retrieve a phone number for her brother, Mahlik.

"How did you remember that name?" Micki asked as Samantha called out the number of Mahlik's home office in Riyadh.

"I have a mind like a steel trap, apparently," he quipped. "I just wish I could remember more. Vic hardly spoke about her. I believe she was much more in love with him than he was with her. He was more enthralled with the fact that a, how did he put it, lug like him could catch the eye of a princess.''

''And he left her to work for you?'' Micki whistled. ''Well, no wonder she's pissed.''

Tilting his head, Bas watched her expression for signs of humor. She couldn't possibly think it reasonable that a woman would hold a grudge after all these years, did she?

A patrol car on regular duty cruised by, the police officers inside obviously unaware of the recent developments. The street people scattered into various buildings and alleyways.

''I thought your street friends would stick around,'' he said to Micki, disheartened. Unlike Brandon, Bas didn't have paramilitary training. He had no doubt they could locate Vic without police cooperation, but he wasn't convinced they could ensure his release without someone getting hurt. Eventually, he might need cooperation from local law enforcement, and if he had to call in every favor from every friend, business acquaintance or relative stranger he had ever crossed paths with, he would do so to retrieve Vic unharmed.

Micki smiled. ''They'll be back. They've just gotta clean up, if you know what I mean. They won't miss the action. Not for what I promised you'd pay them.''

Bas arched his brow, but knew he'd gladly shell out whatever she'd pledged if the information they'd provided helped them find Vic. He dialed the number Samantha had conveyed and waited for the international call to go through. It wasn't lost on Bas that Micki had ventured across the street on her own, putting herself at risk to help him find his friend. Once again, he was indebted to her, and as soon as they had Victor back safe and sound, he knew exactly how he would repay her.

He patted the pocket of his jacket. All it would cost him was one gold coin.

TARAH LEAPT OFF the couch the minute her phone rang, the birdsong not the least bit soothing this time. She didn't know when Victor would awaken, but until she had a new vehicle—one freshly stolen and not yet reported to the police as missing—she couldn't risk escape. Soon, she'd be home again. Never until this day had she allowed herself to miss her homeland. But now that she had Victor back, she couldn't wait to inhale the mesmerizing scents of the desert, the spiced perfumes that lilted through the home she missed so dearly.

For the past five years, no one from her family had known her location, except that she was in the United States. She missed her home, her privileged life, but not the loneliness. With Victor, she'd never feel alone again.

Not completely wanting to alienate her family for when she needed them, Tahrah had allayed their fears by remaining in contact by telephone. But her pleas for privacy often went unheard. They called constantly, begging her to return to the proverbial fold, reminding her of the disgrace of her disappearance.

The trilling continued, causing Victor to stir from where he sat, tied to a chair in a back room, the windows draped with dark cloths. She nearly didn't answer, but she expected a call from her accomplices. She needed their cooperation and their silence, at least long enough for her to spirit Victor out of the country.

Nonstop birdsong shattered the quiet of the house. Victor mumbled, sleepily tugging at his binds. Damn, the phone! She answered, prepared to placate yet another of the *sharmute* she'd been forced to employ in her quest.

"Tahrah?"

She didn't recognize the voice, and those who worked for her had no idea of her real name. She glanced at the tiny screen, but the origin of the number was blocked.

"Who is this?"

"Sebastian Stone," he answered.

Tahrah's eyes narrowed. How did he get her number? How did he know who she was?

"I have nothing to say to you," she said, preparing to end the call when his shout caught her ear.

"Then you'll talk to the police. They don't know your location, but I can give it to them. I'm right outside."

"You lie."

"Look out the window."

Tahrah scuttled into the front room and glanced between slats in the splintering shutters. Across the street, Sebastian Stone stood, cell phone to his ear, a dark truck parked beside him.

"How did you find me? Is this a trick?"

Stone paused. She wondered if she'd insulted him. She knew her brother once counted Sebastian Stone as a trusted business associate, but their connection ended long ago. Mahlik wouldn't care if she took what belonged to Stone, not when Victor would make her so happy.

"No tricks," he claimed. "But you must release Victor."

She laughed at his audacity. "He's mine. He would have stayed with me, married me, if not for you!"

Bitterness boiled in her belly and Tahrah had to stop and remind herself to breathe. Sebastian Stone had lured Victor away from her, filled his head with promises of wealth and decadence that she, so young at the time, could never have countered. But now, things were different. She'd taken what she could from her wealthy family, absconded to the United States and spent her time learning, studying. She understood computers, the Internet. She'd spent hour upon hour delving into the records she could find about Sebastian Stone and his loyal manservant, Victor Campisi. Her Victor. Her love. At first, she'd sent the threats out of anger and spite. But when she realized her notes only kept Victor closer to Sebastian, she'd changed her tactics. Sought to divide and conquer.

"I'm coming in," Stone claimed, crossing the street with long, purposeful strides.

"I'll kill you," she said, wondering if her men had left any weapons about. Damn! She should have asked for a gun, but she'd never imagined anyone would track her down.

She grabbed the hypodermic needle on the table, the one she'd used to ensure Victor remained docile until she removed him from the United States. Sebastian pushed through the rickety gate and climbed the steps to the bolted front door.

"Stop! I said I'd kill you," she screamed, backing toward the room where Victor groaned with increasing volume.

"I'll take that chance. But how many chances will you take, Tahrah? You know I know where you are. You know the truck behind me has people who will help me. You're outnumbered. Of course, what you don't know is that the police have your accomplices in custody. It's only a matter of time before they reveal your role in this, attempt to trade with the police for their freedom. If you don't hurry, I can't ensure your escape."

"Escape?"

She watched his silhouette through the greasy window on the door. He stood tall, steady, his cell phone to his ear. "If you talk to me, I can arrange for you to leave the country safely. But I can't do that once the police are involved. I have no power here.''

Tahrah's mouth dried, her legs shook so that she nearly stumbled toward the door. Why should she listen to him? Why, when he'd taken from her the one thing she'd ever really wanted? But the sound of sirens injected ice and fear into her veins. What if he wasn't lying?

She shoved the bolt and chains out of the way, then tore the door open and dragged him inside. She knocked the cell phone from his hand, then held the hypodermic needle to the base of his throat.

''Talk, Mr. Stone. Because you have only moments before I kill you.''

BAS HELD PERFECTLY STILL while Tahrah kicked the door closed behind him. He thought he heard a shout from across the street, but trusted Micki would stick to their plan. He'd trusted her to deal with the men who witnessed Victor's abduction. She had to trust that he could work similar magic with Tahrah bint Yarin, even if the stakes were decidedly higher.

''You're a fool to come here,'' she said, her voice shaky, her eyes darting rapidly from him to the needle to the back of the house. A groan from the back room injected Bas with both relief and terror. Yes, Vic was here. But in what condition?

''That remains to be seen. Mahlik suggested a face-to-face negotiation would fare better with you than a telephone contact. He's wanted to see you himself for quite some time.''

''Mahlik?''

Her hand shook and the sharp tip of the needle retreated an inch or two. Bas blinked, a droplet of sweat skimming the corner of his eye. If the house had an air conditioner, it wasn't doing much against the New Orleans heat.

"Mahlik gave me your number," Bas explained, knowing his most valuable card was his connection to her brother. He'd learned during his phone call to the Saudi sheik that Tahrah had not entirely cut off her family during her strange escape to the United States. More than likely, she planned to return to them. Bas could use this to bargain for Vic's release. "Mahlik told me he's been begging you to come home for months. He'll welcome you with open arms, if you let Victor go."

"I cannot," she said, shaking her head so that her dark hair streaked across her face. "Victor belongs with me. I've done all this to take back what you stole from me. You!"

She shoved the needle close, but didn't prick his skin. Bas surmised that if she wanted to hurt him, she would have. She was scared, desperate. But her violence had always stopped short of true cruelty.

In her desperation to have Victor all to herself, she'd obviously left the house unguarded. The men who'd witnessed the abduction had counted four thugs in the van, likely the same four the police were now questioning. Sooner or later, one of them would tell the police about Tahrah, and then Bas would lose his main negotiating point. In return for Tahrah's phone number and confirmation that she was in the United States, Bas had promised Mahlik he'd convince Tahrah to leave the country before she was arrested. And Sebastian Stone did not renege on a promise.

Bas watched Brandon Chance's shadow flicker in the back window. He was in place, prepared to break inside if Bas's preferred method—calm negotiation—didn't succeed.

"Think, Tahrah. If Victor had wanted you, he would have stayed all those years ago."

"What?"

Sebastian stepped forward, forcing Tahrah to retreat. In

the back room, he could see Victor bound to a chair and semiconscious. What had they given him? Victor grunted, shook his head, then started to cough.

"Tahrah?" he rasped and his heavy lids widened, then dropped again.

His friend was alive, but who knew what the effects of the drug would be? He needed medical attention. Now.

"How long will Victor stay with you, Tahrah?" Bas asked, his tone even, but insistent. Now was not the time to lose his cool. But she had to understand the urgency of the situation. "Right now, you have him drugged, tied up. Will you keep him that way forever? Is that how you treat someone you claim to love? By hurting them?"

"He hurt me," she cried, backing toward Victor, the needle tumbling from her fingers.

Sebastian hid his relief. "Yes, obviously he did. But if he loved you, truly loved you, he would have stayed with you, no matter what. No matter how much money I offered him. He left, and that hurt, but by taking him, you've made yourself a criminal. You won't keep him docile forever, Tahrah. You know that. He'll leave again. And you'll be hurt again."

Tahrah dropped to the small couch beside Victor, tears splashing down her face. Sirens sounded from outside, distant but growing nearer. Reality of her plight played on her exotic features and Sebastian allowed himself a moment of sympathy. She had her Victor, but not her victory.

"Tahrah, listen to me," Sebastian continued, knowing his time was limited. He had no idea if the sirens were for them, but he could take no chances. "Your brother has agreed to pay your debts and accept you back into the family with open arms if you leave now. If you avoid arrest. If you don't harm Victor any further."

Tahrah stared at her hand, watching as her fingers started to quiver, then shake uncontrollably. Bas took the moment of her distraction to retrieve her purse, phone and veil. He forced them into her hands.

"Go now, Tahrah," he insisted. "Take the car across the street and go directly to the airport. The people there will not stop you. There will be a ticket at the counter in your name." Bas dug into his pocket and retrieved the paper where he'd hastily penned the details. He abhorred the lack of justice in allowing her unpunished release, but as long as Victor was safe, Bas would accept the woman's escape. He trusted that Mahlik's emissaries waited at the airport to take her home. He trusted that the Saudi sheik would ensure Tahrah never bothered them again.

Seconds later, Micki burst through the front door. Bas felt his heart freeze, but Tahrah didn't seem to notice. Her gaze, wet and blurred with tears, remained locked on Vic, who'd stopped moaning and sat with his chin on his chest.

"The cops are on their way," Micki said, darting straight toward them. "I guess her friends have looser tongues than we thought."

Tahrah didn't move. Sebastian considered pushing her toward the door, but he and Micki and Brandon were already skirting the aiding and abetting laws. Technically, Tahrah wasn't yet a fugitive. If they could get her out now, they might have a legal leg to stand on if the police didn't take kindly to their interference.

"She won't go."

Micki knelt down in front of Tahrah and took her hands in hers. "Tahrah. Tahrah?" Micki forced her to make eye contact, then gave her a half smile. "You really threw them for a loop, you know? If this guy over here ever breaks my heart," she nodded to indicate Sebastian, "I may have to take a page or two out of your book."

Tahrah blinked rapidly and, after a moment, she returned Micki's smile. But the grin didn't last. "I wasted so much time."

"We all waste time on men who don't deserve us," Micki assured her. "You aren't the first woman to get screwed by some chump. You won't be the last. But do you have to spend the next ten years in an American jail to prove your love?"

Bas knew he was scowling, but he also knew that Micki was trashing Vic—and men in general—to gain Tahrah's trust.

And when Tahrah's black irises finally found a focus, they brimmed with unadulterated disgust. "Men are pigs," she spat out.

"Some clichés are clichés because they're true," Micki replied soothingly, her tongue so firmly in her cheek, Bas could see the lump beside her mouth.

Taking only enough time to turn and spit at Bas and Victor's feet, Tahrah sprang off the couch and sprinted out the door. The minute she crossed the threshold, Bas started untying Vic's bonds.

Micki leapt over the couch to release his ankles, but stopped and pressed her ear to his chest instead.

"His breathing is fairly steady, but he needs a hospital."

Brandon barreled through the door and used a pocket knife to slice away the ropes on Victor's ankles. "An ambulance is on the way. Sam's following your princess to make sure she gets to the airport as agreed."

Bas nodded, and the banging of his heart against his ribs lessened. It was over. Victor was safe. Once again, Micki had played an invaluable role in the rescue of someone he cared for deeply. Once again, he'd pay her back.

Only this time, the stakes were through the roof.

17

"SHE GOT AWAY?" Victor asked from his hospital bed, blue bruises on his chin and cheeks. He'd put up quite a fight against the thugs who'd yanked him off the street.

Micki laid her hand over his, careful not to dislodge the IV near his wrist. "Bas had to help her flee before the police arrived. That was the deal. Her brother agreed to help us in exchange for her escape from prosecution."

Vic rubbed his hands over his face, causing Micki to wince. His fingers pressed tightly into his eyes in an obviously futile attempt to alleviate the lingering pain—not to mention the drowsiness of the drugs the doctors had given him, despite his protests. "Win-win, I guess."

Micki rolled her eyes. She didn't think the concept applied this time, not when the woman who'd threatened her sense of safety had gotten off scot-free. Sure, Tahrah didn't get what she'd spent a significant number of years trying to attain—namely, Victor—but she had her freedom. Such as it would be once she returned to the family compound in Saudi Arabia.

"Personally, I think win-win's a crock. Somebody always gets the raw end of the deal."

Vic chuckled, but the action obviously caused more pain, so Micki bit back her own laughter. According to the doctors, he'd been hit with a heavy dose of chloroform, or a chloroformlike substance, followed by injected doses of Seconal. The fact that he had regained consciousness only after a few hours was a testament to Vic's iron will and great medical care. He'd cooperated as a model patient, after Bas commanded him to do as the doctors ordered.

Micki had thought the dictate a little rough, but had kept quiet. She'd spoken just as roughly to Danielle from time to time, for her own good. She'd witnessed the hell Bas had gone through in the last five hours, thinking Victor could be hurt, even dead. Just as he'd moved heaven and earth to ensure Danielle's safety and recovery just four days ago, he'd done the same for Vic. The best thing about Sebastian's power was that he could and would wield it to help the people he loved.

"Where's Bas now?"

Micki scooted a little closer. "Attempting to explain to the police why he tipped Tahrah off before they could arrest her. Talk about a hard sell. Anyway, I think they would like it very much if we left New Orleans as soon as possible."

Vic's grin injected a little color into his pale face. "Didn't exactly play by the rules, did he?"

"Yes, he did," Micki insisted, proud of how Bas had manipulated the situation so that no one got hurt. "*His* rules."

Vic followed the line connected to his arm, turning to watch the drip from the bag hooked beside his bed. He didn't make eye contact, even when he posed a question. "You still leaving at the end of the week?"

Micki pressed her lips together. This time, she heard clear regret in Vic's voice. He didn't want her to leave. And, frankly, she didn't want to, either. But the fairy tale had to end. She had her life to live. On her own. She planned to make peace with her grandmother, who she'd unfairly blamed for her own immaturity and stupidity. She wanted to continue getting to know her sister better. She wanted to start her new job, make her own way—maybe complete her education. As Bas continually pointed out to her, she was excellent with people and had a sharp mind. She'd likely make a great social worker. Or maybe even a cop, if she could stand the irony.

"Yeah, I am," she confessed.

Vic opened his mouth to speak, but then shut it the minute Bas strolled through the door.

"Welcome back to consciousness," he said, drolly.

"Thanks, boss. Took four of them and drugs to take me down."

"I'm surprised it didn't take five," Bas said, grinning. "The doctor wants to keep you here overnight, for observation."

Vic immediately started shaking his head. "I need to get out of here, keep an eye on you two."

Bas strolled to the edge of the bed and braced his hands on the footboard. "Brandon has arranged security while we remain in the city. And I spoke with Mahlik after I finished with the police. He assures me his sister is with friends who are, at this very moment, escorting her back to Saudi Arabia."

Vic continued to shake his head. Micki knew from their earlier conversation how he'd struggled with grasping that a girl he'd had what he considered a mild flirtation with could have spent so many years plotting this revenge. "She was a sweet kid. Kind of quiet."

Micki clucked her tongue. "It's always the quiet ones."

Vic chuckled, and even Bas cracked a smile. Micki had truly felt sorry for Tahrah once she heard the whole story from Bas, who'd spoken at length with the brother before and after his sister's escape. The eldest of five daughters and six sons, Tahrah had been the dreamy one, the romantic. Victor didn't deny that they'd flirted and spent some time together years ago when he'd worked Mahlik's security detail, but where the idea of marriage or even a future had come from, he had no clue. Mahlik insisted his sister often confused fantasy and reality—and, right there, she'd won Micki's sympathy. When a sexy man was involved, it was easy to blur the lines between the two.

"Now, you need your rest," Bas ordered Vic, gesturing toward the door so Micki would join him.

"Yeah. But could I talk to you a minute, boss? Alone? No offense," he said to Micki.

"None taken," she answered, patting him on the hand. "Want me to sneak you in a burger from The Camellia Grill tomorrow?"

"I'll be your slave forever."

Micki and Bas exchanged quick wordless glances, and Micki decided she'd better hightail it out of there before she blushed. She knew Vic had no idea of the significance of what he'd said.

She exited, closing the door of the private room behind her. Brandon had a man posted at the door and one down the hall, so Micki sashayed to the corner of the wing to grab a drink from the water fountain. When Bas still hadn't emerged from the room, she wandered to a nearby window and checked out the view. A parking lot. Great. She had nothing to offset the antsy nerves rippling under her skin.

The danger was gone. Vic was safe. She couldn't deny the relief she felt. She'd faced the ordeal they'd been through with surprising resilience and calm—and she knew that Bas's presence had contributed to her strength under pressure.

Together, they made a great team. She'd used the fast-talking skills she'd learned on the streets to gain the trust of the men hanging out on the corner and again with Tahrah, while Bas had employed his powerful contacts and expert negotiation skills to ensure Victor's release before any real damage had been done. Even in the stressful situation, neither one of them had snapped or lost their tempers. Not that she didn't imagine that two high-maintenance personalities such as theirs wouldn't clash from time to time, but damn, for now, they rocked.

Too bad it would all be over in just a few short days.

"Micki." Sebastian's handsome face poked from the doorway.

Micki? He never called her Micki. She wondered if, maybe, he was finally opening himself to the woman she was—the woman he'd only started to truly get to know.

She hurried down the hall, smiling as an old adage slipped into her mind. She didn't care what he called her, so long as he called.

"Ready to go?" he asked.

"Should we leave him?" She remembered her own extended stay in the hospital, the isolation and boredom, the temptation to push the nurses' call button just so someone would come in the room, even if she couldn't make herself talk.

Bas nodded. "He's half-asleep, which is good. He needs a break. I'm thinking about sending him to Aruba for a week. Maybe Belize. I'll let him choose."

"Very generous of you," she said.

"I can be a very generous man. I didn't know that until recently, but, thanks to you, I'm convinced."

She smiled and took his hand in hers. They strolled down the hall toward the elevator, and Micki was surprised that the two bodyguards posted outside Victor's door made no move to accompany them.

"They aren't coming with us," he told her, when he caught her staring.

She eyed him with wary expectation. "Really?"

"Do you want them to?"

"No! Frankly, if Tahrah bint Yarin wants to come after us, I say bring it on. I wouldn't mind a chance to show her up close and personal what I thought about her ruining my funky purple boots."

"I can buy you new boots," Bas reminded her.

"So not the point," she insisted.

He chuckled, gesturing for her to enter the elevator when the doors swooshed open.

"So where to now?" she asked as the elevator descended.

"Where would you like to go?"

"Everywhere! Nowhere. I don't care. But," she said, remembering how little time they actually had left, "you did promise me a real tourist's tour of the city, remember?"

A slightly disappointed cast clouded his eyes. "I did."

She eased her arms under his, snuggling against his chest. "New Orleans is supposed to be the sexiest city in the world, you know. What do you say we go find out if that's truly the case?"

Bas swept her into his arms and kissed her. His arms locked around her waist with ultimate possessiveness and his tongue explored her mouth as if this had been their first kiss. Even after the door sliced open at the lobby and some guy in scrubs cleared his throat so they'd stop kissing long enough to disembark the elevator, Bas didn't let her go. He merely swung her outside, lips still locked, and continued kissing her until she could barely breathe. When he finally released her, she had to hold tight to his sleeve, fearing she might lose her balance.

"Wow," she said, taking in a gulp of air.

He grinned mischievously. "Consider that an appetizer."

She grabbed him by the lapel of his jacket and tugged him toward the door. "Good, because I'm starved."

TWO DAYS LATER, Bas determined that they'd explored just about every square inch of the French Quarter, the Garden District, the Arts District and a considerable length of the Mississippi River. He experienced a particular rush of pleasure remembering that excursion, mentally patting himself on the back for renting out an entire riverboat just for them. He'd nearly balked when Micki suggested they don period clothing and work out a little Scarlett-Rhett fantasy on deck—despite that he yet again won the toss of the coin, he'd indulged her.

Indulging her fantasies had become his preoccupation. Except for checking on Victor, who was now convalescing in a suite at the Windsor Court, Bas consumed himself with making every moment he had left with Micki count. She never ceased to amaze him with her fearless attitude toward life and loving. She tried every delicacy he set before her, from oysters to crawfish to alligator tail. She'd danced on the street with a jazz trio jamming in Jackson Square. She'd stolen not only the reins from the hansom cab driver who'd taken them around the city, but his shiny white top hat, too. And though Bas would have imagined being horrified if any other of his lovers ever did anything so publicly free-spirited, with Micki, it only increased his desire to have her in his life for more than just one more day.

But he couldn't ask her to come with him on his worldwide journeys. She had every right to the life she'd carved for herself back in Chicago—every right to take a stab at success on her own terms. In fact, he figured she was finally ready for the power she'd so desired at the start of their fantasy week. And when she slipped out of her room wearing a barely-there miniskirt in soft blue leather, a hand-woven turquoise halter top and spiky sandals, he knew he'd do whatever she asked, whenever she asked—coin flip or not.

"Ready to go?"

He nodded, unable to speak. She strode past him on a scented cloud, luring him toward her with the cool florals and crisp citrus. She grabbed the handle of the door.

"Wait," he said. "Where are we going?"

Her devilish grin lit her eyes with sapphire facets. "Out."

"You've been quite secretive about where you wish to go tonight."

"Have I?"

He slung his hands into the pockets of the loose-fitting khakis she'd picked out for him this afternoon. He felt a bit ridiculous in the trendy, casual outfit she'd chosen for him, but it made her happy, so he'd bought it. And if allowing her to keep her secret a little longer also brought her joy, he'd do that, too. But his habit of always knowing where he was going and with whom and for how long was tough to break.

"Yes, you have."

"Can't stand it, can you? Not knowing what's going to happen next."

He crossed the room and indulged his need to hold her flush against him, inhale her alluring scent from close up. Very close up. "I have to stand it. With you, I never know what's going to happen next."

A thrill shimmied up her spine. Bas enjoyed every quiver, thanks to her skimpy outfit and their tight proximity.

"Then hold on to your loafers, Bas baby. Cause tonight is going to knock your socks off."

He glanced down at the tan leather shoes she'd picked out for him to go with the khakis and the simple silky button-down shirt in celery green. He snagged the pants at the thigh, and lifted so she could see his bare ankles.

"Per your request, I'm not wearing socks," he informed her.

Her grin bloomed fully. "Oh, good. Less clothes to remove later."

With that, she swung open the door. Bas had no idea what she had in mind, but he didn't give a damn. So long as they could spend this last night together, she could take him anywhere and he'd be one happy man.

18

MICKI WATCHED BAS'S FACE as the cab eased to the curb in front of Club Carnal. He watched the scene outside with his usual cool expression, spawning her secret smile. *Enjoy that control while you have it.* If her plan succeeded, he'd soon be French-kissing his aloof composure goodbye.

At least one hundred people, all dressed to kill, chatted, flirted and scoped out the action from the line that snaked around the building outside New Orleans's hottest nightclub. The pounding bass undertones of some unidentifiable song jammed into the air through the glass doors, creating a pulsing beat that matched the strobe of Micki's excitement. Large muscled bouncers guarded the entrance, their black attire burnished red from lights lining the sleek entryway. Electric anticipation surged through Micki, just thinking about what would happen soon after they crossed through the doorway. Bas thought he was the expert on fantasies? Ha!

Through Reina, Micki had connected with Chantal Dupre, the owner of Club Carnal. Fulfilling fantasies was the top goal in her business plan. The gleaming glass-and-chrome entryway would lead them into a world that was much more Micki's turf than Sebastian's—the perfect playground for their final game.

Tomorrow, he'd fly her back to Chicago, deposit her on her brand-spanking-new doorstep and jet away to his next big deal. She knew he'd ignored his business longer than he ever had in his life. The incident with Tahrah and Vic had sent some of his business associates into panic mode and he'd spent a good amount of time over the past two days putting out fires and scheduling meetings in London, Tokyo and Jakarta. Though she guessed that they'd likely see each other again because of Danielle, at the end of the day tomorrow, the fantasy would be over.

The fact that she loved him made no difference. She'd grappled with that private acknowledgment since they'd left the hospital and embarked on fantasy after fantasy. How could she not love a man who was willing to ignore his business to give her a week of fun? Or a man who would eschew legal justice to ensure he secured his friend's quick and safe release?

Yes, she loved him. But in twenty-four hours, he'd go back to his world and she'd dive headlong into hers. What they shared this week would be nothing more—and nothing less—than a spine-tingling memory. And Micki wanted to make sure the memory would last a long, long time—for both of them.

But composed as he was, Bas didn't allow the briefest glimmer of discomfort show on his handsome face as he opened the door and stepped out of the cab, offered her his hand, paid the driver and escorted her to the entrance.

He opened his mouth to speak, but she pressed her fingers to his lips.

"Micki Carmichael," she told the bouncer, who immediately swung open the door, then pressed his hand to a communication device strapped to his belt and connected to his ear and mouth. He announced their arrival to someone inside. Micki caught a quick glimpse of Bas's eyebrows as they raised in surprise, but otherwise he didn't say a word.

Club Carnal was everything she'd imagined...and more.

Theatrical fog curled out of vents in the floor, misting the crowd on the dance floor, which glowed red and then blue and then red again from lighting built underneath the tiles. Crystal balls swirled above them, dipping and swinging like yo-yos in time to the pulsing beat of the music, shooting sparkles of color to every corner of the four-story-high building.

Bodies pressed, swayed. The bar area flowed with a constant stream of people flashing cash and credit in exchange for Club Carnal's infamous Hurricane Punch or any of the hundreds of other libations they served in generous portions.

If Bas had spoken to her, his carefully controlled volume would never make it over the din of pulsing music and sinful flirtation all around them.

Chantal Dupre promptly bounced over to them, her strong voice, contained in a petite body topped by wild brunette hair frosted to a burnished red, booming over the riot.

"Micki? Welcome to Club Carnal!"

Micki smiled and shook Chantal's hand, then glanced conspiratorially at Bas. Their hostess offered greetings to him, then directed them toward a private elevator off to the side. After Chantal keyed in a code, the brushed metal doors swung open. Once all three of them were inside, the sounds of the club muted and they ascended in relative quiet to the third floor.

"My brother owned the club originally," Chantal explained. "Except for the catwalks, he used the third floor for storage. When I bought the place, I converted some of the storage areas to VIP rooms. Just opened them, but I don't advertise. It's word of mouth and invitation only. But once you're in, whatever you want, you get," she said, winking at Micki.

''Sounds illegal,'' Bas noted, his tone aloof and wry.

Chantal feigned deep thought. ''Not last time I checked.'' Then her face lit up. ''But wouldn't a raid be a kick?''

The doors sliced open and the music slammed them once again. Chantal handed Micki a shimmering key ring, motioned the direction and shouted for them to have a great time. Like Reina, Micki liked Chantal instantly. She'd been kidding about the illegal part, mostly. What happened in the VIP rooms was entirely up to the people who reserved them. But after meeting Chantal, Micki knew one thing for sure—the women in this town knew how to party.

The third floor of Club Carnal consisted of a wide, steady catwalk surrounding the entire club, caged by six-foot steel gates. From here, guests could watch the dancers below or admire the well-known, expertly lit collection of erotic art displayed on the walls. And once they passed through an arched doorway kitty-corner to the elevator, they entered the hush-hush world reserved for those with the influence and money to pay for privacy in a very public place.

In the first room they entered, a bar stretched across the wall. Unlike downstairs, only the most exclusive brands of alcohol were served in the finest crystal glasses. Small televisions caught the action downstairs from a dozen different angles, sending a bluish glow over the dozen couples or so enjoying the private lobby. Micki immediately crossed the room and ordered drinks. Bas remained where she'd left him, but a quick glance over her shoulder confirmed that the decadence of the VIP lounge had caught his interest.

She returned with two tall glasses, filled to the rim with a pink blend of liquor and juices. Tropical and potent. She handed one to Bas, who eyed the concoction warily.

''It's the specialty of the house. Carnal Hurricane Punch. I should probably steal the recipe for Dixie Landings,'' she said, wishing she hadn't mentioned her new job right now. Tonight was about tonight. The fantasy. And only the fantasy.

He nodded, but didn't take a sip. Micki drew the straw to her lips and sucked the cool liquid into her mouth slowly, making sure every decadent flavor reflected on her face as it danced over her tongue and slid down her throat. Despite the air conditioner injecting coolness into the sultry air, her flesh already glowed with a light sheen of perspiration. She drew the tall, thin glass between her breasts and allowed the iced drink to cool her feverish skin.

A chill shimmied through her, coiling around the tips of her breasts. She glanced at Bas's assessing eyes. He watched her body react to the music, the heat, the drink. He watched everything, missed nothing. Which was good, because she was ready to start the show.

Though they hadn't known each other for long, Micki knew Bas wouldn't balk at any challenge she threw his way, including enjoying himself at the club once she got him to warm up to it. The night they'd spent at the Preservation Hall, a sparse building known for hard benches and first-class jazz, he'd told her about the upscale nightclubs he'd visited in Europe. He never quite took to the scene the way his friends had, though. The crowds threw him off-kilter. She guessed the constant eyes on the private man challenged his ability to retain control of everything associated with his image.

That realization had given Micki the idea to explore their last fantasy in Club Carnal. She needed Bas out of his element before she could loosen his iron grip on his self-control.

After a second long sip, Micki closed her eyes and tuned in to the music pounding all around them. She swayed, rolled her shoulders, rocked her hips to the electric rhythm.

God, how long had it been since she'd danced? Since she'd surrendered her body to the beat? The brief appetizer of movement injected her with a need for more—much more. She captured Bas's untouched glass and slid both drinks onto a nearby table, then grabbed his hand and tugged him onto the intimate dance floor already writhing with warm bodies.

He opened his mouth to speak, but she kissed him instead. "Don't bother claiming you don't dance. I don't give a damn."

One eyebrow slashed upward over his suspicious eyes. "Maybe it's time for us to flip my coin again."

She laughed. "Are you so confident that you'll win the toss again? Your luck has to run out sooner or later."

"According to whom?" he asked, seemingly oblivious to the way she rocked and swayed only inches from his rock-still, rock-hard body.

She snaked her hand up and down his chest, loving the shirt she'd chosen with the silky slick material. "Law of averages."

Any other man would have felt like a fool allowing his woman to dance around him without joining her, but any other man wasn't Sebastian Stone. Micki surrendered to the music, inviting the smooth, steady cadences from the drums and guitars to wrap around her skin and inject lust into her bloodstream. She lifted her arms over her head, arched her back and allowed the rocking rhythm and gravity to slowly pull her arms down to her sides. When she finally shook her hair out of her eyes, she saw that she'd caught Bas's interest. He watched the sultry melody take over her body. She rocked closer, then glanced into his eyes. From this close, where her sleek skirt brushed against his slacks, she could feel the hardening flesh and muscle straining underneath. She watched his irises darken, his tongue dart across lips moist with sweat.

"Dancing isn't so bad, is it?" she said, rising on tiptoes so she could direct her words straight into his ears.

"You're very good," he said.

She backed up and accidentally bumped the man dancing behind her. Bas's eyes flashed with warning, but the man didn't seem to notice, having succumbed to the seduction all around him. He grinned at Micki and wordlessly invited her to join him and his partner as they gyrated on the dance floor.

She did.

Bas didn't move, but watched vigilantly as Micki formed a threesome with the writhing couple. Micki threw her inhibitions aside, willing to do whatever it took to lure Bas into her trap. She smiled at the woman, who grinned back then smoothed her hands over Micki's shoulders and matched her rhythm. Micki swung around, her bottom nestled against her new partner, their thighs touching, hips rocking. The guy then moved around them, taking the rear to his partner, stealing touches on Micki's arms, hips, legs. They formed a sexy train, and the steam they generated caught the attention of everyone in the room.

So Micki wasn't the least surprised when Bas's possessive hand grabbed hers and dragged her out of the musical menage.

"What do you think you're doing?" he demanded, his voice so close to cracking with rage, she almost stepped back. His grip tightened around her arm, nearly cutting off her circulation. Yes! This was what she wanted. To push his buttons, shove him outside his ever-present calm into a realm he couldn't control.

Even when Victor had been shanghaied or when he'd first seen his sister thin and ravaged by her drug use, Bas hadn't lost it. Anger wasn't the emotion she'd been going for, but it was the first step. And she trusted he could rein in his rage before things got out of hand.

"Dancing," she answered.

Instantly, his fingers loosened. "That man touched you."

"We were dancing." She glanced over her shoulder. The couple had meshed with another twosome and the four of them created some ultraerotic moves on the dance floor. "They don't even know I'm gone."

"I don't want another man touching you," he said simply.

She leaned against him, pressing her body close to his, slipping her hands into his pockets so she could squeeze him, letting him know exactly what she wanted. "Then you're going to have to do the touching, Bas, because I need some. Right now."

She swung around, strode purposefully toward the beaded curtain behind the bar. In one hand, she held the key to the private VIP room she'd reserved. In the other, she clutched the red velvet pouch containing the erotic gold coin that she'd snagged from his pants.

She wasn't the most experienced pickpocket in Chicago, but she wasn't half-bad. She'd never used such sensual means to distract a mark before, and she likely never would again. But so long as she had what she wanted, she didn't care.

The private room she'd reserved was small, intimate. Like the bar, the corners sported small televisions detailing the action downstairs, along with small joysticks so voyeurs could zoom in and out at will. Incense burned on a small, low table, surrounded by dozens of soft, thick pillows in various shapes and sizes. Micki nearly lost her balance as her heels caught on the thick, plush carpet, layered over enough padding to construct a mattress. She kicked off her heels and wiggled her bare toes in the soft warmth.

Canister-style fixtures hung low from the ceiling, casting dim golden circles of light on the floor. The music seeped into the room from hidden speakers and more erotic art graced the walls. Before Bas could shut the door behind them, a waiter appeared with another round of pink Hurricane Punch. He set two glasses and a full pitcher down on the table, then disappeared without a word.

"Like it?" she asked.

"I prefer the privacy."

She shrugged, pretending not to care when she most certainly did. Then she dangled the red pouch from her fingers, erasing all other thoughts from their minds.

"Thief," he said.

"I've been called worse."

"Not by me," he said.

"True. But it's my turn to flip the coin."

He nodded. "I was wondering when you would suggest that."

She smirked, knowing that if he had wondered, he certainly hadn't wanted her in charge of the coin. And now that she had the disc again, she knew why.

This wasn't the first time she'd possessed the coin without his knowledge. Just yesterday, while he'd used the phone, she'd reached across to the bedstand and snatched the coin for closer inspection. She'd flipped the coin a dozen times, ending with equal results of heads or tails. But when she cradled the coin in her palm, she realized the weight of the circle wasn't evenly distributed. With practice, she'd figured out how she could determine the outcome of the toss depending on the amount of spin and height of the throw.

Bas had been pulling one over on her, and she was about to return the favor.

"I'm suggesting it now. This is my last chance at winning," she said innocently, revealing nothing about her secret knowledge.

Guilt descended on his expression as clearly as a shadow at noontime. "There's something I've been meaning to tell you about the coin," he began, but stopped when she expertly flipped the disc and caught it on the back of her hand. With a short toss, she retrieved the coin between her fingers, then flipped it from one side of her hand to the other with her knuckles. Another useless skill she'd learned on the street, but one that wiped the smug expression right off Bas's face.

She grinned, bit her lip, then balanced the coin on her thumbnail. "Just to be fair," she said, pausing so he could think about how unfair he'd been to her all week, manipulating the coin so he could win every toss, "I'll let you call it."

In reality, she'd been miffed for all of about fifteen minutes, quickly realizing that Bas hadn't abused his role as master. He'd used his authority to force her to experience unforgettable pleasure she might not have otherwise known. He'd commanded her to beat down the walls of her own sexual repression—walls she would never in a thousand years have suspected had been built within her free-spirited body. The last bricks would tumble tonight, thanks to the coin. Her walls. And his.

19

"HEADS," HE CALLED.

Micki clucked her tongue, wondering if he was falling into her trap on purpose. "You always call heads. That threw me off, you know. Made me think the coin would only land that way. But if I flip it like this..." she said, and sailed the disc into the air. She didn't allow it to fall to the ground, but caught the coin in her palm. "Ah, tails. I win."

He didn't contest her flip and she didn't think he would. Bas had a few barriers he needed demolished as well, though he probably thought he'd figure out a way to avoid truly losing his hold on command.

Poor bastard. He was in for quite a shock.

She sat on the cushions, arranging the pillows to her liking. He bent his knees to lower himself beside her, but she stopped him with a flat palm.

"I didn't order you to move, did I?" she said, feeling a slight twinge of guilt for her harsh tone. He'd never used his position to degrade her. She wouldn't, either. But that didn't mean she wasn't going to enjoy telling him exactly what to do—or better, telling him exactly what he was going to allow her to do to him.

"Yes, Mistress," he answered, standing so straight and tall, she felt her breath ease out of her lungs on a sigh.

"I'm thirsty," she said.

He eyed the drink, but didn't move.

She nodded, and without another word, he retrieved the glass and knelt beside her, bending the straw toward her mouth.

She took a long sip, then indicated with her eyes that he should return the glass to the table.

"It's still rather warm in here," she said, fanning herself with her hand.

"Shall I adjust the thermostat?" he asked.

"No, I like it hot. But you don't look like you do. Take off your clothes. Slowly. I want to watch."

She thought back to their first night on the airplane, when he'd made quick work of doffing his clothes. On their second night, he'd made quite a show of watching her remove her dress. And on each night after that, she couldn't really remember precisely how they'd gotten naked—when they'd bothered to remove their clothes at all. Tonight would be different in so many ways.

He touched the top button of his shirt first, pausing with arched eyebrows, seeking her approval. If not for his perpetually cocky grin, she might have thought he was throwing himself fully into the role of love slave. If he wanted to believe he was still in control, that was fine with her. He'd learn.

He undid the buttons slowly, never breaking eye contact with her. With a shrug that showed the power in his strong shoulders, the shirt fell to the floor. He pressed the heel of each shoe to the carpet, and toed off his loafers. Then he removed his belt. The button of his pants. The zipper. With undeniable male grace, he stepped out of the trousers, folded them at the crease and draped them over the corner of the table. With only his boxers remaining, she commanded him to stop.

"Stand still."

She crawled forward, stopping when her face was level

with his knees. With as much catlike grace as she could muster, she slinked behind him and rewarded his braced stance with a long lick on the sensitive skin behind his kneecaps.

"Michaela," he rasped.

"Silence!" she commanded. "You made a mistake when you won those coin tosses, Bas. You had the chance to command me to please you, but instead you wanted me to please myself, or allow you to do all the work. I'm taking a cue from you. You're mine to savor. So stand still and enjoy yourself."

"You don't have to do this," he said.

She suckled a tiny spot at the base of his thigh. "Oh, yes, I do."

For the first time, Micki had carte blanche to explore Bas's body. She hadn't realized completely how restless he could be until her hands attempted to roam. Allowing her to touch him for more than an instant gave her too much power over him. And now that she'd figured out his secret, his fate had been sealed.

She untied and removed her crocheted top, but left her skirt on. She stood up straighter, pressing her bare breasts to his back, her pebbled nipples hard against his tense muscles. She smoothed her hands over his taut backside, digging her fingers into his hard flesh, then yanked his boxers down to his ankles.

"Kick them aside," she ordered. "I need room to work."

He did as she asked, then stood completely still as she kissed a wet and wild path across his shoulders, her hands kneading and massaging his butt. She suckled a line from the top of his spine to his waist, then snaked her hands around him so she could stroke his sex.

"So hard," she murmured. "Long and thick. You fit so

perfectly inside me, you know that? God, I'm getting wet just thinking about it. Reach around, baby. Touch me. See for yourself."

He obeyed, and she hooked one leg around his hip for easy access. He probed her with his fingers. She aroused her breasts by rubbing them against his back, all while she encircled his erection with her hands, pumping him to rock hardness.

Leaning her cheek to his back, she could hear his heart pounding, feel his lungs struggle for steady breathing. No matter how delicious his touch, she moved so he lost his access. She swung around in front of him and lowered herself to her knees.

"Oh, have I been waiting to do this," she said, licking her lips.

"Michaela," he began, but before he could form a complete protest, she took him in her mouth, feeling not degraded or secondary as other lovers had made her feel, but powerful and in control. She drank in the taste of him, explored him fully with tongue and teeth and hands. She cupped him, stroked him, sucked him until she felt the telltale shiver of his imminent climax.

She broke away and retrieved her drink. While he waited, still as stone, she eschewed the straw and filled her mouth with punch and ice. She moved back to him, swallowed, but kept the ice in her cheeks when she wrapped her mouth around him again.

This time, he nearly jumped out of his skin. But instead, he widened his stance, allowing her fuller access. She stopped, swallowed the remaining slivers of melted ice, then murmured as she suckled heat back into both of them. He was harder than he had been before. Needier. He'd thrust his hands into her hair, softly but surely inviting her complete exploration. He chanted her name, his voice deepening as climax threatened again.

She stopped, grinning, wiping the moisture from her mouth as she stood straight and witnessed the sweat beading over his upper lip. Pressing her hands to his shoulders, she pushed him down, then lifted her short skirt.

"My turn."

Boldly, she hooked her leg over his shoulder, and he wasted no time in obliging. The act was raw, lusty, needful. And he wasn't slow or careful as he had been all the other times he'd tasted her so intimately. This time he suckled her like a desperately thirsty man. She nearly went over the edge but stepped back, out of reach, denying them both what they wanted.

Wild desperation darted in his eyes and Micki knew they'd reached the precipice she so wanted to find with Bas. His control was a thing of the past. Power was what they shared. Equally. She tore off her skirt, holding him at bay with her outstretched palm.

"You want me?"

"Yes," he answered.

She stepped over to the wall, which was lined with soft velvet paper. She glanced up, not surprised to see what she'd been told she could find in this particular room at Club Carnal. Straps. Lost in the darkness dangling from the ceiling, thick cuffs lined with soft fleece. She slipped them around her wrists, tugged, tested the strength.

Bas took a tentative step forward, stopping himself, but just barely. *Perfect.*

"How badly?" she asked.

"Micki." He breathed her name dangerously. Took another step closer. She considered drawing this out, making him beg her to climb atop him and release the pent-up passion drawing them both close to insanity, but she couldn't deny herself the pleasure she knew his untapped wildness would soon give her.

"There's a condom on the table. Put it on," she ordered.

He turned and ripped the packet, but she stopped him from donning the latex with his back to her.

"Turn around," she commanded. "I want to see your hands on your cock. I want to watch you wrap that package up for me like a slick, hot present."

He spun around and her raunchy talk pushed another set of buttons that set his eyes on fire. He did as she asked, and once he was ready, she beckoned him to her side.

Eye to eye, her arms locked above her head, her breasts thrust forward, she knew the time had come.

"Pick me up," she ordered.

He complied, buoying her with his hands under her buttocks. She wrapped her legs around his waist and, their gazes fastened, she wriggled her body until he slid deep inside her.

"Don't move," she said.

His eyes flashed with denial, but he didn't say a word. Didn't move a muscle.

Using the straps for leverage, she pulled herself up, then lowered herself again. Her nipples were so close to his mouth.

"Lick me," she said. She nearly lost her mind when he complied, swiping sweet moisture over her sensitive breasts as she lifted and lowered herself on his hard sex.

Her arms tired quickly and Bas compensated by holding her tighter. "Michaela," he murmured, finally speaking the words she desperately wanted to hear. "I can't stand it. Please, let me have you. Please."

"Against the wall, baby. Hard and fast."

Her words shot like a starter pistol and, in seconds, Bas had her bolstered against the wall. He drove into her like a man possessed, frantic and fired. She let go of the straps, locked her arms around his neck, allowed the full breadth of his power to pump into her with hot, wild strokes.

The first streak of fire was his. He cried out her name, slamming his entire being into her, rocking her into an orgasm that turned the dim light to blackness. Stars exploded inside her eyelids and she clutched him so tightly, she felt her nails dig into the flesh around his shoulders, neck and back. He didn't seem to notice or care, he only captured her mouth with his and rode the wave of their orgasms until they practically fell onto the pillows.

After several long minutes, Bas drew her atop him so he could gaze into her eyes.

"Did you get what you wanted?" he asked, breathless, his deep tone hinting at humor.

"You lost control for a minute there. For that one instant, I had the real Bas Stone inside me, focused only on us, together. How did that feel?"

He swallowed and, with surprising gentleness, he kissed the top of her forehead. "Liberating."

Micki's entire body filled with joy. That's what she'd wanted to give him—precisely what he'd given her. Freedom. Pleasure. Happiness. All in just one delectable week.

"You'll remember that feeling? When I'm not around?"

Bas rolled her over, pinning her between the soft collection of pillows and his hard body. "Don't leave."

She laughed, but she felt her throat tighten at the same time. "I have to go home, Bas. I have more unfinished business there than you have all over the world."

"Go home, take care of your business, but then be with me. You can see the whole world, Michaela."

She shook her head. The offer was tempting. And impossible. No matter how she cared for him, loved him even, she had to stay on the road she knew she needed to travel.

The road that would lead to her discovery of her own self-reliance.

"I want to, Bas. It's so tempting to think there's more out there for us to discover together, but I have to make my life work on my own first. I need to start my job, keep my place, go back to school."

He nuzzled his nose to her cheek. "You could study the world firsthand, Michaela. No term papers. No tests. No rules. Just us. How can you say no? Or if you can, tell me how can I make you an offer you won't refuse."

She turned her face aside. How could she say no? Just a week ago, she'd promised Danielle that she would use this time to find out what kind of man Sebastian Stone truly was. She'd learned he was indeed as powerful and strong as he portrayed himself to be, but he was also caring and kind and selfless. She could love him, *did* love him. Truly, madly and deeply. But that didn't change the path she'd chosen for her future—the path she knew she had to take before she could commit to anyone.

"You can't, unless you offer to wait for me," she admitted, then pressed her hands to his lips to keep him from making that promise too quickly. "But I won't ask you to wait. What if we just see how things go?"

"I love you, Michaela."

Her throat froze. Her heart ripped. She opened her mouth and pulled air into her lungs so quickly, she nearly choked. She forced herself to swallow so she could speak. "You don't know that, Bas. We've only been together a week."

"I'm not a man who needs a great deal of time to see what is inherently obvious. Do you know yet if you love me?" A speculative look flashed in his eyes.

He knew she did.

He knew. Just like he knew everything about her in such

a short time. He'd made it his business to know—and once Bas set his mind to doing something, he succeeded.

Except, of course, tonight.

"Of course, I know I love you. How could I not? You didn't give me much choice."

He chuckled, and swiped another path of kisses along her cheek, her chin. "So where does that leave us?"

She rolled out from under him, crawled to the table and retrieved their drinks. She handed him a sweaty glass, then jumped when a droplet of condensation splashed down onto her bare breasts. "It leaves us with about twelve more hours together to worry about nothing but who's going to win the next coin toss."

Bas picked the straw out of his glass, then downed half the drink in two thirsty swallows. Yes, they were amazing together. So different, yet so alike. But they could no more blend their divergent lives than she could remember where she'd left the coin after the last toss.

"Now, where did I put that coin anyway?"

Micki had no intention of losing the gold disc. When they parted tomorrow, she wanted the coin with her. She'd wear it around her body like the mistress it had been created for, a souvenir of the best week of her life.

She slid her drink onto the table and started tossing pillows in her search. Bas, on the other hand, relaxed into a mountain of cushions he'd stuffed underneath him. His gray eyes flashed with humor, even while his smile quirked sardonically.

"You're cold," he said.

"What?"

She spun around, struck by the sight of him lounging so decadently and with such an impudent look in his eye. "I said, you're cold."

She had no idea what he was talking about. She crawled

toward him and he made a hissing sound. "Oh, yes, much warmer."

Shocked, she sat back on her knees. Bas Stone was playing the hot/cold game with her? Bas Stone of the wry, sophisticated sense of humor? If she'd doubted before that she'd affected his outlook on life, she didn't anymore. Which made her all the more hot to find that coin.

"I CAN'T LET YOU GO."

Micki allowed Bas to pull her into his arms, their nude bodies slick and exposed as the dawn broke over the terrace. They'd returned to the hotel late in the night and made love until the wee hours of the morning. The scents of the garden enveloped them, injecting the air with a sweetness that contrasted with the bitter breaking of her heart.

"You don't have a choice." Her heart ached with each word, each syllable. "I have a life and so do you."

"Our lives don't have to be separate, Michaela. I didn't accumulate all this money and power to lose the one woman who's ever meant anything to me."

He whispered the words directly into her ear, holding her tightly. Thank God, or else her knees might have buckled right out from under her.

"Your money and power can't buy what I need, Bas. For once in my life, I have to make it on my own. If I don't, how will I know if I can? I'd end up dependent on you or some other guy for the rest of my life. How could I live with that?"

He dropped his forehead onto her shoulder, and she knew he understood. Just as she knew he loved her. Because only a man who loved her would have worked as hard as he had to comprehend and respect the choices she'd made.

"I'll miss you," he admitted, another three words that tore at her heart.

"Aw," she said, trying to lighten the conversation with humor. "You're just bummed because I'm the one treasure you couldn't possess, no matter how fat your bank account may be."

He nipped her shoulder with his teeth. "Don't be so sure about that, Michaela. Our week might be over, but I may not be done with the game just yet."

She pushed back, intrigued and slightly frightened by the determined look in his pewter gaze. But she let the subject drop, kissed him sweetly, then led him to the bedroom so they could pack.

Epilogue

MICKI MARCHED DOWN THE STAIRS at the "L" train station, untucking her blouse as she hit the humid, Chicago summer air. Even amid the miasma slightly reminiscent of boiling asphalt, the odors of the Dixie Landings bar from her clothes wafted to her nose. She loved her job, but she could do without the sticky scents of fried green tomatoes, spilled beer and sweat. Crossing the street to the block in front of the house she shared with Rory and Alec, she toed out of the short-heeled ankle boots she'd bought—purple of course—and walked barefoot, the leftover heat on the concrete massaging her feet. She'd thought the boots would be both attractive and comfortable during a ten-hour shift. No such luck. She made a mental note to invent such a shoe in the near future. She'd be richer than Bas Stone in no time.

Bas Stone. She leaned back her head and grunted, chastising herself for allowing him to creep into her thoughts for the hundredth time that day, especially now, when all she wanted was a hot shower and a soft bed.

Not true. All she wanted was a shower and bed with Bas.

Why she even tried to keep him off her mind was beyond her. She usually wasn't up for impossibilities. Yet ever since fantasy had become reality with Bas, dreaming alone held very little appeal. She passed the refurbished brownstones and town houses on her block, wondering where he was, what he was doing. They'd been apart now for a month. Just yesterday, she'd called France and had spoken to Danielle, who'd made slow but steady progress. In two weeks, Micki would be sitting yet again in a first-class airline seat on her way to Paris—this time to check on her friend. Would Bas be there? What would they say to each other when they met again? To hell with what they'd say, how would she feel?

Like an idiot, more than likely. His last offer had been so tempting—the chance to educate herself with world travel, the rare opportunity to learn about business from the master himself—but like the stubborn brat she'd always been, she'd decided to stick to her original plan. And yet again, she'd been seduced by her ideal image of independence. Living on her own. Working her way through school once she passed her GED. Saving up her cash tips to buy a car, maybe even a cool, two-seater convertible that would be totally useless during a Chicago winter. Idiot!

Micki stomped around an orange construction cone, then cursed when a strip of yellow caution tape blocked her path. She started to step around the break in the sidewalk when she noticed a path of flower petals leading up to the house.

What the…?

She knelt, lifting white petals of jasmine into her palm. She glanced up, noting that the house undergoing renovation was her favorite on her street, a gothic structure in dark gray stone, with pointed windows and even a few tasteful carvings along the top.

As far as she knew, the house was owned by one of the many societies that called this part of town home. But by the looks of things, they were about to make some changes. She shrugged, figuring they'd probably ruin what was the most interesting building on the block.

She stood to head home, but the front door of the house opened and a stream of colored light from the stained glass windows captured her attention. A man stepped into the jewel-toned rainbow. A man dressed all in black.

Micki caught her breath. She knew that silhouette. She'd know him anywhere.

"Sebastian?"

He held out a bouquet, and she stepped over the tape and toward the entrance in a daze. Amid a collection of jasmine were pale lilac plumeria and miniature white magnolia with dark glossy leaves and bold yellow centers. Micki deeply inhaled the sweet essences of the South, not yet sure that she wanted to look up into his eyes. Her mind flew back to New Orleans, back to the memory of the terrace at the Windsor Court hotel. Back to their goodbye.

She broke out of the reverie and fisted her hands on her hips. He was supposed to leave her alone, supposed to let her do this independence thing.

"What are you doing here?"

"Settling in," he answered.

"Excuse me?"

"I've always liked Chicago. Victor and I decided to open a corporate headquarters. We'd toyed with the idea from time to time, but up until now, seemed like a wasted expenditure." He put the flowers onto a nearby bench seat, snagged her around the waist and drew her flush to his body. "Funny how your business sense changes when you fall in love."

Bas bent his head and inhaled the scent of her shampoo, fresh with tart apples even amid the odors from the club. Despite her less-than-enthusiastic greeting, she hadn't tensed or pulled away. She remained still in his arms, but slowly her muscles melted against his and he heard a tiny sigh escape from her lips.

"I missed you," she confessed.

"I'm glad, because I missed you, too." Despite his need

to feel her close, he pushed her back a few inches just so he could look into her eyes, those glossy aquamarine irises he'd longed for throughout his four unbearable weeks apart from her. He'd gone about his business, flown across several continents and worked a dozen lucrative deals, but the payoff had paled in comparison to the rewards he now received gazing into her eyes. He loved her. He wanted her. And to get her, he'd had to undertake the toughest negotiation of his career with his most dangerous opponent—himself.

"You can't be serious about the corporate office," she said, her laugh shaky, as if she couldn't allow herself to believe, even a little bit, something so preposterous.

"I'm dead serious. After I finished graduate school, I moved out of my apartment and, since then, haven't lived in one place for more than a few weeks. Leased homes. Hotel suites. Hell, sometimes Vic and I bunked on the jet. Now that I think about it, even my home in Lansing was never much of a home, thanks to my parents' obsessions. But our week together showed me that where I am doesn't matter so much as whom I'm with. I want to be with you."

She snagged her bottom lip with her teeth and he could see the conflict playing across her eyes. Yes, she'd missed him and wanted him in her life, but she also desperately needed her shot to make her own way.

But they could compromise. As foreign as the concept was to him when it came to lovers, he was willing to try.

"I'm still going to work. Go to school. Do all the things I need to do, on my own terms," she insisted, her tone resolute, yet light enough that he knew she was open to bargaining.

She'd laid down the nonnegotiable points. Now it was time for him to sweeten the deal.

"Absolutely. I'll still be busy. I'll still have trips to take, though I imagine I'll be cutting most of them shorter than usual. And when you have time, you can come with me. And when you don't, I'll be right down the street.''

Her brow lifted over her wide-eyed stare. ''You really bought this place?''

''Cost me three times its worth, but the style held a certain appeal. Reminds me of this fantasy about an overbearing lord and a headstrong princess.''

Micki laughed. ''You do remember that the princess had that lord completely under her control by the time she was done with him, right?''

Happiness bubbled from deep within him. Like the princess, Micki owned him. And he relished the sensation. ''I'm willing to take the chance. In one week, we fell in love. Who knows what delights we'll discover when we spend more time together? I don't need promises, Michaela—not beyond your vow to see this through with me. Honestly.''

Her eyes sparkled and Bas knew that he'd made the right choice. He didn't deserve the fortune of finding Micki, but he'd be a certified fool to let her go.

''I should have known from the flowers that you were up to no good, Sebastian Stone.''

''Are you accusing me of nefarious purposes?''

He hooked her arm through his and led her through the impressive entrance of the place he intended to call home. She could live here if she wanted, or she could remain three doors down. He didn't care. They'd find time together. Now that he'd found the woman of his dreams, of his fantasies, he would build a life. A real life. With Michaela.

''Nefarious? Not exactly. But you've got something planned for me tonight, don't you?''

He slipped his arm around her waist. ''We'll start with

the bath I've drawn for you upstairs. Do you still have the coin?''

She grinned, flipped the necklace from beneath her shirt and dangled the coin like a hypnotist's instrument—only he already had the power of suggestion working on his libido. With anticipation dancing in her eyes, she dashed into the house, unbuttoning her blouse and disappearing beyond the door.

Bas raced after her. Her expectant squeal was all the invitation to seduction he needed—now and for always.

HARLEQUIN BLAZE COVER MODEL SEARCH CONTEST 3569 OFFICIAL RULES
NO PURCHASE NECESSARY TO ENTER

1. To enter, submit two (2) 4" x 6" photographs of a boyfriend or spouse (who must be 18 years of age or older) taken no later than three (3) months from the time of entry: a close-up, waist up, shirtless photograph; and a fully clothed, full-length photograph, then, tell us, in 100 words or fewer, why he should be a Harlequin Blaze cover model and how he is romantic. Your complete "entry" must include: (i) your essay, (ii) the Official Entry Form and Publicity Release Form printed below completed and signed by you (as "Entrant"), (iii) the photographs (with your hand-written name, address and phone number, and your model's name, address and phone number on the back of each photograph), and (iv) the Publicity Release Form and Photograph Representation Form printed below completed and signed by your model (as "Model"), and should be sent via first-class mail to either: Harlequin Blaze Cover Model Search Contest 3569, P.O. Box 9069, Buffalo, NY, 14269-9069, or Harlequin Blaze Cover Model Search Contest 3569, P.O. Box 637, Fort Erie, Ontario L2A 5X3. All submissions must be in English and be received no later than September 30, 2003. Limit: one entry per person, household or organization. **Purchase or acceptance of a product offer does not improve your chances of winning.** All entry requirements must be strictly adhered to for eligibility and to ensure fairness among entries.

2. Ten (10) Finalist submissions (photographs and essays) will be selected by a panel of judges consisting of members of the Harlequin editorial, marketing and public relations staff, as well as a representative from Elite Model Management (Toronto) Inc., based on the following criteria:

Aptness/Appropriateness of submitted photographs for a Harlequin Blaze cover—70%
Originality of Essay—20%
Sincerity of Essay—10%

In the event of a tie, duplicate finalists will be selected. The photographs submitted by finalists will be posted on the Harlequin website no later than November 15, 2003 (at www.blazecovermodel.com), and viewers may vote, in rank order, on their favorite(s) to assist in the panel of judges' final determination of the Grand Prize and Runner-up winning entries based on the above judging criteria. All decisions of the judges are final.

3. All entries become the property of Harlequin Enterprises Ltd. and none will be returned. Any entry may be used for future promotional purposes. Elite Model Management (Toronto) Inc. and/or its partners, subsidiaries and affiliates operating as "Elite Model Management" will have access to all entries including all personal information, and may contact any Entrant and/or Model in its sole discretion for their own business purposes. Harlequin and Elite Model Management (Toronto) Inc. are separate entities with no legal association or partnership whatsoever having no power to bind or obligate the other or create any expressed or implied obligation or responsibility on behalf of the other, such that Harlequin shall not be responsible in any way for any acts or omissions of Elite Model Management (Toronto) Inc. or its partners, subsidiaries and affiliates in connection with the Contest or otherwise and Elite Model Management shall not be responsible in any way for any acts or omissions of Harlequin or its partners, subsidiaries and affiliates in connection with the contest or otherwise.

4. All Entrants and Models must be residents of the U.S. or Canada, be 18 years of age or older, and have no prior criminal convictions. The contest is not open to any Model that is a professional model and/or actor in any capacity at the time of the entry. Contest void wherever prohibited by law; all applicable laws and regulations apply. Any litigation within the Province of Quebec regarding the conduct or organization of a publicity contest may be submitted to the Régie des alcools, des courses et des jeux for a ruling, and any litigation regarding the awarding of a prize may be submitted to the Régie only for the purpose of helping the parties reach a settlement. Employees and immediate family members of Harlequin Enterprises Ltd., D.L. Blair, Inc., Elite Model Management (Toronto) Inc. and their parents, affiliates, subsidiaries and all other agencies, entities and persons connected with the use, marketing or conduct of this Contest are not eligible to enter. Acceptance of any prize offered constitutes permission to use Entrants' and Models' names, essay submissions, photographs or other likenesses for the purposes of advertising, trade, publication and promotion on behalf of Harlequin Enterprises Ltd., its parent, affiliates, subsidiaries, assigns and other authorized entities involved in the judging and promotion of the contest without further compensation to any Entrant or Model, unless prohibited by law.

5. Finalists will be determined no later than October 30, 2003. Prize Winners will be determined no later than January 31, 2004. Grand Prize Winners (consisting of winning Entrant and Model) will be required to sign and return Affidavit of Eligibility/Release of Liability and Model Release forms within thirty (30) days of notification. Non-compliance with this requirement and within the specified time period will result in disqualification and an alternate will be selected. Any prize notification returned as undeliverable will result in the awarding of the prize to an alternate set of winners. All travelers (or parent/legal guardian of a minor) must execute the Affidavit of Eligibility/Release of Liability prior to ticketing and must possess required travel documents (e.g. valid photo ID) where applicable. Travel dates specified by Sponsor but no later than May 30, 2004.

6. Prizes: One (1) Grand Prize—the opportunity for the Model to appear on the cover of a paperback book from the Harlequin Blaze series, and a 3 day/2 night trip for two (Entrant and Model) to New York, NY for the photo shoot of Model which includes round-trip coach air transportation from the commercial airport nearest the winning Entrant's home to New York, NY, (or, in lieu of air transportation, $100 cash payable to Entrant and Model, if the winning Entrant's home is within 250 miles of New York, NY), hotel accommodations (double occupancy) at the Plaza Hotel and $500 cash spending money payable to Entrant and Model, (approximate prize value: $8,000), and one (1) Runner-up Prize of $200 cash payable to Entrant and Model for a romantic dinner for two (approximate prize value: $200). Prizes are valued in U.S. currency. Prizes consist of only those items listed as part of the prize. No substitution of prize(s) permitted by winners. All prizes are awarded jointly to the Entrant and Model of the winning entries, and are not severable - prizes and obligations may not be assigned or transferred. Any change to the Entrant and/or Model of the winning entries will result in disqualification and an alternate will be selected. Taxes on prize are the sole responsibility of winners. Any and all expenses and/or items not specifically described as part of the prize are the sole responsibility of winners. Harlequin Enterprises Ltd. and D.L. Blair, Inc., their parents, affiliates, and subsidiaries are not responsible for errors in printing of Contest entries and/or game pieces. No responsibility is assumed for lost, stolen, late, illegible, incomplete, inaccurate, non-delivered, postage due or misdirected mail or entries. In the event of printing or other errors which may result in unintended prize values or duplication of prizes, all affected game pieces or entries shall be null and void.

7 Winners will be notified by mail. For winners' list (available after March 31, 2004), send a self-addressed, stamped envelope to: Harlequin Blaze Cover Model Search Contest 3569 Winners, P.O. Box 4200, Blair, NE 68009-4200, or refer to the Harlequin website (at www.blazecovermodel.com).

Contest sponsored by Harlequin Enterprises Ltd., P.O. Box 9042, Buffalo, NY 14269-9042.

HBCVRMODEL2